A NOVEL

DANCING
WITH THE BOSS

CLARE GUTIERREZ

LIVE OAK
BOOK COMPANY

Published by Live Oak Book Company
Austin, TX
www.liveoakbookcompany.com

Distributed by Live Oak Book Company

For ordering information or special discounts for bulk purchases, please contact Live Oak Book Company at PO Box 91869, Austin, TX 78709, 512.891.6100.

Design and composition by Greenleaf Book Group LLC
Cover design by Greenleaf Book Group LLC

Publisher's Cataloging-In-Publication Data
(Prepared by The Donohue Group, Inc.)

Gutierrez, Clare.

Dancing with the boss : a novel / Clare Gutierrez. -- 1st ed.

p. ; cm.

ISBN: 978-1-936909-38-4

1. Gangsters--Southwestern States--Fiction. 2. Mafiosi--Southwestern States--Fiction. 3. Man-woman relationships--Fiction. 4. Southwestern States--Fiction. I. Title.

PS3607.U85 D26 2012

813/.6   2012932155

First Edition

Each new day dawns clear and bright, and all things start anew.
—Frances L. Newkirk

This book is dedicated to my mother, whose love of books filled our evenings with adventures on cold winter nights. A kind and gentle soul, I miss her still.

PROLOGUE

An abandoned small frame house, its doors falling away from their casings in a vain attempt to escape the loneliness, a fence that long ago descended into disrepair and thus allowed access to a dark vacant alley. All perfect for this otherwise dangerous Saturday night visit. Headlights off, Tina maneuvered her Jeep into the overgrown hedge and parked. Here in Aguilar, Colorado—a town the size of a village—every activity outside the norm drew attention. Unwanted attention.

The moon hung precariously in the night sky, casting an eerie glow around itself. The air was just shy of cool on this spring night. Carefully surveying the area, Tina hurriedly walked the two blocks to the rear of the town's only health clinic, slipped along in the shadows of the dilapidated cinderblock wall surrounding it, and let herself in the back door. She moved silently up the hall and entered the office marked "Doctor." She closed the door and placed her sweatshirt across the gap at the bottom. Taking a deep breath, Tina sat down in front of the computer, pulled up her list, and began to work.

The sound was so slight, she wasn't certain at first that she had heard anything. But caution pressed her to close the program and sign off. The only light in the office came from the monitor. As she shut that down, too, she felt them enter the room. Tina held her breath. The first voice was vaguely familiar.

"Working late, aren't you? Maybe you need to catch up a little? Maybe we can help."

"What do you want?" she asked. Still not turning, she sat with her hands resting on the computer keyboard, barely breathing.

"Like you didn't know." The man flipped the light on. "You're going with us this time."

Tina brought the computer back to life. She knew better than to look at him. The second man, snapping her head back by her hair, spoke menacingly. "You thought we wouldn't find you? The boss isn't happy and we don't have all night, so move it."

Data rushed across the screen as she began to run through the clinic's programs instead of hers. She needed to hedge for time somehow. If she could just figure out who had sent them.

"What the hell is all this?"

"You asked for the files, I'm getting them. Unless you would like to do this." She gambled that neither knew how to access the files without her. Tina stalled for time as inconspicuously as possible, trying to think. They were getting impatient. Surely they wouldn't kill her and risk losing several years' worth of her data. The second man shoved a gun against her head. "Why don't we just settle this now?"

The first pulled him off and pushed him away. "Not yet," he declared.

With those words, Tina made her decision. She calmly shut down the computer.

* * * *

Miles away in the mountains, at the bottom of a steep ravine, three men worked with a slaughtered steer. Jacko watched the men pulling entrails from the animal. Several large lanterns cast a garish light around the area. Blood covered all three men as they worked diligently, but slowly; none of them had ever butchered a steer, or anything else for that matter. They would need to speed it up or the corpse would stiffen, making it harder to stuff inside the carcass. Jacko spoke to them harshly, and they tried to move faster. He studied the face of the young man lying in the mud. "This kid wasn't as tough as everyone thought," he muttered to himself.

When the body was forced into its final resting place, the men began brushing away traces of their activities. It was a pitiful effort, but Jacko didn't pay any attention. No one ever came up this canyon anyway. It lay deep within the boundaries of a private ranch, where there were no other riders. If things went as usual, the steer and young man would be eaten cleanly, bones scattered about the area. Jacko rode away, calling back in perfect Spanish, "I'll call when I need to."

Heading up the ravine, Jacko wore a crooked smile. "That makes the last one. All three are gone, without a trace." He felt a slight rush; it was finished, by his direction. In his mind, he played the scene over and over: "Señor Saldivar, your son is gone, vanished; no sign or word." The old man would go crazy and would blame the feds, of course. The three illegals would also vanish, but in a well-planned accident. None of these men had identification or family this side of the border. No one would be the wiser.

Time for him to make his move. He, Jacko, would be unbeatable; he knew both sides too well. His eyes, gray with a malicious glint, searched for the mouth of the canyon, leading out. A bitter man, he cared about nothing except his own ambition. A childhood spent running loose on the streets of the barrios in Los Angeles had given him survival skills beyond any the government could have provided. He had changed locations many times over the years; always a core of bitterness stayed on inside him, growing. That core drove him, pushed him beyond any limits he could set for himself. Power. That is what he wanted now. His position with the feds allowed him access to information he used to this end. Slowly, he would rid his world of problem people.

CHAPTER 1

Annie Kirk drove to the modest, sleepy town of Aguilar nestled in a small valley surrounded with gentle hills; a gateway, of sorts, to the Spanish Peaks and San Isabel National Forest. A lazy creek, so lazy it was dry most of the time, wound its way carelessly through the town and beyond. Annie passed through the town on its one main street, bound for her family's 22,000-acre ranch, headquartered at the base of the West Spanish Peak and continuing up to its timberline. Five years earlier her parents had died in an auto accident, leaving the Clear Water Ranch to Annie and her three siblings.

Clear Water was now home to her older brother, Allen, retired from a career with a Special Ops unit of the federal government. He enlisted at seventeen, right out of high school, and never looked back. Annie, the second of the four children, was a successful gallery owner and rare art dealer in Sedona, Arizona. Leaving the day-to-day operations of her antique store to a close associate, she now spent most of her time finding art for special clientele. Their sister, Lynn, had a home in Wyoming. She kept the books for the oil and gas company left to the family by her grandparents. Thanks to her sharp business head, monies generated from this endeavor provided a more than ample income for all four. The youngest of the family, Earl, owned a trucking business that was one of the largest independent companies in operation. His trucks ran from Canada to the tip of South America, and all parts in between.

Allen had been pleading with Annie for months to join him at Clear Water, and she finally agreed to come home—uncertain how long she would stay. She had never been particularly successful as help for her father, possessing a wandering heart that led her thoughts away from the jobs at hand. She could not imagine why Allen would think she could be of some use now, but the timing was great. Having a responsible manager for the antique store freed Annie's time. With a computer and answering service, she rarely stayed in Arizona anyway. It would do them both good to spend some time together. This would prove, however, to be a bittersweet homecoming.

As she drove toward the Spanish Peaks, she felt a quiet contentment. Leaving Aguilar's "city limits," she sped along, only slowing down when the road became dirt. Rounding a long curve, the peaks exploded into view. Bluish with snow still capping their great summits, they stood as enormous sentinels. Even now commanding the role of landmarks as in years gone by, they boldly led travelers toward their wild, unmarred beauty. Vegetation was changing, as scrub brush and piñon reluctantly gave way to pine, spruce, and tall quivering aspen. Easy rolling hills were becoming edgier mountains with buck brush, sand rocks, and glimpses of barbed wire fences marking man's ownership. Mountain flowers flashed across the countryside, small sparklers creating childlike patterns amid the rougher flora.

Lowering the windows, Annie let the smell of spring's arrival fill the Escalade. Passing ranches with budding hay fields, grazing cattle, and occasionally a smattering of horses, the country spoke of a tranquil time. Nothing like the hustle and bustle of city life she had been immersed in for so long. As the county road snaked toward the West Spanish Peak, higher and higher, the air became cooler. Large groves of aspen filled spaces between ancient evergreens. Oak brush struggled to grow in the thinner, colder air. Higher up, mountain flowers were just pushing up through the ground.

Crossing a large rapidly flowing creek, Annie could see the ranch's hay field on her right. It had been irrigated and was beginning to sprout alfalfa.

Evening would likely find the field full of deer. Beyond the field, stone walls rose from the ground. Formed by intrinsic igneous rock, pushed by magma from deep beneath the earth's surface hundreds of years ago, they had slowly moved up into any space they could find. These large rock walls stood from one to one hundred feet high and one to more than twenty-five feet wide. Like spokes in a wagon wheel with the Peaks as the hub, the rock walls soared and dipped, great static waves. Beneath one such wall nestled against the hillside sat the ranch headquarters.

As she turned off the county road and drove toward the house, Annie felt the familiar awe the beauty of this place inspired. Work buildings, implement sheds, and the bunkhouse were situated on an island of sorts. A large creek split north of the bunkhouse, and other buildings, to join below and continue along the edge of the hay field. The creek was lined with groves of tall aspen shimmering with quivering leaves.

Crossing both of these creek arms, Annie pulled up to the front of the main house. Along its east side, a mass of lilac bushes had begun to bloom. Wild roses tucked about the perimeter of the house were also blooming, as were sweet williams, crowding into every free space in the flower beds and adding their cinnamon scent to the mix. The house was a sturdy rock bi-level built in harmony with the mountain slope. One rear entrance led to the kitchen. A large covered patio with access from a guest room and the master suite continued along the back. From the patio area, occupants had easy access to the barns, corrals, and stables. In the front, two ancient pines stood guard on either side of a long, wide cement stairway that led up to a front porch running the length of the house at the second story. The stately evergreens were nearly as tall as the house itself; their branches, thick and full, served as a restaurant for chipmunks, a home for birds. As the nightly breezes wove their way through the boughs, the evergreens provided gentle music.

The familiar sights and smells filled Annie with a feeling of elation. She slowly crossed the grand porch to the French doors, through which one entered a large room. She stepped inside and called out a greeting. Her voice echoed in the empty house as she surveyed the familiar room. The wall along the porch was filled with massive windows, allowing the sun to flood the house. To the left of the great room was a dining area, and beyond, the kitchen. It was here, tacked to the doorjamb, she found a note from Allen. He had gone to Denver for something they needed on the ranch and would not be back until Sunday, two weeks from today.

Returning to the porch for another taste of home, Annie listened to the whip-poor-wills call, crickets begin their dance, and frogs announce to the world they were out in force. Off in the distance she could hear an owl. She knew the coyotes would begin to stir soon. Their yelping would add to the reverberation. "I'm here, Allen," she spoke into the silence.

Annie's stomach reminded her she had not eaten since early morning. Rummaging through the fridge, she found what was left of a roast, made a sandwich, and wandered out back to the patio. Nibbling, she glanced up and spotted a large dog standing just beyond the brush line. He never moved. At attention with his ears up, he studied her intently, his bright eyes fixed on her sandwich as much as on Annie herself. When she finished eating, she walked toward him; as he stepped cautiously back, she set what was left of her sandwich down and backed away. He finished the meal and trotted back into the brush. The dog reminded her of a wolf, though not as large. Nothing about the animal suggested he was lost or unkempt. His coat was shiny, he looked well fed, and he was alert. He was at home.

As she unloaded and cleaned out the Escalade, she saw that the dog had moved around the lilacs and continued to study her. She finished her chore, went back inside, and began settling into her parents' old room. The spacious room featured an antique four-poster, which stood several feet off the floor. A small step stool was kept beside the bed. Opposite the door that opened into the bedroom sat a deep oversized tub and an equally large shower stall. The right wall held a built-in desk with drawers. Computer and phone lines lay in wait. The left wall of the room was full of windows that ran from the ceiling to the floor. In the middle of the windows were French doors that opened onto the back patio. Her new companion stood watching her through the French doors.

When night fell, Annie filled the tub with hot water and bubbles. After opening the French doors to the patio, now void of the dog, she stripped and sank into the tub—large enough to allow her to stretch out her legs. She leaned back and nearly fell asleep. Opening her eyes, she was startled to see that the dog had returned and even ventured into the doorway. She watched him, but stayed still. Slowly, he moved into the room. "Guess you aren't a stranger here, are you?" The dog just stood, as if waiting for the next command. "Okay, come here, you." Annie spoke softly as she stretched out her hand. The animal moved to her, carefully nosing her hand, then lay beside the tub. He remained in the room while Annie readied for bed. When she awoke the next morning, the animal was asleep on her bed. "I have no idea what you've been called, buster." Annie smiled to herself. "Guess I'll call you Buster." She rubbed his ears while he laid his head on her leg. "Well, Buster, time for coffee."

* * * *

For the next several days, Annie roamed the immediate area, reacquainting herself with the house and barn in particular. The dog followed her everywhere. Each time she entered the house, he followed her in without hesitation.

The downstairs part of the home had been remodeled, and it was easy to tell that was where Allen lived. The colors in the heavy tapestries, thick rugs, and oversized stuffed furniture were strong: red, gold, brown, and green. The area was comfortable and peaceful. It was definitely Allen's place.

As she turned to leave, Annie caught sight of something on the bottom shelf of a side table. It turned out to be a photo album. Plopping into an armchair, she pulled the lamp chain and sat back. Most of the photos showed people she didn't recognize. As she casually flipped the pages, one stopped her. Frowning, she studied the print. Her brother was leaning against what looked to be an army Humvee. He was armed and dressed in camouflage. Another man stood next to him; neither looked happy. In the background, barely visible, she could see a line of people who appeared to be handcuffed together. Stamped on the lower left corner was the date. Shocked, Annie noted the photo was from six months earlier. "I thought he was retired," she thought. Slowly, she went through the rest of the album. Each page held photos that looked like they'd been taken in a different place, yet the same man was with Allen in every one.

* * * *

After a week of roaming the ranch, Annie decided to visit Aguilar for a change of pace. Driving into town and turning onto Main Street, she slowed in front of the small post office. Annie pulled over and parked as a black Hummer slid in behind her. Pausing for a moment on the sidewalk, she turned in a complete circle, surveying the street and surrounding area. Taking note of the familiar businesses she felt a stab of nostalgia. The feeling was the same. Annie looked skyward, watching a flock of birds call to each other as they graced the sunny skies, in the heat of mid-day. Her hair swung freely, shining with the sun's rays bouncing off her bared head. It felt good to be back.

Stepping through the post office door was like stepping back in time. The small receiving area was filled with friends of her parents, catching up on all the gossip. Few recognized her at first. Suddenly, one patron gasped and shrieked at her. "You've come back! Your mother would be so proud that you're *trying*, Annie."

"I assume it's no secret how 'useful' I was on the ranch," Annie mused. She smiled at them all and tried to catch everyone's name as they reintroduced themselves. She finally worked her way to the attendant and asked for the mail. Fishing in her purse for her ID, she realized the building had become silent. Turning, she watched as a well-dressed man went to a large lockbox, removed the mail, and walked out. He nodded respectfully to Annie and the women, all the while surveying the area. Annie watched as he got into the Hummer and handed the mail to someone in the back. He then turned forward in the driver's seat and drove the vehicle away.

"Who's got the Escalade?" asked the man in the backseat.

"I'm thinking she must be Allen's sister since he doesn't have a girl-friend right now. That's his dog with her," answered the driver.

Looking around at the people gathered, Annie silently wondered who the man was and why everyone seemed subdued in his presence. Turning back to the attendant, she retrieved her mail and left. The group in the lobby was beginning to resume its chatter, and many waved as Annie walked out. "Are you here for a while, Annie?" called one woman.

"I think so," Annie answered, smiling over her shoulder at them. They nodded in approval.

Annie decided to do a little sightseeing before heading back to the ranch. Her next stop was at the corner grocery store. As she had seen in the post office, shopping was also a social occasion. When she finally got into the SUV, Buster grumbled his discontent with being left so long. "I guess hunger has you irritated," Annie said with a note of sympathy. "Let's grab a hamburger at the soda fountain and finish our little tour." She rubbed his ears affectionately.

Annie wasn't certain she should bring a dog into the soda fountain but decided to try. Nothing had changed in the eatery. The counter at the front provided seating on six red vinyl and steel swivel stools. Past the counter were four booths, two on either side. In the middle sat an old jukebox. Flipping through the list, Annie was surprised to see that most were still old songs from the '50s and '60s. "Are you new here?" the woman behind the counter asked while taking Annie's order. "Your dog is sure well behaved. Don't usually let 'em in here, but he looks kinda official like, you know?" The woman smiled at Buster.

"I'm visiting my brother. I used to live here. Well, not here exactly, but up the canyon. My name is Annie Kirk. This is Buster," she said as she patted him.

The waitress studied her for a few moments. When the cook called for the order, Annie heard her tell him, "That's Allen's sister there. She come to visit." Both looked at her, smiling. Giving a friendly smile in return and taking her lunch sack, Annie drove toward the football field, where she and Buster sat to eat.

After lunch, Annie continued to roam around. She turned onto a back street named Constitution and came upon the only health clinic in town. She had noticed an ad at the post office earlier seeking volunteers to help out at the clinic. At one time it was a small home, but now it had been converted into an active facility. Several cars were parked in front. Annie walked up the sidewalk. Although cracked and patched several times over, the walkway was clean, with a short neat hedge running along each side. Within the building, a small waiting room full of patients greeted her.

"You don't look too ill," a perky receptionist smiled at her. "May I help you?"

Shaking her head, Annie replied, "I was thinking of helping you. Do you still need a warm body? I've never worked in a doctor's office before, but I do know Quick Books." Annie grinned. Enthusiastically, the girl grabbed her hand and pulled Annie around to meet the office manager. Annie agreed to return the next Wednesday, to assist with the billing activities.

Leaving the clinic, she drove northeast, toward the road leading home. Passing by the older homes, she noticed a black Hummer parked in the front of one of them. There was no activity, and although the house and yard looked well tended, she got the feeling that whoever lived there must be quite elderly. A wheelchair ramp led to the front door, and hand-rails were placed along the steps, porch, and throughout the yard.

* * * *

At the ranch, Annie decided to check up on her two businesses. Her part-ner, George, could handle the antique store quite capably on his own. It was her art brokerage business—locating and buying fine art for her clients—that took more time. The answering machine was full of mes-sages, and it was early evening before Annie finished all of the follow-up paperwork and closed down the computer.

As she did so, Annie heard the sound of an approaching vehicle. She walked to the front window and smiled as her brother stepped out of his pickup. Not having seen her brother for a long time, Annie took stock of their likenesses and differences. Both good-natured, they had an easy way about themselves. Allen was six feet tall to her five feet, eight inches, but in contrast to his thick blondish graying hair, which curled anywhere it wasn't clipped, she had glossy brown hair that hung straight, just beyond her shoulders. Both brother and sister were tan, with wrinkles that hov-ered around their eyes and mouth. Allen's hazel eyes were not as green as Annie's, but they were surrounded with the same long thick eyelashes. Allen moved with the careful stride of one who is accustomed to going undetected.

Allen and his passenger were so busy talking they failed to notice the front door open until Annie called out her hello.

"Hey, my long lost sister returns," he called up to her. "Jacko, meet Annie. Annie, this is my partner, Jacko. When did you get in?" Allen hugged her, pushed her back at arm's length to look at her, then hugged her again. "It's been WAY too long, little sister." With Allen's arm still draped around her shoulders, Annie shook hands with Jacko, who nodded but did not speak.

Allen launched into what he and Jacko had been discussing as he walked through the great room to the kitchen. "For some time now, ranchers up and down the canyon have lost cattle. Only one or two at a time, but it's steady. The cattle never turn up. Not dead that we can find, not at the stockyards, not in someone else's pasture. Not anywhere. No one has seen anything. We've gotten leads on cattle, loaded trucks, stuff like that, but nothing has panned out." He threw his hands up. "Anyway, enough about us, how about you?"

Annie smiled. "Just the same old thing for me. The store is going great. I really like my partner; I can leave whenever I want. My life is dull compared to yours."

"If you were a cattle thief, Annie, what would you do with the steers you lifted?" Allen asked, smiling at her.

"I wouldn't take them anywhere around here to sell. I'd use something like a camper pickup or something that wouldn't look like a trailer." Annie was laughing. Jacko smiled at the siblings, but the smile did not extend to his eyes.

"I think I'm headed to bed. See you two in the morning." With that, he was gone.

"How did you wind up with a partner?" Annie asked her brother after Jacko had left the room.

"It's a long story. I honestly need you, Annie. I need another pair of eyes here whenever I'm gone . . . and I'm gone a lot. Jacko is someone I'm keeping an eye on. Don't hang around him alone. Don't talk around him. Other than that, I think he's benign as far as you're concerned." Allen grinned.

"Wow! Hope you take him with you when you go wherever it is you go, Allen." Annie shuddered slightly. "What about you? I thought you had retired."

"Not exactly. I don't work with the government. At least, not that they would acknowledge. I'm doing under-the-radar sorts of things. Mostly like I did before, but . . ." he shrugged. "Can't discuss it. You know the rules. I found out retirement is not all it's cracked up to be. I missed the action. Besides, this way I never have to deal with the suits. They pay no attention to me."

"Okay, I've got it. Don't ask questions." Annie laughed.

The brother and sister sat at the kitchen table over coffee for hours, catching up. "I'm sorry I'll be gone again in the morning. It's like this a lot, I hate to say. I need you to keep an eye on anyone coming on or off the place, gates opened—stuff like that. Going into Aguilar every week will be good. You could just drive up the canyons occasionally." Allen noted Buster stretched on the kitchen floor at Annie's feet. "Glad you've made friends with the dog. Poor thing, he doesn't even have a name," Allen laughed.

"Oh, he does now. I call him Buster," Annie corrected him. "He's good company." Allen hugged his sister goodnight before heading down the stairs to his room.

* * * *

As summer rustled around, Annie's time settled into a routine. She drove up the canyon every morning. Each day found her traveling a different road, covering the large ranch. During the afternoons, she walked, roaming the trails and roads closer to the house and barns. As promised, she spent Wednesdays in Aguilar, at the clinic.

She found she enjoyed volunteering so much that she soon started to spend more than Wednesdays at the clinic, making small operational changes to ease the computer worries of the crew. The health care providers were comfortable working with computerized medical records, but the business office staff was drowning under an antiquated system. Slowly but surely billing was updated under Annie's direction. Before long, Annie had made friends with the clinic staff.

The clinic was under the oversight of a larger health care company out of Pueblo, sixty-eight miles away. Physicians were usually sent down one day each week, but Tina, a physician's assistant, worked every day, spending the week in Aguilar then going home on the weekends. It took little time for Annie and Tina to become friends. Both single and independent, they instantly enjoyed each other's company. Tina's ready smile, upbeat attitude, and relaxed manner made her a favorite with the patients, too.

On the days when Annie worked, after the last patient had left, she and Tina walked the short distance to the drugstore to grab a hamburger or to Tina's apartment, where they shared wine and cheese and crackers.

The post office, drugstore, and grocery store were gossip havens. Time spent in these places was rewarded by someone invariably broadcasting the latest happening to everyone within earshot. Since Tina lived in Aguilar five days of the week, she was a walking newspaper. On more than one occasion, Annie had laughed her way through lunch, listening to Tina's comic review of the past week's events. Several times the ladies had watched the Hummer cruise the streets, having just left the older house where it lived. Twice, Annie had seen the same man she noticed in the post office her first day in town. He was always polite, but aloof.

One afternoon, she and Tina passed him leaving the drugstore. "He's certainly not very friendly," Annie observed. "He is, however, a very good dresser. Love the shoes."

"Rumor has it they are all in the Mafia," Tina offered. She shrugged her shoulders nonchalantly. "Could be. They're always with the guy in the backseat. They obviously work for him. His mother lives in the house, but you never see her anymore."

Suddenly Tina laughed. "I did see something funny two nights ago, though. I sometimes roam the streets in the evenings, to wind down. I was just passing the house when the Hummer drove by me. It backed into the drive and no less than five men got out. As soon as they got out, the Hummer pulled out and drove back in, front first. I see that Hummer roaming around town a lot. Not headed anywhere, just roaming. You have to wonder what they're doing."

"That *is* strange. Just what could Aguilar offer people like that?" Annie wondered aloud.

CHAPTER 2

I t was Saturday, a great time to review the books, balance the bank statements, and send out patient invoices, uninterrupted. And, because Annie had already installed the new computer program, this chore would go quickly. But by the time she finished her own personal paperwork and Blue Dawn invoices and finally left the ranch, the sun had set.

Annie drove within two blocks of the clinic's back alley but was forced to park and walk the rest of the way because debris from tree trimmers blocked her way. The office was dark; even the guard lights were out, but she took little notice. Using her employee key, she let herself in.

She had walked nearly half the length of the hall when she stopped. The doctor's office door was closed at the far end, but she could see a light under the door and hear voices . . . angry voices. A muffled slam sounded, as if someone hit a desk with his fist, and the clinic fell silent. Annie held her breath. Typing began, and it sounded as though two men continued to argue.

Fearful of being seen by people who probably did not want to be seen, Annie started walking backward down the hall to leave. She couldn't imagine what information would be so important that someone would come into the clinic during off hours. An uneasy feeling gripping her, she scurried as best she could, keeping an eye on the closed door all the while.

When the light from the office suddenly went out, she panicked. Pulling Buster with her, she slipped into a nearby cleaning supply closet. Annie could feel him begin to stiffen; fearful he might growl, she gently moved her hand down to his muzzle and held her breath. Scuffling noises and a closing door echoed in the empty building. She heard heavy footsteps move down the hall, then the back door was opened and closed. For a long time, Annie stayed in the closet barely breathing, afraid someone might return.

Convinced the intruders would not return, she slowly opened the door. The hall was dark. Buster pushed his way past her and headed for the kitchen, growling. Annie followed and hesitantly tried the door, but it was locked. She went down the hall and found the office door locked too. Evidently whoever had been in the office had keys. She decided tonight was not the time to work on the books. Shaking and dragging a protesting Buster, she quickly left the clinic by the back door.

Annie nervously surveyed the darkened yard before rapidly moving into the alley along the old cinderblock wall separating the clinic from the home next door. Now the absence of the guard light was alarming. She hurried to her vehicle, scrambling to get in. With her heart in her mouth, Annie locked the doors before starting the engine. Driving without lights until she came to a regular street, she sighed with relief when she moved onto the well-lit Main Street.

The twenty-seven-mile ride to the ranch was harrowing. Repeatedly looking in her rearview mirror, Annie promised herself she would never venture someplace alone at night again. She kept replaying in her mind what had just happened. She couldn't imagine why someone would sneak into the clinic. Although the two voices were not familiar, she could still hear them. Annie knew the physician's computer had full access to patient health records and financial information; she surmised the intruders must be after someone's medical records. But she couldn't envision information in a medical record warranting this kind of secretive action. After mulling things over, Annie decided to visit the clinic the following morning after church. Perhaps she could tell what the men had been looking for.

When she was safely inside the house, she locked every door. Buster merely wandered into the bedroom, jumped onto the bed, and settled in. "Okay, if something were amiss, that dog would not just lie down," Annie reassured herself. And with that thought, she went to bed.

* * * *

Leaving St. Anthony's church the next morning, Annie drove by the clinic. The little building appeared to be deserted and so peaceful she decided the cloak of night had played games with her. She changed her mind about going in and drove home. Besides, she had a lunch date with Tina tomorrow and could tell her then about the adventure Saturday evening. It would also feel safer retelling the story when more people would be around.

Monday Annie headed into Aguilar. She met the receptionist unlocking the back door. Annie went on to unlock the lobby while the receptionist headed toward the kitchen to get the coffee going. Annie had just pushed the door open for a couple waiting outside when a bloodcurdling scream ripped through the air. Rushing toward the source, she found the receptionist shaking and pointing to a body—*Tina's* body. Moving quickly, Annie touched Tina's wrist to feel for a pulse. Nothing. Tina lay face down. Blood had pooled around her head. In the back of her skull, what looked to Annie like a gunshot wound was clearly visible. Tina was cold and stiff to the touch. Annie stood up and ordered the receptionist to "Call the police." She looked around the room then back at the prostrate form.

"We don't have police here," a voice from the small crowd now gathering answered.

"Then call the sheriff. Call 911!" Stunned, Annie stood still. "What could be worth killing someone over, in this place? That could have been me! I was here," thought Annie with a shudder.

Annie was not certain what to do next. "We'd better close up again. Get everyone out of here; lock the front door. Call the office manager."

She looked at Tina again. "This can't be. Who would want to kill someone like Tina? Why?" she wondered, her heart in her throat.

The sheriff and his deputy arrived, as did the coroner and an ambu-
lance with siren blaring. The officers ordered the few patients still standing around in the waiting room to leave. Then the sheriff began to
interview the staff at the clinic while the deputies searched the building
and grounds. Annie heard one officer ask the coroner when Tina most
likely had died. His best guess was Saturday evening. He would know
more after the autopsy. Annie knew she had not heard a gunshot; that had
to mean Tina came in after Annie had been there.

"What do you do here?" the sheriff asked while jotting down her personal information.

"I just volunteer. Mostly billing, sending patient invoices, things like
that." She did not mention Saturday night's visit.

When he had finished questioning everyone, the sheriff suggested
they could leave but asked them to stay in town until told otherwise. "I
have everyone's phone number; I'll call if I need to. Here's my card if
anyone remembers anything else and needs to reach me."

As she started out the door, Annie suddenly remembered that whatever the men had been after, they had been searching for it in the doctor's
office. The receptionist was already driving away. Quietly, she returned
and spoke to the deputy, who nodded. It was a busy health clinic—the
only one in town, she reminded him—and patients would need to make
other arrangements for care. It would be necessary to notify them that
the clinic would be closed at least through the end of the week. He agreed
to allow Annie to do whatever she needed to do, to alert them.

Tina had been taken away, but the kitchen area where her body had
been found was taped off. Blood still pooled on the floor. "That's why
Buster wanted into the kitchen. Tina must have been there. Maybe she
was already dead." Annie shivered at the thought.

Annie sat at the computer, took a deep breath, and began to type. She
immediately saw that someone had tried unsuccessfully to get into Tina's
file—repeatedly. The computer had shut down. The screen flashed its
usual warning: Log on incorrect; last attempt 10:15 pm, with the date.
She knew from staff mistakes that if someone tried to log in with the

incorrect user name or password the computer would automatically shut down after the fourth attempt, displaying the last time and date.

Annie typed her own password and the screen filled; apparently Tina had been working on the computer when she was interrupted; the computer opened with its last entries. Scrolling down through reports and notes, Annie became increasingly confused. None of the names was familiar. Additionally, the addresses were not even remotely close to Aguilar. The data was not the usual patient information. Annie had not worked with very many, but she had, at the request of the office manager, begun to enter laboratory reports and other patient specific information in the records. She knew this was not billing information. Just what it was, she couldn't tell. Frowning, she noted that several names were marked as "done." Curiously, each name on the list owed a rather large amount of money.

Annie quickly copied several documents onto an extra flash drive she found in the desk. The sound of voices moving down the hall prompted Annie to close Tina's files. She was printing patient statements when the receptionist entered. Annie stopped working and turned to talk with her. The receptionist suggested she clear appointments for the next week too.

"It's creepy here," the receptionist noted, still weeping. "Why would anyone kill Tina?"

Eventually the sad little troupe of staff drifted out the back door. The sheriff's deputy, still moving about, requested the office keys, which the receptionist gladly gave up.

* * * *

The drive home afforded Annie time to decide how much to share with Allen. When he came into the house with Jacko for dinner, Annie was bursting to tell them all about her awful day. Choosing not to mention her role on Saturday evening or what she had discovered on the clinic's computer, she described the gruesome scene the receptionist had uncovered. Annie noticed that although Allen was shocked to hear about Tina, Jacko was indifferent about the news.

"You don't seem surprised, Jacko. Did you already know about Tina?" Annie asked pointedly.

"She probably got into some fight with her boyfriend. I didn't know her, so I don't really care," he replied, shrugging his shoulders. Annie glanced at Allen, disturbed by Jacko's cold response. She could tell Allen was also bothered by Jacko's indifference.

While the two men were out riding the next morning, Annie studied the information on the flash drive she'd taken from the clinic. The list meant nothing to her, nor did any of the notations. As she read more closely, she noticed the dates of many entries were from more than five years earlier. Tina had not worked with the clinic that long. "Who are, or were, these people?" she asked herself. Annie struggled with the feeling she should turn the information over to the sheriff.

If only Jacko would leave the ranch, Annie could hash this all out with Allen. He and Jacko were coming and going all hours of the day and night. But even to Annie's untrained eye, they seemed to be getting on each other's nerves.

CHAPTER 3

Most ranches, including Clear Water, were divided into smaller pastures, each with its own name, to allow ranchers to account for all their steers more easily. Annie remembered that Allen mentioned he and Jacko were going to check cattle in the Gonzalez pasture. As usual, she had received a late call from her brother, letting her know they would not be in for a couple of days. He offered no further information. Annie decided to investigate Gonzalez herself.

After packing a lunch and water, Annie headed for the barn. Entering the tack room, she found their unused saddles mounted on rails. "The next time they leave, I'm checking to see if the saddles are gone, at least," Annie muttered. Not having ridden much lately, she wasn't certain how well she could stay with it, but she headed out, with Buster trotting along. After entering the Gonzalez pasture, she closed the gate behind her and continued northward. Heavy snows from the previous winter had assured there would be plenty of grass. Numerous creeks running throughout the ranch were full. The weather was beautiful, the country lush, and the ride soothing.

Buster was the first to notice something had died farther up the canyon. The dog had stopped trotting and stood, half crouched, fixated on something. Following the softly growling animal and horrendous odor,

Annie found a dead steer lying in a ravine. It appeared the poor beast had been dead for several days. Much of the hide and flesh had been eaten away, but the air was thick with the smell. Covering her face, Annie dismounted and slid down the bank toward the animal. Perhaps she could tell how he died. It did not look as if he had fallen down the ravine, more like he had slid down. Brush and vegetation were mashed in a path as wide as his girth.

As she moved down the bank, Annie noticed a footprint from a boot. Someone had come down after the steer had fallen. As she drew closer to the carcass, the stench was horrendous. She walked around the steer and abruptly stopped, dumbfounded. At first, she was not certain what she was seeing. Slowly, it dawned on her. The internal organs of the steer had been removed and in their place was a body. At least what was left of a body. The skull was clearly human. There were chunks of rotting flesh still hanging on portions of the skeleton. The smell was ghastly. Buster growled menacingly, every hair on his back standing straight up.

Horrified, Annie was already moving up the embankment. Anxiously, she called to Buster and mounted. She had to call him several times before he would come with her. He was uneasy and kept looking back. Now Annie was frightened. "How awful! Does Allen know about this? Are he and Jacko involved in some way? As much as they talk about Gonzalez, maybe they are." Annie rode home fast, all the while realizing that she couldn't call the sheriff, especially if Allen were mixed up in this somehow. Her best hope was to talk to Allen alone.

Back at the house, hours ticked by while Annie paced nervously, waiting for Allen's return. She finally sat down at the computer, thinking she could distract herself with the flash drives from Tina's computer. Loss of sleep during the weekend took its toll. Annie was soon sound asleep at her desk.

* * * *

Awakened by the sound of Buster whining, Annie shook the sleep off. Stumbling, she made it to the French doors in her bedroom and peered out. Horrified, she recognized Allen. He was leaning against one door, bloody and weak. Pulling it open, she caught his arm as he staggered into her room. Helping him to the bed, she laid him down. "What happened?" she gasped.

He had no time to answer, though, because the ringing of the phone startled them both. Hesitatingly, Annie picked it up, watching Allen. He looked at her, shaking his head and placing his finger over his lips.

Before she could even say "Hello," Allen's voice came on the phone. "Hey, sis, I'm calling to say sorry but we're going to be late getting back to the ranch again. Jacko and I should be home by next Friday, though, I promise. Need anything?"

"Not a thing, Allen, but thanks for asking. See you then." A frown deepened between her brows as Annie set the phone down. Shaking, she looked at Allen. His face and upper body were soaked in blood, and she was not sure what injury he was bleeding from. He obviously needed medical attention.

"Allen, I need to get you to Trinidad. You need a doctor. Can you stand?" She tried to get him up.

"No! I can't go to a hospital. Need someplace where no one would look for me." He tried to stand but wobbled against Annie. "I've got to get away from Jacko."

"Can you travel?" Annie asked doubtfully.

"I got here. It's not as bad as it looks. Not all this blood is mine," he explained, smiling weakly. "I did fight back, you know. Help me clean up a little, but I need to get out of here soon, before Jacko comes back."

Working quickly, Annie cleaned him up the best she could. "I'll drive you to Lynn's house, Allen. Jacko wouldn't know to look for you there, would he?"

"No, I've never mentioned Lynn. Good idea. Now, just wipe up in here so he can't tell I was ever here. Sorry this puts you in the middle, Annie, but it'll be far worse if he knows for certain I'm not dead."

Trying to hurry, Annie scurried about, cramming anything that had been bloodied into a large plastic garbage bag, and finally packing extra clothes for both of them. After she had pulled the Escalade up to the rear of the house, she helped Allen struggle out of the house and into the backseat.

"Are you sure you'll be okay without medical attention?"

"A lot better than I would be with it, kid," he replied with a crooked smile.

"I'll be right back. I want to check the house one more time."

Annie moved about the bedroom wiping down the area where Allen had been, throwing everything she had used into the same trash bag. Any sign he might have been there was gone. Setting the coffeemaker on a timer, she filled it half full, left a cup in the sink, called to Buster, and ran to the vehicle.

"Just for conversation's sake, how long is this going to take?" he inquired from the backseat. He was lying with his head on a pillow, covered lightly with a blanket.

"I'm not certain. I haven't driven this way in ages. Can you make it okay?" Annie hoped she didn't sound too worried. As she started down the driveway, Annie looked at her brother in the rearview mirror. He had already closed his eyes, and lay quietly. "Should I talk to him? I won't know if he's unconscious or sleeping," she thought, giving vent to her anxiety. Frowning, she kept looking back at him. Once he raised his hand to pull the blanket closer. "I have to think, he's going to be fine," she reassured herself.

Heading northward toward their sister's home in an isolated part of Wyoming, Annie mulled over what she could do to protect Allen. She also wondered whether his being attacked was connected to Tina's murder—or that of the corpse packed inside the steer—somehow. It seemed that only Allen held the clues and the answers, and as of yet, he couldn't help much. Each time she looked back to see whether they were being followed, Annie tipped the mirror to check on her older brother too. Buster sat patiently in the passenger seat, watching her. She soon forgot about the dead steer.

* * * *

Annie drove as far as she could before stopping for gas. She estimated Buffalo—the town nearest Lynn's—was about five hours north of Fort Collins, which meant she and Allen had about a nine-hour drive, total, and it had to be driven quickly. The night passed like the miles did—fast. Although no closer to understanding what was happening, Annie did have a plan of action in mind.

As the sun rose, she pulled up to Lynn's house. Though she was a tiny woman, standing five feet on her tiptoes, Lynn had laid many a man to waste assuming her spirit and drive were defined by her size. With short thick wavy blonde hair, deep blue eyes, and a sprinkling of freckles over her face, Lynn was at once engaging and comforting. Her smile was the same as Annie's, open and free. Unlike Annie, with her free-spirit attitude, however, Lynn was levelheaded and all business. Most things were black or white to Lynn; she did not see much gray area when it came to life's major decisions.

Lynn was making coffee when Annie knocked. She was shocked to see her sister, but she immediately let Annie and Buster in. Without preamble, Annie said, "I need to get the Escalade into your garage, fast. Allen is with me and he's hurt."

Lynn grabbed her keys, and within minutes she had backed her pickup out of the garage to make space for Annie. Together they got Allen into the house and onto Lynn's bed. While the sisters set about making him comfortable, Annie confessed, "I'm not certain just how badly he is hurt. Let's get him settled, though, and while he sleeps, I'll fill you in."

Between the two of them, they finally were able to remove Allen's shirt. He had been beaten about the face and head; he appeared to have a broken nose and his lips were swollen. He had abrasions and bruises over much of his torso, though by now, the bleeding had stopped. Cleaning him up, Lynn tried to get him to take a deep breath. He shook his head. Lynn feared he might have a fractured rib. After his chest was wrapped, his wounds cleaned, and dressings applied, she talked him into taking a pain pill she had left from a tooth extraction.

True to her nature, Lynn kept quiet, preferring to speak up after she had heard just what was going on. After listening to Annie describe the recent events in Aguilar, Lynn was taken aback to think all this could be happening to Allen and at the ranch.

"Do you think Jacko suspects you realized it wasn't Allen who called?" Lynn finally asked.

"I don't think so, because I smiled while I was talking to the 'other' Allen. I think I convinced him."

"What? You actually smiled?" Lynn gaped at her.

"Well, it took me by surprise. I just knew, somehow, that I couldn't let on that I was upset, so I smiled. You know, if you smile, they say it comes through in your voice on the phone. Come on, I couldn't think of anything else to do. It worked." Lynn shook her head.

"Like old times?" Allen grinned at his sisters. "Sorry I didn't call first, Lynn," he joked and then lay back on the pillows.

"Just what in the heck is going on, Allen?" Annie demanded. "Can you help a little?"

As his story unfolded, Annie became aware that she was shivering in fear. The cold touched her as it slowly seeped into her heart and mind.

* * * *

Allen propped himself up in bed as he began to talk to his sister-rescuers. The ranch, it turned out, was a ruse to allow him to move about the region easily and without suspicion.

"The investigation started when ICE, the Immigration and Customs Enforcement agency, chanced on some monies being sent to questionable characters. My team, unofficially working with the CIA, was called. Shadowing these guys led to drugs and human smuggling, but even this wasn't the real issue. This organization is not like any we've had experience with. They're not using the usual drug cartels. So far, gangs from several countries are involved. We think a guy we've been following for three years may be directing some of the activity. He is a suspected terrorist. So far, he has been able to skirt any real evidence tying him to anything. It's pretty evident he has something to do with this. We don't want to blow things up yet, until we can tell what or where they are targeting. They are bringing men in from countries such as Iran, Turkey, Pakistan, and even Africa. They are all slipping into the U.S. by way of the Mexican border."

Allen shook his head. "Of course, we now have intelligence proving other organizations are watching to see just how good we are. Including our government, which keeps insisting the borders are secure and denying any problems exist with the influx of human cargo. Our government thinks we need to offer broad amnesty. They don't understand these guys are dangerous. They aren't your usual illegal immigrants looking for work."

Allen paused a moment, leaning back against the pillows and frowning up at the ceiling.

"Jacko definitely can't be trusted, but I don't believe he works with the group from South America, one of the gangs my team follows. I'm certain we are getting closer to the real issue. We just haven't had time to put him in the right peg yet. When Jacko realizes I'm not dead, you know what's going to hit the fan. I'm sorry to have brought you in on this, but despite that, you two need to stay out of this as much as possible. I'm not certain if Tina was connected, but the organizations that we're uncovering are connected, to everyone . . . and I mean everyone."

"So what happens now?" asked Lynn.

"I was on my way to the Red Tie Gala in New York. It takes place in a week or so. One of the men on my team secured an invitation through his contact in Iraq. Unfortunately for him, he'd be recognized by the people we think are going to be attending. None of them know what I look like. The Gala started as a front for the bosses from New York, Chicago, and so on to get together. I'm talking the Mafia bosses. As a group, they don't meet often. People think the mob is defunct," he noted sarcastically.

"What really seems to be happening is the American Mafia is not fond of the invasion by criminals from other shores, especially when those guys are uncontrollable and horning in on old businesses. We hoped to identify other boss types that might be there. Although the Gala is an annual event, not every gala is a cover for their meeting. This one will be, we're certain. I'm positive Jacko didn't know I was headed for New York. He must have decided I'm getting too close to his operation, which we think is tied to one or two of the outside groups. Annie, you have to be certain he doesn't suspect you know about me. As far as you— and Lynn—are concerned, you haven't seen me. I'm not certain what happens now. I need to think on that and wait to hear from the rest of my team." He closed his eyes.

"The caller from Denver," Allen continued after a moment, looking at Annie, "is an expert at reproducing voices. Agents have used him for years. He can imitate almost anyone. I'm surprised he's still in business; according to the rumor mill, he died. No one has used his services for several years," Allen shook his head slowly. "It's taken us five years to get this far and it's clear things are heating up. Hell of a time for me to take a vacation."

Knowing the "voice" on the phone had been someone in Denver was a little comfort to Annie. That meant Jacko had not been around to watch her load Allen into the car nor to have had them followed. Annie wanted to ask Allen how he had gotten from Denver to the ranch outside Aguilar, and if it was Jacko's blood on his clothing, but he was fading. She would have to wait until later to get her answers.

Lynn gently fluffed the pillow beneath Allen's head and asked him, "Are you certain you wouldn't consider letting us get a doctor for you?"

Allen shook his head. Lynn took a deep breath, "Just sleep, then. We'll all talk more later."

* * * *

"Is there anywhere he can go where no one knows him?" Annie wondered aloud as she and Lynn huddled over the kitchen table. "I think he should just hole up somewhere and heal. He's a mess, you know. He was beaten pretty badly. Worse, he's a sitting duck." Annie was worried about them all, now. "I suppose we could make it a family affair. Do you think Earl could take Allen out of the country? Or if not Earl, maybe someone he could trust. What do you think?" Annie looked hopefully to Lynn.

"Let me get him on the phone and you can explain all this to him." Lynn dialed Earl, the youngest of the siblings.

Earl's happy voice was reassuring. Like Allen and Annie, he was easygoing and good-natured, but he had a level head, too, just like Lynn. Driven by a work ethic defined by his father, Earl never stopped, yet he would help anyone and kept in touch with every friend he ever made. His drivers had all been with him for years. At Annie's request, he immediately agreed to help, interrupting her explanation to say, "I'm on my way. See you sometime this evening."

Slipping his phone back into its holster, Earl poured another cup of coffee and tried to think how best to handle this latest twist. He and Allen had worked together for nearly ten years. Earl's business had proved an invaluable avenue to move people around whenever the need arose. Many of the drivers he paid were actually working with Allen's team. The operation was almost becoming too big. Earl knew when Allen had been dropped off at the ranch; he just didn't know what should happen now except to get Allen to safety, fast. Earl would leave it up to their elder brother to tell the girls.

Meanwhile, Annie worried aloud to Lynn, "I need to go back. I can't let anything seem like it's out of the ordinary. I just need to know Allen is okay. He's a government guy, so someone will have to talk with us. When someone does report to us he's missing, can you come down?"

"Yes, of course I can come."

"I haven't had a chance to tell Allen what I found when I went riding," Annie added. Briefly, she described the "hiding cache" in which she found the body. "Do you think Allen had anything to do with that?"

"Allen has the answer to that one, maybe, but whatever he says, I think it's going to get ugly. We need to do what we can to help Allen. If these people are what Allen says they are, Annie, no one in this family is very safe. *Please* drive carefully, and call me when you get to the ranch. Wish you were not headed to an empty house." Lynn gave a faint smile and hugged her sister tight.

As Annie drove away, she reached over to rub Buster's ear. "Well, looks like it's going to be a long vacation for you and me, fella."

CHAPTER 4

Juan Saldivar, head of one of Mexico's struggling drug cartels, was a handsome man with an evil face. His eyes were expressionless and cold. His hands were bent and knotted with arthritis. An old gunshot injury to his right leg had left him with a severe limp. No longer agile, he seldom left his house. In keeping with his reputation for violence, he still wore a gun.

Everyone knew that Saldivar's only pleasure in life rested in his son, Junior. The father's drive for power was an addiction that gripped his every waking thought. He was determined to become the main cartel. If what he was working on now turned out to be successful he would rise to the top—and bring Junior with him.

On this particular night, Saldivar's lieutenant stood in the doorway of the study, uncomfortably shifting from one foot to the other. He would have given anything not to be the one to come with such news. It was to have been a quick trip. Junior and three or four of his best men would meet with their contacts in Houston and leave most of the drugs, then on to New York, where they would drop the rest. From there, with cash in hand, home.

"Señor, we used our usual contacts, same drivers, commercial planes, all planned. New York never met with him, or so they say. Houston put him on the plane as planned, so they claim. Junior is gone. Like a wisp of smoke. They are all gone. Nobody has heard from any of them. Nothing." The man slowly walked across the room to stand, hat in hand, waiting.

Juan looked at the man in disbelief. Anger grew inside him, erupting with a fury. The patrón threw the coffee cup in his hand at the wall. He kicked over a small table, sending papers and an ashtray crashing to the floor. He raged at the man and slammed his fist on his desk.

"Find him!" he screamed, gripping the man by his neck. Even as he gave the order, he knew it was hopeless. "I will find him and anyone who had anything to do with it. They will suffer. They will pray for death." In his heart, the overwrought father knew his son was dead. In their line of business, people didn't just run off or disappear; they died. "Everyone will pay," he vowed bitterly. "I need to call Junior's woman. Maybe she knows something." Saldivar's mind clung to the hope Junior was alive, maybe with the woman, but deep in his soul he knew it was not so.

Saldivar thought briefly of the boy's mother, dead these long years. She had been a beauty. A wild little thing, captivated by Juan's dangerous personality. He had loved her obsessively, even more so after their son was born. Then, in a twist of fate, she had died young. He never knew a moment's peace after that awful day except when the child was around him. Now the child was gone too. The patriarch was alone again, the same way he had started. His eyes were dimming, as was the light outside. Shaking his head, he stood at the window, unbelieving. "Everything is gone."

CHAPTER 5

The drive back to the ranch seemed to go on for years, not hours. Annie stopped frequently for coffee and to let Buster run. Arriving at the house, she could see no sign of any disturbance. Locking up after she had unloaded the few things from the car, she headed for the bedroom. The blinking red light of the answering machine caught her attention, and when she pushed "play," she was taken aback to hear Allen's voice. He had left two messages, and in the second message, he sounded concerned. Since the calls had been made about an hour earlier, Annie decided to call back.

Jacko picked up after the first ring. "Where have you been?" he demanded, his voice angry but also relieved.

"What's the matter? I slept in, went for my usual walk, and just hadn't checked messages until now. I suppose you're going to tell me you two aren't going to make it back on Friday, as planned."

When "Allen" came on, Annie found herself searching for any little slip. "Since when do you worry about me during the day? I thought you only worried about older women at night." They visited a while longer before he bid her goodnight.

Annie slept soundly until Buster's cold nose woke her. Letting Buster out, she returned to bed and lay staring at the ceiling. "I have to do something. I'll go nuts just waiting around. I'm going to town."

Arriving at the clinic, Annie felt a wave of sadness thinking about poor Tina. Though the clinic remained closed, a few employees were on duty to handle emergency calls and requests. Annie suggested she should probably send monthly statements, as usual—at least the oldest ones—and keep monies coming in to pay staff. The office manager agreed.

Once at the computer, Annie checked the user history and was relieved to see no one had logged on or used anything, including Tina's records, since Monday. She found three more files and transferred them to a flash drive. After running off the appropriate patient accounts, she shut down the computer. "Do we know when the clinic might open back up?" Annie wondered aloud.

"They plan to open this coming Monday," the receptionist replied.

"What about funeral arrangements? Have we heard anything?" Annie continued.

"Someone out of New York signed for the body and it has been sent there," the office manager informed them. Then he added, "I've been thinking. I'm going to make a boxed rose bed here and fill it with roses in Tina's name." Someone else suggested placing a plaque there too. The staff all agreed to contribute. After donating money, Annie left, driving slowly around town to clear her mind.

Crossing Main Street and heading toward the high school's football field, Annie noticed the black Hummer behind her. It followed her until it became clear just where she was going and then, with a shark-like movement, it turned away. Annie remembered Tina's countless tales about the Hummer's owner, Anthony Tuscano, and his crew. Annie felt it was no accident that she had been followed; it had to be because of Tina and the clinic and Annie's friendship with her. Walking aimlessly around the field, she tried to remember every detail about Tina. Nothing about her behavior had ever seemed different. Now, though, Annie remembered how skittish Tina always seemed when she and Annie went to her apartment. Tina always looked around the rooms and glanced out the door before closing it. At the time, Annie just chalked it up to a habit Tina had picked up from living alone. "I live alone, and I've never done that. And I've stayed in some large cities before. Why worry about Aguilar?" Annie mused.

Back at home, Annie walked around the house, trying to understand Tina's murder, still unable to make any sense of the information on the flash drives. "I have to be missing something. But what?" She tried to recapture every conversation with Tina. Frustrated, she found herself downstairs in the rooms Allen used. Everything was neat and orderly, even his closet. "So like him, I can almost hear . . . what's this?"

Sitting against an outside wall, its edge just visible, she found an odd-looking briefcase. It was small and thick. When she picked it up, she was surprised how heavy it was. The case was locked with a round padlock, the type used to prevent cutting the lock. Forgetting Tina, Annie set about trying to unlock the case. She remembered keys hanging behind the bar in Allen's study. None fit. "Where would I hide a key? Better, where would *Allen* hide a key?" Plopping down in his recliner, she let her mind wander. Suddenly she knew where the key was.

Dashing up the stairs, she called to Buster and ran to the barn. Annie climbed up the ladder, into the old hayloft. Crossing to the space over the milk barn, she carefully ran her hand along the beam between the roof and wall. Where they used to hide cigarettes, the keys lay waiting for Annie.

This time, the briefcase opened. Inside, she found notes. Stacks and stacks of notes. She couldn't make any sense of what she saw: maps, data on people, lists of dates, and on and on. Locking it back up, she knew the safest place to keep it. Annie returned to the hayloft.

Back at the house, Annie gave up trying to understand anything. "Maybe tomorrow," she mused as she stepped into the shower. The phone rang just as she was drying off.

The welcome sound of Lynn's voice greeted her. "I thought I'd call and let you know Earl got here and picked up Allen. He's doing some better. Not a lot, but some. Do you want me to come on down? I could leave in three days."

The memory of being followed by the Hummer—added to everything else that had happened—prompted Annie to agree, "Yes, please. The sooner the better."

CHAPTER 6

Tony set the phone down on his desk, leaning back in his chair. Closing his eyes, he thought about Allen. Picking the phone up again, he dialed another number. "Still nothing from Sam or Allen?" he asked. Nodding, he listened for several minutes. "Maybe it's time we visit the sister. Let's go for a ride, Lou."

It was late evening, and Annie and Buster went out for their usual walk. They passed a field of flowers in full bloom. Indian paintbrushes, "Mexican hats," and flax danced gracefully. The soothing sound of the creek nearby as it tumbled over rocks along its way provided tranquil background music mingled with the whisper of a gentle wind through the aspen groves near the road. She found the weight of the past days lifting a bit.

By the time they returned, Annie was relaxed. The breeze from the patio felt so good Annie decided to leave the doors open. She filled the tub and added bubble bath. Undressed, her hair piled loosely on top of her head, she stepped into the hot water and bubbles. Buster lay at the foot of the bed sleeping. Annie stretched out, leaned back, and closed her eyes, and she, too, drifted off to sleep.

* * * *

As the Hummer turned off the county road, Tony's eyes took in the house. "Drive around back, Lou. I don't care to have the car sitting out in the front."

"Do you see that, Tony?" asked Lou. A wide unbroken swath of light illuminated the patio at the back of the house; it was certain there was a door open.

"Yes. Door wide open, lights on . . . Stop here." A large retaining wall beneath the barns cast a deep shadow over the road. Both men got out of the Hummer. "Surely she wouldn't leave the door open, after seeing what happened to Tina," he thought.

Buster bounded up to Lou. "Hey, fella," Lou clucked softly as he rubbed the dog's ears. Touching Tony's arm lightly, Lou nodded toward the front of the house and, with gun drawn, moved quietly around the house.

Tony pulled his weapon out as he silently stepped onto the patio. The soft lights from the bedside stand and tub area cast a warm glow around the room. Annie still lay sleeping as Buster led Tony into the room. Annie's eyes flew open, however, when a deep voice quietly spoke to her. "Do you always leave your doors wide open?"

Startled, Annie started to rise, then thought better of the idea. Her towel was lying just beyond reach. Taking a quick breath, she answered, keeping her eyes straight ahead. "I don't have much company out here." She could hear the man laugh softly. Her initial surprise was replaced with anger and humiliation. "Are you going to stand there all night?"

"Maybe," he responded. "It's a nice evening, don't you think?"

"It was until just a few moments ago," Annie replied sarcastically. "I suppose you have a reason for being here?"

"What were you doing at the clinic the other night?" His voice was still low, but now it had an edge to it.

"I was going to work on the accounts. I didn't know anyone was there until I was already inside." Annie paused. "I didn't see anything or anyone because I hid."

"You hid? Why?"

"Because I was scared. What kind of question is that?"

He was quiet for a moment. "Where did you hide?"

"Under the bed, where do you think? I hid in the cleaning closet."

"Look at me. This is not a game. If anyone knows or even suspects you were there, you'll meet the same fate as Tina. I can't protect you if you're not honest with me. What's going on?" Tony studied Annie. He needed to be certain she was telling him the truth.

Annie forced herself to remain composed, hoping the encounter would end quickly. For the first time since he had entered the bedroom, she lifted her eyes to look at the man. Long thick black lashes framed his dark brown eyes. He was looking at her intently, though without hostility. She took note of his strong well-defined jawline, slight Roman nose and head of neatly clipped curly hair, just beginning to gray at the temples. His expression was serious. He stood watching her calmly and in control, waiting.

"Honestly, I don't know. I never even knew Tina until I started to work at the clinic. I volunteered to have something to do. It's easier to work on the accounts when the clinic is closed." Annie's voice was now quiet. "Who are you? What would you protect me *from*? Why would you *want* to protect me?"

He studied her for a moment, glanced at the receding line of bubbles, and smiled . . . ever so slightly. Annie felt herself blush as she sank deeper into the clearing water. Stepping back, he nodded to the man now waiting outside the door and started for the patio. "Lock these doors."

"Wait, what if I remember something? How do I get in touch with you?" Annie quickly called after him. He left without answering. Annie jumped from the tub, wrapped herself in a towel, and closed and locked the patio door. Buster was watching her, wagging his tail. She sat next to him and scolded, "Great protection you are. You let them in and didn't even bark. What's with that—unless you know them. Is that possible?"

Annie sat in bed, huddled under the comforter, hugging her knees. Uncertain just why, she was not worried about her visitors. That had to have been Anthony Tuscano, the famous Tony, because he fit Tina's description. His dark eyes were intelligent and not unfriendly. What he said during his visit, however, was troubling. "How did he know I was at the clinic that night? And if he knows, who else does?"

With a persistent idea in her mind, she pulled on a robe and slipped into sandals.

Grabbing a flashlight, she headed to the barn and retrieved the briefcase. Back at the house she tried to make some sense of the information she read. After several hours, she discovered that names she found on Tina's lists were usually names with the greatest debt. To whom? Other names were listed without any monetary notations; those names sounded Saudi, Pakistani, Iraqi, and Iranian, among others. Annie also found numerous dates matched between Allen and Tina's lists. She didn't know what the dates signified. Allen knew Tina. He said as much when he learned that Tina had been killed. Would he know why she had the same information? Annie also wondered if Tony knew Allen was connected to Tina.

Unable to sleep, Annie cruised the Internet. When she finally closed down the computer, the sun was rising. The few names she had looked up were all connected with crime: some Italian American Mafia, some from Columbia, Venezuela, and Mexico. She also found names listed as Cubans. Several were found in articles regarding past brushes with the law, including citizenship disputes and deportation issues. Annie tried to focus on anything that could tell her who might have shot Tina. Who, besides, Allen would know? Maybe it was time to visit Tony, and she knew just how to get his attention.

CHAPTER 7

*T*ony walked around his mother's yard, listening to the sounds of a sleeping town. Dogs barked occasionally, a few cars were out, but generally the night was silent. A little like his mind. Where could he go for answers quickly? Who would know? Tina was only a bit player. He wished Allen would call in—soon.

How did the lady in the tub fit in, or did she? He felt she was being honest with him, but with everything at stake now, he couldn't take any chances. Years' worth of work at risk. Could there be another reason why she was at the clinic that night? A smile settled on his face. She sure was easy to look at, and obviously intelligent and on the independent side.

Tony entered the house and went into the sitting room. Looking along the shelves, he studied the framed photographs of his family. For years, his great-great-grandfather, great-grandfather, and grandfather had run a tight organization. They had done what few families like his had ever managed to do; they moved freely between Italy and America. His father had been a shrewd man who recognized that the old ways were being eroded by America's drug business and greed. Honor was becoming a thing of the past. He had begun to move the Tuscano family toward legitimacy.

Then, his father died. Of "natural causes" so the death certificate said. When Tony's father died, the power and might shifted to his mother. Though grief stricken, she resumed implementing his father's plan. As other families were arrested and successfully tried, she looked to uncharted avenues trying keep the family solvent. When she turned everything over to Tony, they were wealthy beyond anyone's wildest dreams. It was at that point Allen had come into their circle, introduced by Sam, the "good" cousin. Tony smiled to himself once more. A master of disguise, Sam worked with the federal government *and* with the Tuscanos, doing both exceedingly well.

Allen and Sam had devised a plan. Since the U.S. government did not acknowledge Allen's team and Tony's family could work without the usual restraints of laws, the two teams would work together and might be able to do big things. At first Tony had been reluctant. But after the earliest couple of projects, as they were called, went off well, he saw how successful both groups were. It evolved from there. In the beginning, projects were suggested by Allen's contacts; as time went on, Tony's contacts fed into the field. Tony wished his mother could understand what the Tuscano family was about now. He knew she would be pleased.

Saddened, he walked into her bedroom and watched her sleep. She was the kindest person he had ever known, but that didn't slow the drive or dull the steel she needed to hold the family together. If she could think, what would she suggest? Wandering back to the library, Tony sat behind his uncle's desk, where he felt a familiar calm and direction.

The beauty in the tub reentered his idle thoughts. He smiled again, surprised at himself. He never noticed women as a rule. At least not in this way. He had noted her gorgeous body. Her enchanting eyes. Stepping out onto the porch, Tony spoke briefly with Lou, his right hand and first cousin, before retiring. With the image of Annie still in his mind, sleep came on easier that night.

CHAPTER 8

Earl had placed Allen in good hands deep within Mexico. At some point, he would have to discuss with his sisters just what he and Allen did. Not yet, though. He had to keep Allen under wraps so he could mend.

Earl touched his quick dial. Sam answered. "He's okay for now. Need to be certain he stays out of commission for a while. I'll have to keep an eye on Annie and Lynn. The less they know, the better." Sam agreed. Whether or not anyone wanted it, Allen had pulled his sisters into the dangerous game he and Tony played.

* * * *

Annie pulled up in front of the clinic and went inside. Today Tony would get the message she needed to talk.

Everything was so public in such a small town. It was time to use that to her advantage. In the early afternoon, Annie abruptly left the clinic and ran to her SUV. After jumping into the Escalade, she gunned it and sped off. Loose rocks on the road flew behind her as the dust flew wildly around the street. Several people working in their yards stopped, watching her race down the road.

Just as she thought, the Hummer was soon following her. Annie drove as fast as she dared to the football field. Without hesitation, she parked the vehicle and walked out across the field. By the time she turned around, a school custodian was walking away from the driver of the Hummer and was now heading her way. When they met, before he could open his mouth, Annie said, "I suggest Mr. Tuscano speak with me." She left the man standing in the middle of the field, returned to the Escalade, and drove away without looking back. Lou sat in the Hummer with his hands resting on the steering wheel. He smiled watching Annie leave. "This is going to be good," he thought. "Tony has his work cut out for him with this one."

It took Tony only a few hours to connect with her. Again, he had Lou park the Hummer in back out of sight. Tony came to the same patio door. This time, Annie had the dead bolt in place. She waited for several moments before opening the door, letting him wait. He paused in the open doorway and leisurely looked her over before he stepped inside. She was dressed in flowing white harem pants and a soft pink A-line knit tee. Her hair was piled carelessly on top of her head. He nodded slightly, obviously approving.

As usual, Tony was well dressed. He moved with ease and was more relaxed this time. Annie noticed that he stood taller than her brothers.

"Why do you always come to the back door?" Annie asked frowning.

"If I came to the *back* door, I'd be in what I assume is your kitchen," he answered quietly, correcting her.

Annie shook her head and followed him into her bedroom. She suggested they sit in the great room, but he shook his head no, slightly, looking around while he strode about the room. Annie stood watching him. He eventually ended up back by the French doors, leaning casually against the door frame. "Am I correct in assuming you are *the* Anthony Tuscano? Does anyone ever call you 'Tony'?"

"Yes, to both," Tony answered shortly. He studied her unhurriedly. Annie waited patiently for him to start the conversation. He asked her about Allen and her family. Slowly, she began to tell him a few things. Not much, but a little. He listened in silence, with his hands in his pockets, his feet crossed, watching her. When he asked what happened to

Allen, she flatly refused to tell him. For a moment he simply looked at her, through narrowed eyes. Then Tony began to tell her about Allen. Annie listened, stunned. But rather than be alarmed, she slowly found herself trusting this man.

"Okay, this is what I know," Annie told him everything she could think of that was fact, including the information she had found on Tina's computer. Tony asked if he could see it. Annie agreed, but stopped short of giving him the flash drives she had copied. Instead, she offered to get a copy of what she had found to him. Tony nodded briefly. When she described the dead steer, he tipped his head to the side, frowning.

"Could you tell how old the person was or how he died?"

Sarcastically, Annie replied, "Age, several days, maybe a week, since almost everything had been eaten and scattered about. How he died, well—"

"Could you take one of my men there?" Tony interrupted, obviously not amused.

"Not without arousing a great deal of suspicion. I truly doubt you or your guys are guests at the ranch very often. No offense, but I also seriously question the ability of *any* of your men to ride. However, I do have a good friend who is a forensic pathologist, of sorts. I plan to take what I can gather from the carcass for him to look over. That may tell us something."

"There is no us." Tony frowned again. "He would have to tell the police. That's *not* a good idea. I do not want you taking anything to anyone. At this point, you're still relatively unknown. We need to keep it that way. There must be another avenue."

"Well, I said this guy is *sort of* a forensic pathologist. He would not care one whit about reporting to the police, or anyone else for that matter. It's not like anyone could take his license away or anything; he doesn't have one. Besides, he knows me well. Perhaps there *is* an us."

"So, exactly how, and how well, do you know him?" Tony asked quietly. He studied Annie carefully. After years of avoiding any serious relationships that would threaten her independence, Annie knew men. And Anthony Tuscano had symptoms of sliding away from the arena of thinking about her on a business level. He already had "the look" in his eye and was sliding faster than anyone Annie had known. This could be trouble. She had no intention of letting it go further.

"Hmmm, I don't think I care to discuss that at this time." Annie saw a strange expression cross Tony's face. "He's just a good friend," she added quickly. "Now, why did I say that?" she thought. "Unless you have a better idea, it's settled," She continued. "I'll have to go tonight, because Jacko is due back Friday. It's an eight-hour drive. I only have two days." Annie paused. "By the way, am I supposed to entice the janitor at the football field to chase me every time I need to talk with you? Again with the frown? You really shouldn't frown so much; you'll get wrinkles, you know."

His smile slipped in and, just as quickly, slipped out again. Tony finally said, "I'll give you a number, but I never answer it. Whoever answers will get me. Seriously, Annie, this is not some Hollywood action movie; people die. Never take anything at face value. Every action taken has a reason. Allen got in over his head because he trusted the wrong person. You're lucky he is alive, if he still is. Call me tomorrow night. I'll see you after you get in." He turned to leave. As he opened the door, he directed her, "Be careful. Keep your dog with you, and lock every door." He left without looking back.

Annie stood on the patio, watching the taillights grow smaller. Tony's parting words about Allen troubled her: "If he still is . . ." She knew in her heart that her brother was alive, but she hoped no one else knew it with certainty. The sky was clear and filled with stars. All this should just be a really bad dream, but it was only too real.

Shaking off the bad vibes, Annie headed for the barn. The horses usually stayed near the creek at night. She quickly slipped the bridle over the head of the first one to approach. He was a large quarter horse/thoroughbred cross, with a calm demeanor. Perfect for her night ride. Annie left the corral, armed with plenty of gloves, bags, and several gardening masks. The moon was not very bright, but she knew most of the way by heart. She had ridden this canyon many times with Allen and Lynn when they were much younger. After nearly an hour, she caught the first whiff of decay.

Buster knew where to go and trotted ahead, stopping at the top of a ravine. He growled and started down the side. Dismounting, Annie grabbed her supplies, a flashlight, and followed. Stopping twice to vomit, she finally had a bag filled with bits and pieces of as much as she could gather. Back at the barn, she wiped down the saddle to be certain she left no trace of her activity behind. Satisfied, she packed the Escalade, and left.

* * * *

As the hours on the road passed, Annie's mind wandered to the man she was going to visit. He took her call to him with elation. He was quieter, however, as she tried to explain what she might need. He agreed to help, but she could tell he was less than enthusiastic.

She and Rhino had first met when they were both in college. She was lost late one night and stopped at a convenience store to ask for directions. Rhino was standing behind her, waiting to pay. Trained as a Navy SEAL, Rhino's nickname indicated his specialty. He worked along the rivers in Nam, exploding boats, hunting snipers, and clearing the way for the U.S. soldiers to safely advance. Nearly all his work was done under water, and he was deadly. Near the end of his tour, he had been badly injured. His face was severely burned and scarred, one ear was missing, his left leg was shorter than the right, and his lung capacity was only 50 percent, causing audible wheezing. He was a grotesque being.

Annie didn't notice. He listened to the clerk confuse her further before he offered simple directions himself. She gratefully took his advice. During the next couple of months, she ran into him on campus again several times. He finally asked her to lunch and she accepted. Annie found someone with a warm sense of humor and soft touch for animals. That first lunchtime conversation began a lifelong friendship.

Rhino was already working toward a degree in forensic pathology. With an IQ of 180, he found little challenge in classwork. Focusing on advances in forensics, he finished with honors. He took a job in New York, working with the NYPD. After two years, he had lost his license and moved out west. When Annie asked about his troubles, he would only say he made poor choices. It was clear he had no desire to discuss it further. Settled into a small scattered community, he faded away; clients found him. Annie visited Rhino whenever she could, spoke with him on the phone frequently, and exchanged emails with him regularly. Rhino never left his compound. At Annie's urging, Rhino began to assist her with her travel arrangements and art research projects. He was a computer whiz, compulsively organized, and detail oriented. All the things Annie needed for her business. Now she needed his skills as a forensic pathologist.

Annie saw the sun coming up before she pulled into Rhino's compound near Las Cruces, New Mexico. He was standing outside waiting, his misshapen form shivering slightly. He seldom left his house except to stock up on supplies. Even then, he had most things shipped to him. Years of listening to snide remarks about his physique, his limp, and badly scarred face left him with no desire to socialize. Annie was his friend, however, welcome anytime she wanted to come.

Annie was always astounded at how different the outside of Rhino's house looked compared to the inside. The small rundown older adobe structure was surrounded by an unkempt dirt yard with several dying cars parked around. The fence boundary lay on the ground or was missing in places. A dilapidated shack sagged near the main house. Its roof had fallen in, and a tree was growing inside the perimeter of the house.

The interior of the adobe structure was another story. Upon entering, Annie found herself in a small reception area. A stairwell near the center of the room led deep down into the earth. Below, in this area, every luxury was provided, including sleeping quarters, a full-service kitchen, and a large sitting room.

Off to one side was a sizable room filled with computers, microscopes, incubators, printers, and other types of equipment Annie couldn't name. It was a well-equipped, self-contained forensics lab. Since Rhino lived alone, he spent hours honing his considerable skill at applying scientific medical knowledge to legal matters. He had studied tissue, skeletal, and computer forensics, along with other specialties.

"I know you're exhausted, Annie, but before you go take a nap, tell me more about what's going on."

It seemed only fair that if she could ask him to help, he should know why. After telling him what her summer had been like so far, she added, "I hope you can tell me something about this person. Like how old you think he is, or maybe how he died. I say *he* because I assume it's a guy. Because I discovered the body at the ranch, I feel I need to remove all suspicion from my brother Allen. I should have brought the computer files and Allen's lists down to you, too, but I can get that stuff to you later, depending on what you find out."

Rhino frowned at her. He was silent for several minutes. His kind of work, done illegally, was not advertised. His usual clientele were not model citizens. Annie had asked him to help her before, but her requests had always meant antiques and fun. She had never asked him to use his real talents. Shaking his head, he reluctantly agreed. "You might be able to leave this evening. I'll tell you what I can, but I'll need more time than you apparently have." He helped her with the bag. Annie shuddered as he began to dump everything out on the worktable in his lab. He donned a mask, turned on a negative air system, pointed to the door into the guest quarters, and began to work. Grateful for an escape from the sight and smells of her specimens, along with the thought of sleep, Annie headed for the room and hit the bed. Buster followed protectively.

After what seemed like a quick nap, Annie felt Rhino shaking her shoulder to wake her up. "Let your hound out, shower, and let's talk," he suggested as Annie stretched.

When Annie made it to Rhino's kitchen, wearing one of his shirts and her jeans, she poured a cup of fresh coffee and sat down. He fed her and visited for a while.

Swirling the coffee in his cup he began, "Well, this is a young man, probably in his mid- to late-twenties. He died from a beating, I think, although with what little I have and such quick testing, I can't tell with certainty that's what killed him. Bones had been broken after death, and he had been chewed by animals. I'll try to get a DNA match on him," Rhino continued seriously, "I don't usually ask questions, as you know, but dearie, this is not a pretty picture, and you are the *last* person I would expect to show up with something like this. I don't have friends enough to lose even one, especially one like you."

"I know. I don't know where this is going," Annie responded, avoiding his eyes, "I may be back with other favors." She stood to leave. "Please take care of yourself and I'll do the same," Annie smiled at her friend as she kissed him good-bye.

Rhino shook his head, "No, Annie. You are the one that needs to be careful. I'm deadly serious,"

Driving home, Annie thought long and hard about Rhino. Maybe involving him hadn't been such a good idea. Putting him in harm's way would be the worst thing to do to him. It was too late now.

* * * *

Annie called Tony about midnight. He was angry she hadn't called earlier and let her know. "Just where are you? I don't recognize this number, and you should have called hours ago. Did I not make myself clear?" Annie was beginning to realize that, as usual, his voice was level, commanding, and firm. Annie's brow shot up, astonished at his scolding tone.

"Calm down. I'll call from home in about five hours. Your answer as to the age of the body is mid-to-late twenties, a male. He was beaten up so badly that's probably what killed him. My friend should have DNA information back in a week or so." Annie disconnected the pay phone and got back in her car.

Setting the phone down slowly, Tony turned to Lou. "I don't believe that. She hung up on me." Tony was known for both his quick temper and his great self-control, not things that generally went hand in hand. "That will be the last time," he noted softly, more to himself than to Lou. Tony was accustomed to speaking and getting what he wanted. He was also a master at "taking care of business" when necessary. Once more, though he had never given a second thought to any woman, he was giving a great deal of thought to this one. Lou watched his boss. He hardly knew Annie, but he knew Tony very well. "If that had been anyone else, they'd be done. When Tony finally fell, he sure fell fast!"

CHAPTER 9

The phone woke her. Stumbling to find it, Annie finally answered. Jacko was agitated. "What's going on? Why did it take you so long to pick up?"

"Well, for starters, I was asleep. What time is it anyway? Where are you? I thought you two would be home by now."

"I need to speak with Allen."

"What do you mean, 'speak with Allen'? I thought he was with you." Annie was surprised at just how worried Jacko sounded.

"That's the problem, Annie. I left to fill the gas tank up, and when I got back to the motel, he was gone. No one has heard from him since. Can you think of anyplace he would have gone before coming home?" His voice was calmer now.

"No. Jacko what's going *on*? You two never come when you say you're going to, don't go where you say you're going, and now this. Someone had better start talking with me."

In an instant, Jacko's voice turned hard and cold. "I don't think that will *ever* happen. Just stay put, and don't talk with anyone. I'll keep you posted if we hear anything."

"Don't talk with anyone? *Don't talk with anyone?* Are you crazy? Allen has two other siblings, you know. I think you need to level with me. What's going on?"

The line was dead. Annie's mind raced. She called Lynn to tell her about Jacko's call that Allen was missing. Lynn decided she'd leave immediately for the ranch. When Annie called Earl, she had to leave a message.

Next, Annie called the number Tony left her. Lou answered the phone after the first ring. "I just received a call from that guy, Jacko. He thinks something may have happened to Allen. No one has heard from him."

"I'll let Tony know."

Closing the patio door behind them, Annie took Buster for their walk. It seemed a safe assumption that everyone thought Allen was dead. The ranch would no longer be a safe haven for Jacko or any of his associates if they had been using it. How long does someone have to be missing before they are declared dead? Worse, how could someone have left him for dead, and not gone back to check? Maybe they already knew he was not wherever he had been left. Maybe that's why Jacko sounded so worried. And what might Jacko try to do to get her out of the picture? With resolve, Annie headed for the house, then Aguilar. "It's time Tony shared information with me, too. This is getting more than a little scary."

* * * *

"Hey Annie, this is Lou. I'll tell the boss you're coming. Just drive slow. We'll meet you somewhere outside town." Annie liked talking with Lou; he always sounded calm and friendly.

The Hummer came toward her but turned off on a side road leading up another canyon.

Without hesitation, she followed. After a while, the Hummer turned onto a little-used winding dirt road, kicking up dust clouds and eventually coming to a stop behind a thick grove of aspen. Pulling up next to it, Annie waited a moment for the dust to settle. Stepping out first, she stood looking around the area. Lou stepped out of the front passenger side, walked around to Annie, and met her with a grin and extended hand. "Hi, Annie, I'm Lou."

His demeanor was not nearly as intense as Tony's. Annie felt he had an edge to him, although he was always friendly with her. Together they walked behind the Hummer and Lou opened the back passenger side door for her. He moved aside as she stepped up and into the large vehicle. He got into the passenger side in the front once again.

"Where to next, boss?" a third man, the driver, asked without turning around.

Annie froze. Her heart dropped. She suddenly had trouble breathing. She had to concentrate hard to keep from making any sound or diving out of the Hummer. Her hands clenched together, she tried to breathe deeply. She could feel Tony watching her as she tried to compose herself, but panic washed over her. She thought, "Oh my gosh, this can't be happening. And I'm trapped in here!"

"Where does this road lead? How far can we go without anyone caring?" Tony asked all the while watching Annie through narrowed eyes, puzzled by the abrupt change in her.

The driver turned to answer. "I'm not sure, but let's just take the road and see."

Annie stole a quick glance at him. His face was hard and heavily scarred; he looked like he would enjoy hurting someone. Involuntarily, she shivered. He glanced at her without any sign of recognition.

"Maybe we'll just stay here." Tony said. He felt the fear in Annie. Certain it was not his presence that frightened her, he made a quick decision. Tony touched Annie's arm and nodded toward her door. He got out, and Annie exited on her side. She walked slowly away from the Hummer, stepping up her pace quickly, hoping no one could see her heart pounding through her shirt. Tony's long stride caught up with her. "What is it? What's wrong with you?" he asked, quiet urgency in his voice.

Without turning, she answered through clenched teeth, "How could you not tell me you were involved with Tina? I suppose you had Allen beat up too. I told you *everything*."

Tony grasped her arm and ordered her, "Come with me."

For an instant, Annie thought of pulling away and running to her car. Knowing the Hummer could easily block her, however, she walked with him as he had directed. When they were in the thicket of the aspen trees, out of earshot of the Hummer, Tony whirled her around and spoke. "You have to talk to me, Annie. Why the change in attitude?"

"Your people were at the clinic. You knew all the time I was there." Her eyes flashed with anger. "I've put Allen at risk by talking with you. I can't beat you, Tony; I just want you to leave my family out of all this. We—"

"Annie," Tony interrupted, "I *did not* know you were at the clinic. Allen is not at risk because of me. Who was at the clinic that night? I have to know."

When she didn't answer, Tony pressed. "You realize you don't have much choice? You can't do anything alone, and Allen is still alive, we assume. This is a lot bigger than you or your family. As I said before, Annie, this is not a game; talk to me."

Annie had to make a decision, and she knew the decision would affect her entire family. "Your driver was at the clinic. I'm positive. I heard him arguing with another man. I'll never forget that voice. Now he knows I know. Where does that put me?" She turned to face Tony, still angry.

"The driver does not know. He's a new man. No one knows except me. Each time I've spoken with you I've been alone. Even the first time, only Lou was with me, but he waited outside, remember? This driver has never been with me around you before. This much I will tell you. My family isn't into drugs, especially, but if the South American families or other foreign families gain a controlling interest, my family is dead. This must be stopped. I need to know for certain who's directing the activity; things have gotten a little complicated. You're certain my driver was at the clinic that night?"

"Yes."

Tony stood thinking for a moment. "Here, from now on, call me from only this phone." He handed her a sleek new phone. "Never from any other. Use your own cell carefully. Your sister will be in later tonight, and your brother Earl will not be in for several weeks. If you need anything, just call. Lou will get me. I don't answer my phone."

"How do you know about my sister and brother?" Annie asked, puzzled.

"It's my business to know," he answered simply. He watched her face for any sign of fear. Nothing. "Why haven't you ever married?"

Startled, Annie looked up at him. "Where did that come from? What makes you think I've never married? Who told you that?" He looked back at her without answering. "I guess that was a stupid question," she noted ruefully. To this, he solemnly nodded in agreement.

"Well?" He could not imagine anyone letting her go. There must be a story there, and he wanted to know that story.

Annie stumbled over an answer. "You know the old saying, I just had lots to do, places to go. I guess I'm too independent for most men. Men tend not to like a woman who can make it on her own. I don't know. Maybe I just never met the right one. Maybe I was too busy. Why are you asking me this, Tony?" She frowned up at him.

Tony smiled briefly, and in lieu of answering, he simply took her arm and led her back to the Escalade. "Lock up."

He stood watching as she backed out and left. Annie watched the Hummer in her rearview mirror. It never followed her; instead, it turned up the canyon and moved out of sight. On her drive home, her mind went into overdrive. She had to have help from someone. It looked like Tony would have to be the one. She set aside the issue of Tony's curiosity regarding her marital status. That would be an item to think on later. The issue of his Mafia ties, now *that* was something else.

Once more at the ranch, Annie walked up the steps cautiously. Buster was waiting on the front porch, and from his demeanor, all was well. Annie went around turning off lights, took one last look around the place, locked up, and lay down. She still wasn't certain what Tony's involvement was, nor could she understand how things tied together. So far, she was only sure that at least three people were of concern: Jacko and the two men at the clinic. She had yet to hear from Jacko, and now she knew the identity of one of the men she'd heard arguing at the clinic. But he was with someone else that night, and that meant somewhere out there was a third guy Annie didn't even know, so how could she watch out for him? In the back of her mind, however, a small voice advised her that she could take Tony's word about his driver. Maybe there were now just two to worry about.

CHAPTER 10

As Lou turned the key in the Hummer's ignition, he glanced back at his cousin. "One issue resolved. I never did like that new guy. He was a lousy driver anyway. You make a point; keep your enemies under watch. That was a good pick up on Annie's part, recognizing his voice."

Tony was more relaxed. "Yes," he nodded, "but our bucket is still full. Lou, keep an eye on Annie. And we need to bring Sam and Dominic up. Still nothing from Allen?"

"No," Lou answered, "maybe Sam will have something to add. Am I keeping an eye on Annie for Allen?"

"For me," Tony answered shortly, making eye contact with Lou in the rearview mirror.

CHAPTER 11

J acko paced. Dragon watched for a while, and then he turned to leave. "Just where are you going?" Jacko challenged.

"Your man is out of pocket, you don't need me anymore. Besides, you are all getting a little boring. I'm going to bed. Let yourself out."

Watching the fat, flabby, and weak body wheel away, Jacko felt revulsion. Dragon weighed nearly 500 pounds; no one really knew for certain. Dragon had been large as long as anyone had ever known him. He made no secret of his talents or his willingness to sell them to the highest bidder. If only Jacko didn't need his services. It would be such a pleasure to discard him. Maybe someday.

Right now, Jacko had a bigger problem. From the way Allen's sister looked at him, he was certain she did not care for him. With Allen gone, she would not likely allow him to stay on the ranch. Shame to lose such a handy graveyard. On the other hand, perhaps he could get a little more mileage out of the situation by pretending to look for Allen. Pretending? Now there is a word. No one had turned up anything indicating he was alive, but no one could find his body either. Jacko should have taken care of the mess himself.

He was certain the sister didn't suspect anything, and Tuscano's men were still running around like roaches. Speaking of which, he hadn't heard from Fish, Tony's new driver, in several days. That could be problematic. Especially given the man's reputation for drinking and talking.

Jacko walked to Dragon's bar and helped himself to another shot. "He's a huge and ugly SOB, but he sure drinks good stuff," he observed to an empty room.

CHAPTER 12

Tony walked quietly into his mother's room. She lay sleeping peacefully, as usual. In sleep, her face wore a tiny smile. "Poor thing, how long will this drag out?" he wondered. He sat down by her bed and leaned back with his eyes closed.

"Are you all right, son?"

Her voice startled him. He couldn't get used to the fact that sometimes it seemed she was in a coma, but at other times, she was lucid and alert. He longed to be able to bounce problems off her, but couldn't trust her mind anymore. As if she read his, she spoke softly, "It's okay. I don't mind. I know you are busy and will take care of our family. That's all I ask. You're responsible for everyone, you know. Answers come from unlikely places and at unusual times. Remember, son, sometimes family is all you have." Closing her eyes, she faded back into her world.

Tony stood gazing out the window, watching evening move silently into the town. Streetlights flickered on as the houses around them settled in for the night. Off in the distance, a dog barked. From somewhere, the air carried the sounds of children laughing. Next door, the old couple sat on their porch, visiting. Neither could hear well. As they had done for decades, they sat yelling at each other in Italian, rocking, holding hands.

As he listened to their chatter, Tony's mind wandered to Annie again.

"Just can't get her out of my mind," he chided himself. For a man like Tony, that was not a good thing. All these years he had never loved any woman. Oh, there had been women, just none that he trusted or even enjoyed talking with. It wasn't a good idea, given his career choice. Better to not give anyone anything to use against him. He smiled to himself. Annie would be a handful. He doubted she took "no" to heart very well. She was so unlike anyone he had ever been involved with, or even been around. She was elegant and refined; at the same time, she possessed an innocence he found he could not resist. She had an air about her. Even at that brief moment when he first saw her standing in front of the post office, the sun infusing her hair with golden light, twirling around so freely and smiling so easily. Her eyes only added to his captivation. To take her into this family would be an unprecedented step. His was not an ordinary family. People came into his family to stay.

His research had revealed she was wealthy, well traveled, and definitely not settled. He couldn't imagine her being dumped into the middle of all this. At that thought, a fierce desire to protect her filled him. But he knew the project was more important. It must not fail; too many people would be at risk. Still, Annie's face and smile drifted in and out of his mind. The image of her pitifully trying to hide in her bubble bath made him smile again. He knew she was going to take someone with patience and a strong hand, and suddenly he realized he intended to be that someone. The prize would be well worth it. She embodied the Italian word for sweetheart—inamorata. He was amazed at how quickly and completely he had fallen victim to Annie.

CHAPTER 13

Lynn turned off the county road slowly and passed the last bridge, driving beyond the barns and corrals. Knocking loudly, she was greeted by a bark. Shortly, Annie opened the door. "You're a sight, girl. Go back to bed. I can make myself at home."

"No, no," Annie yawned, "I think I've run on empty a little too long."

The guest room was situated at the top left of the stairs, next to the master suite. Smaller, but with an elegant bath and French doors leading onto the patio, it looked like a luxury suite in Las Vegas. Lynn threw her suitcase on the bed and began to unpack.

The smell of fresh coffee drew her into the kitchen. The sisters were just sitting down when a phone rang. It was not a familiar ring to either, and it took a moment for Annie to surmise it must be the phone Tony had given her. She ran to answer and was surprised to hear his voice. "How are you doing?"

"I'm fine. Lynn just got here." Annie was intoxicated by his sexy voice and realized she could get used to his late-night phone calls.

"I know. Thought I would let you know that guy who was driving is gone. Oh, I had your house cleared of bugs," he added.

Annie laughed, "When did you do that? I mean, that was thoughtful of you, but it's too cold and high for most bugs. Why on earth would you do that?"

Tony paused, smiled to himself, then explained, "I mean listening devices, Annie."

"Are you serious?" The smile left Annie's face. Did you find anything?"

"Yes. It was not active. I would guess Allen left it. I'll talk to you tomorrow. Lock up."

"Bye, boss." Annie grinned into the phone.

"There's a novel idea," Tony thought. "That would be okay too."

Annie was bringing Lynn up to date on everything when her cell rang. She was relieved to hear Rhino. "You wanted two tickets to the Red Tie Gala. It wasn't easy, but I'm sending you a couple of airline tickets and passes to the Gala overnight. It takes place next week. Doesn't give you much time. I also did a little research. It's a big shindig. I don't like the idea of you getting into this, Annie. Be careful. By the way, don't trust your friend Jacko; he works for the guys from Columbia. Can't get into details, but he's not a nice guy. He would be the only one there who would recognize you, I think. It'll be a full house, girl . . . wish you would change your mind. I'm glad you're taking someone with you; take care, Annie." The line went dead.

Annie shared with Lynn what she had asked of Rhino. Immediately attracted to the idea, Annie was already planning on how they could get their hands on more information. "I don't know how he did it, but he did. Maybe we could find out what Jacko is up to, or who is really after Allen. It could be someone other than Jacko."

Lynn was more wary. "Do we want to find out who is after Allen? And just what do we do with that information, if we get it?"

"I'm not certain. Honestly, I don't know how we would even know if we happen to run into someone of interest. I think we should go anyway. Just think, we'll do a little shopping, eat at some great restaurants . . . this is going to be fun, Lynn. I want to stay near Central Park. Do you have any idea how many art galleries there are in New York?!"

CHAPTER 14

Jacko left Dragon's suite and headed for his favorite hangout, Welby's Bar and Grill. The liquor was expensive, but good; the women were too. Tonight, though, it wasn't the liquor or the women he was interested in. He entered the lounge unnoticed, and as he moved up the stairs, he paused to survey the crowd. He never noticed the man sitting under the edge of the stairwell, but the man noticed him.

Jacko couldn't get used to having to knock and be admitted to the office, but for now he went along with the games. The office was large, its décor reflecting the taste of José Hernandez, the head of the gang from Venezuela. Every man in the room was a new member; they all knew José. No one knew the gringo, Jacko. None trusted the gringo. Jacko's Spanish being excellent, he knew he was the subject of conversation. Some guy found a body while fishing in the river near Zacatecas, Mexico. The body fit the age and date of death; the man reporting believed it was Allen Kirk. The victim had been beaten and shot. Jacko hoped it was Allen. "You're lucky we finally find your job. By tomorrow, *you* would be the next job," commented one of the men. The others sitting around laughed.

Jacko ignored the comment and made a mental note to check with

Fish. He didn't remember anything about him shooting Allen, but the date and location made sense. When Allen failed to turn up in Denver, Jacko had him traced to Mexico. The last sighting was in the area where the body was found. Fish was to contact someone he used in Mexico to finish Allen. "Where will we meet next week?"

Several men turned to look at him. "You're not invited, Jacko. You're not a boss," said one of the men, sneering. Jacko clenched his teeth. One day very soon, every man in this room would wish he had been more respectful. Jacko wouldn't forget. He listened to their talk for a while, then left.

Cece was a small, slender woman. She had worked the bar for five years. With her flashing black eyes and ready smile, she was the pet of the usual crowd. While the place didn't advertise women, Cece would never turn down a good thing. Jacko looked like he had money. When he took Cece to the room, he was in a sour mood. She paid . . . he didn't.

* * * *

The woman with housekeeping was worried. Cece had been a favorite of the men who had their secret meetings upstairs with the patrón, José Hernandez. Someone would be sorry for this act. She knew Hernandez was fond of the spirited Cece, keeping her for himself as much as possible. Timidly, the maid climbed the stairs and knocked on the door. "Yes?"

"Señor, pardon, pero Cece es—"

"Yes?"

"How you say . . . dead. Someone beat her very bad, last night. I think I should tell you before I call the police."

As soon as he was summoned, the young man stepped into the room and spoke quietly. "Please, let me make it right for Cece. Let me take the gringo." From his post beneath the stairs, he had witnessed who had been the last one to leave her room. The men looked at the boy and recognized the face of hate and revenge. This one was always in the background, doing whatever was asked of him. Maybe it was time for him to move up. A fitting end for the gringo. The leader nodded.

"He disappears, do you understand? No more on this earth. Today!"

"With pleasure, Señor."

* * * *

For the first time in his life, Jacko felt fear. As he looked into his rearview mirror, he didn't recognize the face in his backseat, but he knew all too well the look in the young man's eyes. Jacko's final night dragged out for an eternity. He screamed in vain. He begged in vain. He had never imagined such pain. Jacko's last conscious thought was of the youth calmly telling Jacko that Cece had been his sister.

CHAPTER 15

Annie spent several hours online, reading everything she could find about the Gala. She also copied every picture from recent events. Armed, she went in search of her sister.

"I just got off the Net. The Gala was originally to raise money for kids in bad neighborhoods. The sponsors are mostly big companies from New York, Chicago, Washington. Allen said the bosses don't always meet during the Gala, but he thought they would this time. It'll be worth going to see, just to watch how they pull it off. It's formal, so you and I need to go shopping."

Lynn cringed. She hated dances. Even having her sister as a date didn't help much, since it would be doubtful two women waltzing would go unnoticed. "Do women still dance together?"

"What? You're kidding!" Annie laughed. "Come on; it's like riding a bicycle or horse. Once you learn . . . and you were the best, bar none. Now, finding a gown for a five-foot midget in the *women's* evening wear department may be a problem, but we'll do the best we can."

"Very funny!"

The sisters spent the day in Trinidad looking for something appropriate to wear.

Driving back, gowns in trunk, Lynn asked, "Just what are you going to tell this Tony guy and Jacko?"

"I'm not going to say anything to Jacko, and maybe I won't have to. Haven't heard from him in a while, so I'm assuming his plans have changed yet again. The problem is getting him off the ranch. Maybe we could change locks. That's always a strong hint you're not wanted." Annie smiled at the thought.

"Tony will be a little harder," she continued. "I don't want him to know what we're doing, but I'm a terrible liar. I'm reasonably certain he would never approve of what we are doing. He is unbelievably bossy, Lynn. Sometimes I have to really work to keep from laughing at him. Don't think he would take that too well. I admit, the fact that he is in the Mafia, is the boss, and has all these men around him all the time makes things a little strange." Annie shook her head. "I still have a hard time with the 'Mafia' piece."

"I should hope," Lynn added sarcastically. "He really is, you know. His name is all over the Internet."

"I know. I looked him up." Annie paused. "But he shouldn't expect me to sit around and hope our family will be safe, Allen will be okay, and Jacko will go away. Finding that poor guy dead sort of sealed our involvement, as far as I'm concerned. Not to mention Allen's being attacked. The ranch is involved, at least, if not the rest of us. Who knows, maybe we might notice something at the Gala that would help Allen."

"So just what are we doing?"

"Maybe when we see him next we can tell Allen who was there. I haven't a clue what he would have been looking for, but we might pick up something just by being observers."

"You honestly think Tony what's his name is going to let you move forward with all this?" Lynn was shaking her head.

"We have to try. What he doesn't know he can't protest, right? Besides, what makes him think he has the right to tell me what I can and cannot do?

Both were silent for a few miles before Lynn suggested, "Let's try Earl. I think we could use some good news."

Earl answered right away and Lynn put him on speaker. Both of his sisters knew instantly things were not normal. Although he was as cheerful as usual, his tone was troubled.

"Hey. How are you two doing? Everything okay?"

"Absolutely. We're just wondering how you boys were getting along," Lynn said. "Is Allen getting better?"

"He's not getting up and around as fast as I'd hoped, to be honest. Guess it's age. I've tried to call you guys a couple of times. Can't get through very well." Earl's call broke.

"Earl, are you still there?" Lynn frowned at Annie. "I think we've lost him—"

"Hello?" Earl's voice came through again. "Listen, I don't have a lot of time, but you two need to know some things. I hate like hell having to do this, but I don't think Allen will be much help for a while. He's contacted a friend who will get in touch with you. I'm—we're—worried about you two. It's a project Allen's been working on for quite a while . . . Listen, you need to stay away from Jacko. Leave the ranch if you have to, but just get rid of him. I'm thinking . . ." The line cracked again and went dead. Lynn and Annie looked at each other, both anxious.

Annie groaned. "This is getting ridiculous. How will we know who the 'friend' is? On top of that, Earl thinks we can get rid of Jacko? How on earth would we do that?" She gripped the steering wheel, "All I wanted was a simple summer vacation."

* * * *

As the Escalade pulled into the drive, Buster greeted the sisters happily. That was a good sign. Lynn stopped at the door and watched Annie, who had walked to the east side of the porch and stood looking out over the fields. "Are you okay?" Lynn asked.

"I guess. I think this has really gotten a lot bigger than Allen planned. I sometimes wish I were still in Arizona, you know?"

"I know what you mean. But hey, maybe this little jaunt will help Allen, like you said. Who knows? Besides, we're in too deep now. We can't let him go on alone; we need to be his eyes and ears while he's in hiding. Anyway, you love to travel, and maybe we can catch a play or something. Come on, I'm starving. So is Buster." Lynn led the way into the house.

* * * *

"Let's see; Buster should be fine. We'll only be gone for a long weekend. He used to live outside all the time." Annie mulled. "We want to be seen around. Let's hit town again on Monday, get the mail, wander around a little, and come on back then we can head out Wednesday. Now, about Tony. Who knows . . . maybe we can slip out without even talking to him."

By Wednesday, the sisters were packed. Annie was beginning to worry about the silence from Jacko. Tony, however, was not silent. He called regularly. She never knew just when he would call, but she heard from him every day. It was a call she enjoyed; however, it would make this trip a tad difficult. "I think the next time Tony calls, I'll tell him you live in Wyoming, and I'll be with you. He wouldn't have to know where we're planning to visit. I'll tell him I will check in with him, since the phone reception is awful in the mountains. I've never told him just where you live, so he can't really check up on me too much. We'll be back by Monday. We can go into town as usual, and he'll be none the wiser. Besides, I nearly forgot, I need to let him know Rhino thinks Jacko is working with the Columbians. Maybe he'll focus on that tidbit. What do you think?"

"Yeah, why not?" Lynn rolled her eyes, shaking her head. "I suppose it could work."

Annie called, but was asked to leave a message, as Tony was not available. She did, adding Rhino's tip regarding Jacko's connection with the Columbians. Then, they were off.

CHAPTER 16

"I've always loved coming to New York to play, but one has to wonder how people live in such a rush." Annie was standing looking out the window toward Central Park. Their rooms were spacious and cheery. "Rhino booked the Ritz-Carlton for me. Only the best."

Lynn joined her at the window. Still uncomfortable about the evening ahead of them, she asked, "Just what are we looking for, Annie, and what do we do if we find it? We need some sort of a plan."

"Well," Annie started, "Rhino and Allen told us the event is a cover for people to meet without causing a stir. Rhino gave me good descriptions of people I 'may find interesting,' as he put it. If we wander around, we may even overhear something. When we get back, we'll check off people we've seen against the photos I printed off from my Google searches so we'll have names to put with the faces."

"Humph!" Lynn turned away from the window. "Sounds like we're just dangling ourselves out like this week's special. At least let's have some kind of story, in case anyone takes the time to ask us who *we* are."

"Oh, we have a story. We're buyers for The Blue Dawn," Annie called to Lynn from the master bath, where she had begun putting on her makeup.

"The what?"

"The Blue Dawn; it's a fantastic art brokerage firm. They only deal with the finest of merchandise."

Now Lynn laughed. "You're kidding, right?"

"No, I'm serious. That's the name of my business."

"I thought your business was *Annie's Loft*."

"It is. But I created a spinoff company I call The Blue Dawn. I discovered pretty quickly the hunt for things is what gives me the greatest kick. At first, I kept specific people in mind as I went about searching for antiques. Before long, I started getting requests. I've studied, read, and listened to everything I can. You wouldn't believe the artists and sellers I've met and made friends with over time. Rhino helped me with the phantom male's voice on the answering machine so clients think The Blue Dawn is run by a man."

"Does this guy have a name?" Lynn was intrigued.

"Yep . . . Leonard. I sort of borrowed Mom's name. You know, Lenora/Leonard."

A while later, when they were ready to leave, Lynn teased, "Okay then, Leonard, I guess we'd better get going."

* * * *

The elegant Broad Street Ballroom was filling with people. Laughter and conversation produced a low hum in the huge venue, and an air of excitement permeated the affair. The lights dimmed near the edge of the ballroom, and it was here that the small table reserved for The Blue Dawn was set. Several other tables had women or men only at them, and so far, Annie could think of nothing that would make anyone take note of her and Lynn.

The evening wore on, and the sisters took in everything. Speeches ended, the meal served, and the remnants swept away before the orchestra started to play and the dancing began. Annie noted several men nodding and talking. She knew at least two of them were in the group of photos she had studied. The men moved about the room, speaking casually to people, but constantly surveying the crowd.

"Those guys are obviously bodyguards or something," commented

Lynn as she followed Annie's glance. "Hope they don't see us and come over for some reason."

Annie nodded, realizing that the crowd was made up of different groups, each sitting close together and watching the others. The effect it produced was strange—and for the first time that evening amid the glitter and gold, she felt afraid.

CHAPTER 17

*T*ony sat watching the people thoughtfully. His table—strategically placed near an exit, out of any direct light, and providing a full view of the floor—was circled by his men; each with a specific assignment. By evening's end, he would know who had attended this affair and, more important, who had not.

His thoughts were suddenly interrupted. There she sat calmly sipping a drink and laughing at something her sister had just said. Tony leaned forward slightly, looking closely in disbelief. A vision of confidence and beauty. A vision he would have never dreamed would be here, in this place. "What the hell is she doing here?" he fumed to himself. Instantly taking charge of his emotions, however, he realized that he had to get them out of the ballroom. Tony watched as they both stood.

Annie leisurely walked across the room, and feelings he was unaccustomed to dealing with forced their way into his mind. Her gown was a soft dark gray material, gently gathered at the neckline and held in place by large pearl clasps on each shoulder. The gown fluttered down to the floor, gracefully draping her slim figure. With each step, the gown swirled around her. Her hair was piled up on top of her head, with wavy wisps escaping on the sides and more slipping down her neck. A triple strand of misshapen pearls encircled her neck; matching pearls dangling at her ears swayed as she moved. She walked as if she owned the room, and from Tony's standpoint, she did.

In spite of the anger at her presence, he could feel his heart swell while watching her. He had learned long ago to trust his instincts. He knew he was completely captivated by this graceful flower, and he also knew the timing couldn't be worse. Tony leaned over and whispered something to Lou. Shortly thereafter, another of Tony's men left through the door behind him. Tony and Lou stood up. His plan began.

The lines at the elaborate dessert buffet and bar had thinned somewhat, so the sisters made their way easily through the line. Slowly, they wandered back to their table. Watching all the activity, Annie sipped her coffee.

Lynn broke into her thoughts. "Annie, you told Tony you were going to Wyoming, right?"

"Yes. The message I left was that you and I were heading out, and that you lived in Wyoming? I never said I was *going* to Wyoming."

"He does know you don't get to Wyoming from Aguilar by going through New York City, right?"

"Of course, silly. He just doesn't know *where* in Wyoming you live. Why?"

"Not that I've met him, understand, but I'd bet my house that's him . . . headed this way. And he doesn't look very happy. Don't turn around."

Although Lynn had warned Annie, she was still taken aback when Tony finally made his way through the crowd and reached their table. She had no idea he might have come to New York.

Composing herself as best she could, Annie quickly introduced her sister. "Lynn, this is Mr. Tuscano and Lou. Lou is Mr. Tuscano's project manager." Annie caught the hint of a wink from Lou at hearing her job description for him. His grin was unmistakable. "Gentlemen, my sister, Lynn."

Lou smiled amiably at Lynn. "Let's you and I dance, ma'am," he said politely. Not waiting for an answer, he pulled her up and stepped out onto the dance floor with her. Lynn looked back at Annie like someone going under water for the third time. Annie had her own issues to deal with.

With narrowed eyes and clenched jaw, Tony extended his hand to

Annie without speaking. Tentatively, she balked. "I . . . well, really, I can't dance to this music, Tony."

He continued staring at her, his hand still extended. As the music started, Annie reached up to slip her hand into his; it was warm, his grasp firm. The moment their fingers made contact, a tremor stirred through her unlike anything she had ever experienced. Ignoring her feeble objections, Tony walked her to the center of the ballroom. The sounds of Strauss's "Blue Danube Waltz" filled the air. He began to dance—gracefully, silently, gently guiding her. Shaking her head slightly in dismay, Annie followed.

"Relax, Annie. I wouldn't wring your neck in public."

"Except for that 'I could kill you' look you're wearing," she thought, "it feels wonderful to have your arm around me." She could never have imagined him holding her so closely, nor believed his touch could awaken in her such a powerful response. And for a fleeting moment, she stopped thinking about the trouble she was certain she was in with this man who whirled her around the room so elegantly. The music filled every corner, and Annie could feel the rhythm deep within her soul. Turn after turn, they danced. To her surprise, she found herself following his lead, flawlessly. Forgetting herself, she smiled, glancing up at him to find he was looking down at her, his gaze penetrating but warm.

"Are you lying to me now, too, Annie?" he finally admonished quietly, breaking the spell.

Annie held her breath, trying to think just what to say. When she didn't answer, Tony continued. "Did you honestly believe I would forget Lynn was with you? Although, technically, you are visiting with Lynn and she does live in Wyoming. Was that it?" His tone was unmistakably reprimanding.

Annie remained quiet for a moment, blushing, praying he wouldn't notice. "I knew you would not really approve of my being here, but I couldn't lie to you, Tony. In truth, I am a terrible liar. It was easier to leave some details out," she admitted quietly, looking up at him. His eyes were kind but somber. As he listened to her, he held her closer. He instinctively knew she would find it hard to lie about anything to anyone.

"You dance very well," he observed softly, adding, "you are so beautiful." That put the issue to rest. He felt her relax within his embrace. She ducked her head slightly, blushing deeply. Tony smiled.

Relieved he was no longer angry with her, Annie let a small sigh escape. "I have never done this before, honestly, but I do so love the music."

"Just remember this dance, Annie." His voice was deep and gentle. "Follow my lead." He could not afford to be distracted. Too many people depended on his direction. She had to allow him to command her, for everyone's survival. He knew she must do what she was told, when she was told. She had not asked for this, but it was hers, anyway. Circumstances placed her in the middle of Allen's crisis, and Tony meant to protect her.

When he started to lead her away, his hand moved to her waist as he pulled her closer. Again, she felt the tremor within her.

Nearing the door where his men waited patiently, Tony paused, turning her face up to his. "Annie," he spoke quietly, "you have to do just what I say now, or I cannot protect you. This is not Colorado." Tony hesitated briefly. His intuition was always on target. He had never felt more certain. Tony was even more confident, feeling the whisper of a tremble from her with his every touch. "I love you, Annie. It will not be easy, and we will be apart many times, but never doubt how I feel. We have a lot to discuss. Our families, our businesses. For now, I'm sending both you and Lynn to safety. I will join you after midnight." His look was tender, but something in his tone ended the conversation. Tony lifted her chin and softly kissed her lips.

As he moved with her out the door, Annie could see a car waiting. She could hardly walk she was so unsettled. As he handed her off to another man—someone she didn't know—Tony squeezed her hand. His touch was gentle. With a nod of his head, he turned and left without a word. Annie walked toward the car, feeling a little like someone caught skipping school. Tony's frank admission of his feelings for her shook her deeply. "How could he feel something like that so fast? What have I gotten myself into now?" she mused.

Sliding into the car, Annie found Lynn already seated there. She was not at all happy at being packaged and sent away. Annie tapped the window between the passenger and driver seats. "Could you take us to the

Ritz-Carlton at 50 Central Park South, please?" The driver—yet another man Annie didn't recognize—just turned and smiled at them.

* * * *

Although neither sister knew where they were, it certainly was *not* the Ritz-Carlton.

They surveyed the small well-used room. It contained a double bed with a sagging mattress, a spartan bath without complimentary toiletries, a wobbly chair, and a small chipped desk. Flowered wallpaper was peeling near the floorboard and ceiling, which bore several large brown water stains. The television was old, mounted on an unsteady metal TV tray, and stood several feet from the wall. The dark brown carpet was worn and shabby. A balcony on which they could see two white plastic chairs overlooked the beautiful city wonderland of lights. For a long time, the sisters stood side by side looking at life beyond the building, neither speaking.

Finally, Lynn observed glumly, "I like our own rooms better."

"So do I," Annie agreed.

"I didn't know New York even had any motels with balconies," Lynn muttered.

Taking her shoes off, Annie tentatively stretched out on the bed after carefully pulling the spread back. "A person could get used to all this, you know," she commented sarcastically.

"Well, was this evening worth it?"

Annie had closed her eyes, still hearing Tony's words. "I think I'm in over my head," she finally admitted. She had not the drive to share Tony's admission with Lynn—yet.

Lynn contemplated Annie's subdued answer. Keeping her own counsel, Lynn turned the television on to catch the news.

"This just in, the Red Tie Gala was raided by federal, state, and local authorities this evening as attendees were waltzing away the night. Stunned patrons of the fund-raiser were shocked as gunfire broke out. News media have been shut out. Further updates will be brought to you as developments come in." Annie sat upright in bed; both sisters were stunned.

"Tony must have known; that's why he hustled us out. We've got to get out of here, Annie. We can't be linked to Tony now. I'm certain he's involved somehow. What if someone were to recognize us? We need to get back to our hotel," Lynn observed with anguish.

She was already heading for the door. Opening it slowly, she peered out into the hall. It was empty. Lynn quickly stepped out. "Come on, it's clear!" She began running toward an exit sign at the end of the hall.

Annie started to follow, then turned back into the room. "Wait, I need my phone!" She ran across the room, grabbed her phone from the bed, picked up her wallet, and slipped into her shoes; as she spun back around, she ran into a man.

* * * *

"Hi, I'm Sam."

He pushed her back into the room, followed by Tony and Lou. "Lock up. Move it!" Tony barked.

Annie struggled away from Sam and ran toward the door. "Lynn is out there. Wait!" Sam pulled her back again.

"We already have Lynn; got her out safe, but no time to get both of you. Too bad for you, you're so slow." He grinned. The door was secured and the lights were turned off.

"What's . . ." She didn't finish. Tony put his finger to his lips and shook his head as he pulled her across the room. Everyone moved away from the door. The sounds of crashing doors echoed. People were running in the halls, yelling.

Annie was already being steered toward the balcony. "They're coming in; we have to get out." Tony's voice was urgent.

Wide-eyed, Annie stood frozen. "*Out! How?* We're toast!"

With lightning speed, Lou opened the sliding door to the balcony. From the eighth floor, with the suggestion of getting off the balcony in her head, the wonderland of lights was turning into a dangerous city sprawled below. Pulling her behind him, Tony followed Sam out, who skillfully slid the catch rod into place and pulled the slider closed.

"I can't . . . really, I can't do this. I'm terrified of heights," Annie gasped, staring at the lights dancing below. Unbelieving, she watched as Sam easily mounted the railing of the balcony and jumped to the next one, about three feet away. Tony went next.

"Your turn," Lou spoke gently but with urgency.

"I can't, Lou, I just can't!" whispered Annie. Her stomach tightened, her pulse quickened, and she felt as if she could not breathe. "I can't do this," her hand went to her throat. In desperation, she turned and looked at Lou for empathy.

"Look at me!" commanded Tony sharply. "Stop looking down, Annie! Look at me! You can do this. Now! There's no time to think about it. You do what I say, when I say! Now, Annie!"

Annie kept her eyes on Tony as she tried to pull her gown away from her feet. Lou pulled out his knife, and with two quick slashes, the bottom half of the dress fell to the floor. Lou tossed it to the street below. His actions staggered Annie. "This gown cost me a fortune!" she wanted to scream. She couldn't get onto the railing in her heels. Pausing only a moment, she tossed her shoes over to follow the remnant of her gown and climbed up barefoot. Keeping her eye on the next balcony, clutching her wallet and phone, she leapt. Somehow, she made it. Tony grasped her, pulling her down from the railing, and slipping his tuxedo jacket around her shoulders. No time for congratulations, though; already Sam was repeating the process onto the next balcony. Annie's fear, manifested as anger, broke through as she snarled, "I can't do this," and jerked the jacket on and buttoned it, stuffing her wallet and phone into a pocket. "I hate heights . . ." she protested, but she followed nevertheless.

On the fourth balcony, they came to a corner. Annie moaned, shaking her head in disbelief. "Great! Just when I get the hang of it, now what?" A large pipe with step stakes was mounted against the wall. Sam immediately began to climb. Tony followed, and Lou pushed Annie forward. Aghast, Annie looked up. Two floors remained. Behind her, she felt Lou pushing. Above her, she saw Tony beckoning her. Then, pointing to Lou, he air slit his throat. The message was clear. She refused to be the cause of Lou getting killed. Annie grasped the small step and began to climb. Concentrating on each step, refusing to look at anything else, she moved as fast as she could.

Reaching the top, she was pulled over the edge and onto the roof, which reeked of old smoke and fresh trash. Tony pushed her down flat, next to him, as Sam helped Lou. Lying with her head on her arms she heard Tony speaking on his phone. Horns honked and cars raced along the streets below. She could hear yelling to their left. Afraid to look up, she kept her head down, praying they would get wherever they were headed.

"He thinks we were never in the room because the safety rod is still in the door. Glad I picked that little trick up, boss. Says they've been duped."

"They have been," Tony answered softly.

"Are you sure Lynn is safe?" Annie whispered. She couldn't stop shaking.

Tony put his arm over her. "I'm positive. She is much safer than we are at the moment. Don't worry." He made another call, spoke to Lou and Sam in Italian, then handed Lou his phone. She could hear Lou, quietly speaking in Italian.

Everyone lay in silence.

* * * *

After what seemed hours, Annie heard a helicopter. Following the sound, she watched the chopper set down. Faintly, over the noise, she could hear sirens in the distance. "Please no, I can't get into that thing. I just can't!" she screamed inside her head. Annie squeezed her eyes shut and willed the chopper to leave. It didn't.

"Come on, Annie, crawl low. Hurry!" ordered Tony, jerking at the sleeve of the tuxedo jacket.

They crawled over spent cigarette butts, smatters of decaying food, and beer cans. As Annie reached the helicopter, she was pulled up and into the belly of the machine. While Tony and Lou were sliding in over the edge, behind her, the chopper rose. "Oh no!" Annie murmured, unable to keep her voice from shaking. Her fear came to the surface as anger yet again. "You have no idea how much I hate heights. I could have fallen!" she yelled at Tony over the noise of the blades. She was still kneeling in the middle of the craft afraid to move.

"You could have been shot, after whatever else they would have planned for you." Tony calmly yelled back, squatting to lean against the inside wall of the chopper.

Turning enough to reach him, Annie hit his shoulder. "The eighth floor? You have to have a high floor! Are you serious? This can't be the first time this has happened to you!" She crawled away from him and leaned back against the boxes that filled the back of the craft. Closing her eyes, she began to shake again. Never in her life had she been so frightened. She felt like crying; instead she glared at Tony.

"Come here," Tony called to her as he stretched out his legs and sat back.

"No! Leave me alone! I'm angry at you!" she retorted, furiously shoving her fallen hair from her face, smearing her cheek with soot from her hand. Trying to clean the dirt and cement debris off her scraped legs and hands, she ignored him. One lone tear found its way down her cheek. Annie brushed her face with the sleeve of Tony's tailored jacket.

"Angry, but not hysterical," Tony mused. He was pleased that she was still in control. He had no idea how she would react to something like this, and she had done well. A smile crept upon his face. "Come here," he repeated, this time more firmly.

"You've *got* to be kidding," Annie snapped back, glaring across the chopper. "You lead me eight stories above ground . . . no . . . above cement, not ground . . . *cement*! I have to climb what I'm certain was a pipe meant for water to run DOWN, not *up*, and now I'm in a helicopter. I can't look! I get motion sickness real easily, and . . . and . . . no, I'm not moving! I'll die before I throw up in front of you people!"

She was certain she heard Lou laugh, but she ignored him. As the chopper began to descend, Annie finally opened her eyes. Tentatively, she looked out. They were coming to another building. Rolling her eyes in disbelief, she leaned back. "Great! Now I'll have to crawl down *off* this roof," she thought.

With her eyes shut again, she asked, "Are you sure Lynn is okay?"

For a moment, Tony just watched her, smiling. "If you come here, we can discuss it."

"When this thing is still, I'll come." She knew Lynn was fine. Tony would never discuss her sister so casually if she were in danger.

"No. Remember the dance, Annie. You do what I ask, when I ask, just like everyone else."

"I'm not like everyone else, Tony. *I'm a normal person!*" she shot back, her voice breaking. Annie could hear someone behind her laughing. "I'm scared. I never asked for any of this. I don't know what's going on, and I have to do things I never thought I would ever have to do in my life. Thanks to you, I won't be able to step out onto a balcony ever again!"

Annie turned to face Tony. "I feel responsible for Lynn and Allen. I may have made everything worse for Allen. It's impossible not to think of all the things that could go wrong . . . like *falling!*" He was watching her intently, with his head tipped slightly to the side, a smile on his face. She knew he listened to each word, yet she knew he probably couldn't begin to understand her feelings. She bet he had never been afraid of anything in his life.

"Come *here*, Annie," he repeated. His voice was still calm, but this time it held an unmistakable note of authority.

Just grateful to be alive, Annie took a deep breath and gave in. She knew this man was not in the habit of having to repeat any request twice, let alone three or four times. She was a little uncertain about pushing her limits with him. If she had not snuck off to the dance, she wouldn't be in this predicament. Glancing out the window again, shaking her head and muttering, she started crawling across the floor of the cargo bay.

"Don't worry, Annie. We have a rope ladder to get off this next hotel, and it's not one floor higher," Sam called to her.

Frozen, Annie slowly raised her head to look at him. Only when she saw his wide grin did she realize he was teasing her. "Funny, Sam! Real funny!"

Tentatively, she stood up. Wobbling, she made her way toward Tony. He sat still, with his hand outstretched to her. Taking his hand, she felt the same tremor. Hoping he could not feel her tremble, she sat down gingerly.

"See, that wasn't so hard, eh?" Lou couldn't resist saying.

"You have no idea, Lou. I hate heights. I *really, really* hate them."

Tony slipped his arm around her and pulled her closer. "You're still beautiful," he whispered.

Annie blushed, but her fear was beginning to subside. "Just like the dance," she reminded herself.

"What happened back there?" Annie asked quietly. She was still shaking.

"I had to get you someplace safe. You were sent to one of our safe houses, but my driver was followed. If you hadn't pulled that stunt, this night might have turned out like we planned. Don't do something like that again, Annie." Although his manner was kindly, his tone left no doubt it was not a request but an order. Annie fell silent.

She was concerned that she may have placed anyone's life in danger. And she was more than a little embarrassed he was scolding her in front of his men. As if he discerned her distress, he held her tighter.

As everyone made their way down the stairs off the roof, Tony and his men began to discuss what could happen next. Annie was too uncomfortable to register what was being said as she tried to limp with dignity beside Tony. She was in what was left of a torn gown, had skinned knees, skinned hands, and was barefoot and bruised. Her makeup was gone, her hair looked like the worst bed head, and she was filthy. But, she was alive and *walking* down. With her head up and wearing a forced smile, she marched on. Inside the building, they were led to a suite. Men stood outside the doors, and although one raised an eyebrow ever so slightly, he opened up the door for them.

"Has to be the penthouse," Annie noted sweetly to no one in particular.

Lou chuckled. "But without a balcony, you'll notice." Annie glanced at him in time to see him grin. At least he didn't think she was awful, even if he did have to scramble up the side of some building because of her.

Sam stepped in first, looking for Lynn, followed by Tony, Annie, and Lou. Lynn jumped up and ran to them. "Annie, are you okay? Oh my gosh, you look like something the cat dragged in!" she exclaimed.

"Thank you. That's just how I feel!" Annie still could not believe what she had just done.

Once everyone was inside, Tony spoke. "We have business to attend to. You two ladies stay put, make yourselves comfortable. I'll have clothes sent up. There's plenty to eat. If you decide to roam, you'll do so with a bodyguard; his name is Spook. He's the boss, understand? We'll keep in touch. Gentlemen?"

Tony paused at the door. Turning, his eyes found Annie's. She met his gaze, shaking her head in disbelief at all she had just done. He nodded back with approval, smiling slightly.

With that, everyone was gone. Lynn had no idea who had brought her to the current suite, nor could she coerce the men with her into talking. Neither sister had any idea where they were.

They took a moment to look around and admire their surroundings. The suite was large, with separate areas for dining, leisure, and sleeping. Colors ranged from soft yellow to soft beige. Accents in olive green and gold complimented the décor. The marble bath offered every convenience. Beneath a thick, soft comforter was a king bed, piled with pillows of every size. Fresh flowers brightened up each room.

While Annie took a long hot shower, Lynn poured them each a glass of wine from the fully stocked bar. When Annie rejoined her, wearing the luxuriant Egyptian cotton robe provided, Lynn proposed a toast. "I'm thinking we're going to be safe for the next day or so." They both began to relax.

"I'm so glad you're all right. Lynne, you won't believe what happened to me tonight." Talking late into the night, each filled the other in on what had happened since they were separated in the motel.

Eventually Annie realized with a start what time it was. "Wow, it's nearly morning! We need to get to bed. Heaven only knows what will happen tomorrow."

"You got it. But there's still one more thing that's weighing on me, Annie. Not that it's any of my business, but Tony *is* a boss. I mean a *real* boss, like in the mob. He's not who you should get involved with, I'm thinking."

"I know. Believe me, I know. I just can't think about it anymore." Annie made a face at Lynn. "My head aches, my knees hurt, and my mind is all over the board. It *is* your business, by the way. You're my sister, you know."

Lynn gave her sister a warm hug then she dragged a chair over to the door and shoved it under the knob. At Annie's puzzled look, Lynn admitted, "You know, just in case. At least we'll hear if anyone tries to get in."

With that, Annie turned off the lights, and they both crawled into the king-sized bed.

CHAPTER 18

After a good night's sleep and another morning shower, Annie felt better even though both knees were scraped, as was one elbow; her shoulders ached, and her neck was stiff.

Bundled once more in the hotel's complimentary robe, Annie checked with the airline about changing their return reservations. Annie was dumbstruck when she heard that their confirmation number was cancelled. Just as she was wondering whether that was Tony's doing or someone else's, a large package arrived from Tony. Inside, she found clothes for both Lynn and her.

She woke Lynn up right away. "Rise and shine girl. I can't believe you slept longer than I did. You'll be pleased to know we do not have to roam around in gowns. Whoever picked this stuff out—and I suspect it was Tony himself—has great taste!"

"Not that you *had* a gown to roam around in," Lynn noted laughing.

"I never even thought about how I must have looked to those guys. I was so afraid of falling!" Annie grimaced, remembering her state of undress.

Dressed and eager to get out of the room, they opened the suite door to find a man standing outside. He was obviously keeping an eye on them.

"Tony said you might want to wander around a little. I hope breakfast is in your plans," he cheerily greeted them. It was, and the newspaper articles they read during breakfast sent them looking for a computer; someplace quiet. They nixed the idea of using the computer stations at the hotel—too public. A library seemed an obvious choice. Spook knew just the place.

He left them at the front door, noting he would be around whenever they were ready to leave. It was late afternoon when they finally emerged from the library. True to his word, Spook sat patiently reading a paper on a bench near the entrance. After a quick bite, all three returned to the hotel.

Annie and Lynn sat down and went over the copious notes they had taken. Every name they looked up had some link to crime families, gangs, and cartels. "I thought Allen said the cartels weren't in on this."

"Maybe he didn't know they were," Lynn reasoned. "From what the paper says, everyone is involved. Don't you think it strange we didn't see anything about your friend, Tony?"

"Guess we can surmise there are others who slipped out too," Annie noted. "You didn't see anyone else watching us, did you? If we saw what we saw, think what someone who knew what they were doing might have seen."

"I was too busy looking at other people to see anyone look at us. I guess we have a lot to learn about this business."

"Well, sister of mine, we'd better learn fast. I'll bet good money the feds have pictures of us leaving. At least they won't know who we are for a while," Annie noted.

"That's not a safe assumption," Lynn corrected. "Remember, they know Allen well. He had top security clearance or whatever it's called. I'm betting they know a lot about us."

A phone rang. It was the phone Tony had given Annie. Impatient to share what they had found out, Annie talked rapidly.

He was silent until she finished. "You have been busy, I see. You're not still mad at me, I'm assuming. Good. My car will pick you and your sister up at ten this evening for dinner. I have a new driver . . . Angelo." The line went dead. Tony already knew all that Annie had shared with him. Her outburst made it plain, she and Lynn would not leave well enough alone. Tony would have to find a way to keep them isolated, at least from the dangers born of this project.

"He's so used to giving orders, it's pitiful! He doesn't even wait for me to accept or decline. We're going to dinner at ten." Annie was irritated.

"Saves us money and I bet it'll be someplace with great food. We only have one more change of clothes, but who cares?" Lynn noted happily.

A knock at the door startled them. Lynn went to the door, but it was not Spook outside. A badge was flashed toward the peephole. Cautiously, she opened the door. Only one man was in the hall. He was dressed in an ill-fitting brown suit. The jacket was wrinkled as if he had worn it for days. His shoes were scuffed, his hair was poorly combed; generally, he looked like someone Lynn would have imagined was a street person. The badge looked official, and his ID, presented at Lynn's request, matched the face before her. Hesitantly, she stepped aside to let him inside the room. "Maybe he's undercover. *Way* undercover," thought Lynn.

"I'm James. Just like the ID. Allen said you'd probably not believe me without it. He's in Mexico, with friends. He's my long-time partner. I don't expect you to understand all this right now, but he needs our help, or he'll wind up in a river somewhere. Have you heard from Jacko lately?"

Annie frowned. The man was obviously nervous. She remained silent. He pushed, but she refused to comment.

He finally warned forcefully, "Listen, I'll give you a day or so, then we need to talk. You can't take forever to decide if you'll help him or not. I'll call you tomorrow, through the hotel. Whatever you do, don't discuss anything with Jacko if you want to protect Allen. Do you understand? You talk only to me." He left quickly.

Waiting for a few moments, Annie opened the door and looked out. The hall was now empty. Shortly afterward, she and Lynn heard voices. Opening the door slightly, Annie saw Spook wandering slowly toward their door. Twice, he glanced behind him.

"What was that all about?" Lynn questioned, frowning. "Do you think he's for real?"

"I have no idea. I'm calling Tony." Annie touched her speed dial.

"I'm taking a shower. What if he moves up our dinner date?" Lynn whispered as Annie asked for Tony.

CHAPTER 19

Someone answered at the number Tony had given Annie after the first ring. "Hi, this is Annie. Sorry to bother you all, but would someone please tell Tony we had a visitor. Some guy flashing a badge, asking questions about Jacko.

Annie heard voices in the background, and then Tony came to the phone. "What are you talking about exactly, Annie?"

"Some guy with the feds just left. He wants to know if we've heard from Jacko."

"Feds?"

Annie told him about the visitor they had had. "What did Spook say about it?" Tony asked abruptly.

"He wasn't here. No one was here. The hall was empty for a while."

"I'm sending Lou for you. He'll be there in less than fifteen minutes. Don't let anyone in, and I mean *anyone*. Stay away from the windows. Leave the lights on and the TV going." Tony spoke rapidly. His voice, as always, was even and controlled.

Moving quickly, Annie informed Lynn of the change in plans. She stopped mid-shower and got dressed. Taking care not to get near the windows, they moved around the rooms searching for anything they might have left. Soon the suite was empty of any trace of them.

Spook was surprised to see Lou step off the elevator. "You've been keeping an eye on this room, huh?" Lou challenged him, walking rapidly toward him.

"Yeah, sure, Lou." Spook was visibly nervous. As Lou drew near, he turned to run in the opposite direction. Sam and two other men met Spook head-on.

"I think you should come with us, Spook. You need to tell me all about the guy you let get up here a little while ago." With his arm around Spook, Sam, and the two with him, left the hall.

Knocking briefly at the door, Lou opened it and entered. "He has a key to our room!" muttered Lynn. "So much for security."

Leaving by way of a stairwell again, Lou and the two sisters moved down to the third floor. From there they moved across to another fire exit, which opened onto the back of the hotel near a service entrance. The three of them climbed into a dark Suburban that headed across the parking lot and entered traffic in the direction away from the park. Lou made small talk as they drove. Annie could tell they were moving out of the city. After about forty-five minutes, the driver pulled up to a large security gate, spoke into a receiver, and drove through. The Suburban came to a halt in front of a charming estate surrounded by well-kept grounds. Only when he turned back to speak with Lou, did Annie recognize the driver. Nudging Lynn, she nodded toward him. "That's the same guy that drove us to the Gala," she murmured.

Entering the house, the sisters were greeted by a uniformed employee who directed them to their sleeping quarters. The three-room suite was beautifully appointed and offered them every amenity.

They hardly had looked around the rooms when a knock came at the door. Tony stood outside. His face and manner were somber. "We need to talk, ladies. Please come with me to the library."

Minutes later, Annie and Lynn sat silently and watched Tony pace. At last he began to speak, slowly. "I'm sorry to have to tell you that it appears your brother Allen was found yesterday. They're trying to get DNA confirmation. The body was found in a Mexican river. You need to contact your friend, Annie, and see if he can verify anything. I wonder if he may have connections who can provide some details for us. Don't call anyone else. Neither of you knows anything, but your brother's 'friends' don't understand that yet."

"How did his body end up in a river?" Annie asked, her voice a whisper; she could hear her heart pounding in her ears. Lynn was stunned. Tony walked to where the sisters sat. Squatting down, he faced them; looking directly into Annie's eyes, he was silent for a moment.

As gently as he could, Tony answered, "Our report indicates he was shot. Whoever started the job finished it. Have you heard from Jacko, Annie?"

Numbly, Annie shook her head, her mind tumbling. "Allen is dead? And Earl hasn't called. Is he okay?" She wondered. Annie looked at Tony, "I need to call my other brother."

"No, you cannot call anyone for a while. Later, you can both use my phone. Your first call must be to that pathologist guy who helps you." He gently touched Annie's knee.

The room suddenly seemed to close in on the two sisters. Annie could feel the tears begin to fill her eyes. She stood, suddenly, and walked to the balcony. "Can I do anything for you?" Tony asked as he followed her out. Annie shook her head. Tony continued, "Annie, I keep telling you, this isn't a game." His hand on her shoulder was gentle. Annie stood silently. "I'll be back in a little while. I'm so sorry for all of you. Stay here in the library and I'll get a phone to you."

After Tony left the room, Lynn joined Annie. Both began to cry.

"Annie . . . what's wrong with him? Why doesn't he want us to talk with anyone? What about Earl? I'm frightened. Are we in too deep to go back to Aguilar?" Lynn spoke with tears streaming down her face.

"Well," Annie took a deep breath, "we do need to get in touch with Earl. Maybe he already knows about Allen, or . . ." she turned to Lynn, her eyes filled with pain, "maybe since Tony doesn't know Earl, he doesn't know Earl was shot too. Tony may be right. I guess Rhino is our best source of help right now."

"Talk to Rhino first, but then we call Earl. What we do after that will depend on what those calls shake up. It's strange for Earl not to have tried to call one of us." Lynn's eyes filled again. "Oh, Annie, I don't want to believe that Allen *is dead*."

CHAPTER 20

Following Tony's advice—his command, actually—Annie realized she really wanted to talk with Rhino. If there was a mistake about the identity of the body found in Mexico, he would know. Picking up her cell phone, she dialed her friend's unlisted number.

Rhino answered immediately. "Where are you? Are you okay?"

"I'm safe, but I'm not okay," Annie's voice cracked.

"You've heard about your brother. Annie, I'm so sorry," Rhino's voice softened. "When I saw the tape from the ICE office cross my setup here, I made some calls. I wish I could change it, but the DNA is a match. As much as something like that from Mexico could be."

"Maybe they're wrong . . . can you do anything to find him?" Annie's voice begged her friend.

"I'm already trying. The raid on the Gala was a setup. Your friend Tony walked out into the night, as did several others; all local gangsters. By local, I mean American. The groups snagged were from out of the country. You're in the soup, sweetie," Rhino added gently.

"Lynn and I need to get home. I'll call you when I can," Annie said wearily. "I haven't heard from Jacko in ages. Of course, I haven't been home, either. I'll let you know after we get to Aguilar. Thanks for everything, Rhino." Annie hung up. Allen was gone, she and Lynn were miles from home, and Earl, if he were alive, could be in harm 's way. Annie needed to get home. At home, she could think. At home she would feel safe.

"So it's true about Allen?" Lynn asked, when Annie ended her call with Rhino.

Annie nodded, asking, "What about Earl, did you get him?" She couldn't remember ever feeling so low.

"No, I left a message. We need to keep trying. Annie, we need to get out of here. I think there is too much Tony isn't sharing, and I doubt if he ever will. Earl can help us. He has to be okay." Lynn watched Annie, waiting for a response

"We have to do something. The sooner the better." With that, Annie began to pace. She felt uneasy about sneaking out on Tony, but he didn't understand. She had a gnawing feeling in the pit of her stomach, that he knew a lot more than he let on. On the other hand, she had always had the same feeling about Allen, and she was beginning to wonder about Earl. She needed to get back home where she could think and where she felt safe. Annie led the way upstairs to their rooms.

"Let's leave. Just walk out. Leave everything here. We can wander around the grounds a little, then, you know . . . keep going." Lynn shrugged her shoulders.

Annie hesitated for only a second. After sliding phones, IDs, and credit cards into their pants pockets, the women stepped calmly into the hall and continued downstairs. Stopping a man walking through the foyer, Annie asked if the grounds had trails or someplace they might walk around. The man paused, then nodded. Without speaking, he pointed to a doorway past the dining area. Thanking him, the sisters walked through the room and out through doors that opened onto a patio. Both held their breath, expecting to hear an alarm. Only the sounds of people talking behind them and birds singing beyond the door greeted them. The sisters casually talked and laughed. Circling the house on a winding pathway, they spotted the service gate.

Annie worried, "So far so good. Is there a guard at that gate?"

"We're going for a walk." Lynn strode on confidently.

There was a guard, but he was busy on the phone as a delivery truck driver waited impatiently, the engine idling. Lynn smiled and nodded to one of the men in the truck.

Once the sisters were outside the gate, Annie whistled. "Unbeliev-able," she said. "It was so easy."

Staying close to the fence, the sisters moved up the road, following its curve away from the house. When the curve took them beyond the view of the guardhouse, they crossed over into a wooded area and began to walk south. Annie still worried about leaving Tony's protection, but the loss of one brother required action. She had no intention of losing any more of her family. Besides, she wasn't certain just what Tony was protecting her from.

Lynn's phone rang. It was Earl's number. "Hello, Earl?"

"Yeah, hi. What's going on with you two? I've been watching the news. You guys seemed to be having fun. Sort of. Is everything all right?"

Relieved to hear him, Lynn quickly filled him in on the latest. A long silence followed. "Earl, are you there?"

"Oh, I'm here all right. Listen."

Allen's voice came over the line. He certainly was not dead. Lynn grabbed Annie's arm and put the phone to her ear. Annie's mouth dropped. "Allen, is that really you? I don't understand. I heard they matched your DNA. What's going on?"

"I can't explain now. Just keep in touch with Earl. Stay out of trouble if you can, and stay safe. Gotta go. Earl will keep you posted." The call ended.

Lynn noticed the low battery warning come on as she flipped the phone off and slipped it back into her pocket and resumed walking with Annie. Only now, it was air they walked upon. The relief of knowing Allen was alive filled both with an exalted giddiness. Eventually, Lynn stopped. "Annie, just where are we?"

"Seriously? You're asking me?" Annie looked around the area, her lips pursed.

"Let me think. We're not lost yet. Surely there's a street around here someplace. I feel so much better knowing Allen is alive and well." Lynn strode on confidently.

"So do I." Annie was nervous now. For one thing, the road lights, a long way away, were barely visible. On top of that, they were outside of New York City in an area totally unfamiliar to them. Now she felt awful about running out on Tony.

"Annie, you've fallen for Tony," Lynn interrupted Annie's thinking. She was still not too concerned about their plight. She was more concerned about her sister. Tony could only spell disaster for Annie. It appeared Annie had enough "disaster" to handle just now. Tony Tuscano? A mobster, a killer, and the kind of man Annie would have never considered. The head of a Mafia family? What was Annie thinking?

"Okay, that's enough. Let's concentrate on getting back home." Annie shook her head. "Damn it! Wouldn't you know? My luck. I'm going to have to call him for help. First the stupid Gala, now we're lost. Is there no end to this?" Annie scolded herself. The sisters walked on in silence, struggling to keep the road in sight.

Both women were panting when Annie finally stopped. With a disgusted shake of her head, she admitted, "This is hopeless, Lynn. We're lost. I don't have any idea where we should go."

"Someone should be able to tell us where we're going. Call your friend, the hippo guy. He seems like the geeky type," Lynn suggested. "We need help. You know New York has *lots* of waterways around it. We could wind up in over our heads, literally."

"First, his name is Rhino, and second, he's not answering. We'll have to do something else."

Taking the instrument from her, Lynn began to work with Annie's phone. "I've got our location with the GPS and it looks like we have water all around us. Maybe we can find the house, so at least we could go back—as humiliating as that would be."

The sisters stood still. What little light filtered through to them from a soft moon slipped around the trees and brush, leaving only ghostly shadows in their little area. Occasional cars passing in the distance were the only sounds finding their way to the two women. Shivering, Annie kicked a decaying tree stump. "I've done it again. We're in the dark, literally, heaven knows where. Maybe we need to stop until it gets light. What were we thinking?"

"I'd say we weren't. I don't like the idea of being in New York all night." Lynn was feeling the tree they stood beneath, images of scenes from muggings in New York running through her mind like a slideshow.

"We'll just have to keep watch. Maybe we shouldn't talk, just in case.

You know? I've got my pepper spray out. Didn't plan on all this," Annie added under her breath.

Without looking at Annie, Lynn replied, "Therein lies our problem. We had no plan for anything. Annie, this battery is going fast." Closing the phone, she delicately suggested, "Maybe it's time to call Tony before the phone goes out."

* * * *

Tony spoke without looking up. "What do you mean 'they're gone'? It would undoubtedly be the worst I've ever heard, but this better be a joke, Lou."

"I mean they left. They went out the service entrance. Camera shows them walking away. We've already started looking. Thought I'd better let you know. It's getting dark."

Tony stood up. He walked to the window and looked out into the gathering darkness. He was angry, unbelievably angry, but he was more worried. "If something happens to her . . ." Scowling, he turned to Lou.

"Lou, don't we have someplace to store them? An island somewhere? I can't believe this. She won't have to worry about anyone else; I'll kill her first. Let me know when you find her."

Shaking his head in disbelief, Tony turned to look out into the night again. "Annie, if it kills us both, I'm going to settle you down," he promised. Tony checked with the control room every fifteen minutes for the next three hours.

* * * *

Annie opened the phone and dialed Tony's number. "What if he refuses to take my call?" Annie asked Lynn in a worried voice.

"Don't hang up, Annie, I'll get Tony," Lou answered quickly.

"Wait, I'm certain he's mad at—"

"Mad doesn't quite describe what he is, but it's a start," Lou replied.

"Lou, maybe you could just tell us how to get back," Annie suggested hopefully.

"Where are you?" Lou already knew they would have no idea where they were; no one knew where they were. At least, not yet, but Sam was working on it.

"I don't know, and my phone is almost out," Annie answered in defeat.

"Hang up, I'll get Tony," Lou instructed, hoping for once his cousin would control his temper long enough to get a signal before Annie's phone battery died.

Annie's phone rang. Tony's voice was quiet and controlled as usual. In spite of that, his anger came through the line, thick and unmistakable. "Stay put, we're trying to locate the ping from your phone. Keep talking."

"Keep talking?" Annie asked halfheartedly. "What can I say? If I weren't lost, this would be a peaceful evening. Not even a dog or car around. Of course, I'm lost quite often," she babbled, but just then, in the background, Annie heard someone yell, "We've got it!"

Tony interrupted Annie. "Don't move." The line went dead.

Sam saw what he wanted. "Got 'em!" With a touch of the mouse, he zoomed down. After a quick study, he was out the door, calling back, "Tony I'm headed out. If they keep going, they'll be into the river, or worse. I'll call when they're in custody." Smiling to himself, he ran, taking two men with him. His Jeep sped onto the road. "Where did they think they were going?" Sam wondered. "Not like Lynn to just take off."

Sam grinned, "Lynn . . . what a woman." Happily for him, life turned Lynn his way—provided he could keep her there.

"Oh, Lynn. He is *really* angry now," Annie moaned.

"Yeah? Well, he'll just have to deal with it."

Annie shook her head dejectedly. "No, I'll have to deal with it." She dreaded seeing him. With her eyes closed, she muttered, "What am I doing? I hardly know this guy. Why do I even care how he feels?"

The sounds of something or someone approaching through the thick vegetation interrupted her reverie. "Listen," Lynn whispered.

"I heard," Annie breathed. Her heart was in her throat.

"Lynn? Annie?" Sam's voice floated out, ever so quietly.

"We're here," Lynn answered, as they both breathed a sigh of relief.

"Seriously, you two *have* to stop this." Sam scolded, as he slipped his arm around Lynn.

"Ya think?" Lynn responded as the three started back toward Sam's Jeep.

CHAPTER 21

Sam took Annie by Tony's office then walked with Lynn back to the sisters' rooms. Annie opened the door and timidly stepped inside. She was not certain what to say or do. "How is it he makes me feel like a child, so often?" she wondered. Tony stood at the window for a long time before turning. "I asked you to stay put. Is that so hard for you to do? Do you have any idea how many people you may have placed in jeopardy by running away like some school girl?" His voice was leaden and angry.

"I didn't run away. But—"

"I asked you to stay put!" he interrupted forcefully, fighting to control his temper. "Stay put, do you even know what that means, Annie?" His hand slammed the desk. "Stay put!"

"Tony, you have to—"

"I don't *have* to do anything! Do you understand me? *I* don't *have* to do anything!" His voice was louder than she had ever heard it. He fought to control his temper. "Lou!" He called out, turning back to the window. Annie hesitated briefly. Crossing the room, she slipped between the window and Tony.

"You have every right to be angry and want to get rid of me, but don't be angry with Lynn too. This is entirely my fault."

Tony looked down on her in silence. His face was set, his mouth hard and his eyes angry. "Get rid of you? Oh, Annie, you have a lot to learn," he thought. His heart would never allow him to stay angry with her, but still he tried. Just the nearness of her made him want to pull her to him, but she had to learn. She was part of a much larger picture now. "I'll speak to you later," he answered firmly. He could not allow this to go without a swift response. Too many people depended upon his direction. He had just added two more; he knew for their sake he could not ignore the incident. They could not simply do whatever they wanted, not anymore. He remained standing with his hands in his pockets. Lou entered the room. "Lou is taking you to your room until I can decide what to do with you two. You will be unable to leave without my specific order."

"You can't do that!" Annie burst out angrily, her temper flaring.

"I just did." He replied coldly, nodding to Lou as he left the room.

"You'd best have a damn good lock on that door, buster," Annie called after him, her hands firmly planted on her hips. He stopped dead in his tracks.

Lou frantically shook his head, frowning at Annie. "Don't Annie, please don't. Give it up while you're ahead, girl. Please don't say any more." Lou groaned.

"Look, I made a mistake. I thought my brother was dead. I wanted to run away someplace! Have you ever lost a brother? If you have, you probably wanted to run somewhere too! Oh, heavens no, what am I saying?" she continued sarcastically. "Not *you*. You probably just wanted to go *kill* somebody!" Annie yelled at him. The words came out of her mouth before she could stop them. Aghast, she stood frozen.

Lou rolled his eyes "Oh shit, now she's done it," he murmured. "Tony . . ." Lou stopped himself. He knew his cousin well; it was too late.

Tony slowly turned back to Annie. She had never seen him so enraged. His eyes were black and flashing. His jaw clenched as he fought to control his temper. He walked back and stood toe to toe with her, his hands in his pockets, glaring down at her. "No, Annie," he answered, drawing out his words. "I didn't just *feel* like killing someone when my brother died."

Annie gasped. Her hand went to her mouth with the realization of what he was saying. Slowly, he turned around and left. Annie watched his retreating back. Horrified, she turned to Lou. "Lou, he didn't."

"His brother was murdered, Annie. Brutally murdered. Yes, he did."

CHAPTER 22

Tony stalked to his room. He walked all around it, cursing. Leaving the room, he wandered the halls of the estate. He wanted to go to his own estate, someplace he knew was secure. He wanted to grab Annie and shake her. He wanted to smash something. Slowly, the anger ebbed; he was calmer. He strode into the kitchen, intent on making coffee. Lou, Dominic, and Sam were there, and a fresh pot had already been brewed. Silence fell over his men when he entered the room. Wordlessly, he poured a cup of coffee, methodically he added sugar and cream. He stirred the mixture, then smiling, he lifted his cup, "Salud!"

The men hesitated a brief moment, then returned the toast. "I thought you handled yourself with a great deal of restraint, tonight." Lou noted. "*I* wanted to shake her. She's going to take some taming. She has a lot of spirit."

Tony grinned. "Why Lou, *I* never wanted to shake her. I wanted to bend her over my knee and spank her! Yes, she does have spirit. I think I need to keep them busy helping us, since she's never going to let it lie. How do you all feel about the two of them helping us?"

Speaking carefully, Dominic noted, "Boss, you're gone—hook, line, and sinker. So it's a given Annie is here to stay. She may not realize that yet, but she will. She's pretty gone, too, from my observations. Now, if Sam gets what he thinks he's after, our help is in the bag. We need someone to work the information line, the computers, news tapes, stuff like that. Someone permanent, in one place. I think they could easily handle that. I'd say the one who will be a problem might be the brother, Allen."

"I've thought of that. He'll have to deal with it. I don't give up what is mine." Tony drained his cup and walked out calmly, in control again. The men sat around talking for a while.

"So, Sam, are you going to have these lovesick problems too?" Lou asked. "Because if you are, I want to be prepared. I think Lynn might be tougher."

"She is, but unlike Tony and the rest of you goons, I work on the right side of the law. That's what gnaws at Annie." Sam noted, grinning.

CHAPTER 23

"He's locking us in?" Lynn asked incredulously, looking up from the television.

"Yes, until he can decide what to do with us, so he says." Annie sank down into a nearby chair.

"What!" Lynn shouted indignantly. "Of all the . . . !!!"

Annie was silent. Lynn was so angry she couldn't speak. Storming into the bathroom, muttering, she slammed the door behind her. Pictures on the wall rattled.

When Lynn finally emerged from the bathroom, her hair in damp ringlets around her head, she smiled. "I feel better. Guess we kinda asked for this. He'll be okay when we have a chance to talk with him. How mad can he be, anyway?"

"More than you can imagine," Annie answered, gloomily. She told Lynn about her conversation with Tony.

Lynn was silent for a long while. Finally she commented, "It is what it is, you always say. This isn't some great revelation, you know? I can't even begin to fathom what's going on in your mind. But it will work out how it's supposed to."

"Hmmm, then why do I feel so miserable?" Annie wondered half-heartedly.

Nothing was heard from Tony the next day.

By that afternoon, Annie was unable to stand the inactivity. She sat at the table and began to design a plan of action to organize the information they had. Annie also shared with Lynn her suspicions about Earl's involvement.

"I've wondered about that myself. You and I are the only ones who don't know what in the heck is going on. Maybe it's time we did something about it," Lynn admitted. She joined Annie in her quest for answers. They wrote down everything they knew, what they would like to know, and where the answers might be found. They began to compare what they remembered about where the faces had been seen first and what the faces really looked like. Anything distinguishing was documented. A scheme was slowly forming.

During the evening, Lou entered the room, followed by Sam. "Annie?" Lou nodded toward the door. "He doesn't have a gun."

"Guess that's a good sign," Annie noted.

Sam crossed the room, stepped out onto the balcony, and called back, "Lynn, you have to come see this. Do you guys have anything good to drink?"

Giving Annie a small nod and half smile, Lynn followed Sam. Annie followed Lou down the hall. She had to wonder how many others had walked this hall to Tony's office. Annie was miserable, and had been, since their angry parting. While she knew she was wrong, she felt abandoned. The pictures along the hall mocked her; the several men she and Lou passed didn't speak. It was as if because of Tony's anger, she had become an outcast. "Not that I was ever in with this bunch. So much for loving me, I guess. There I go again. It's not supposed to matter, right?" her thoughts jumbled round in her head.

"I suppose I'm still at the top of Tony's shit list," Annie commented solemnly. She dreaded this meeting. Her long black skirt swayed as she walked. The cowl neck of her black silk sweater draped gently, exposing a single heavy silver cross suspended on a white gold chain. Her hair, longer now than when we first met, hung sleek, straight and shiny. Lou smiled to himself.

* * * *

"Shit list? Yeah, and I'd say you're moving down it. Slowly but surely, Annie, slowly but surely." He stopped walking and grasped Annie's arm. Turning her around to face him, he looked directly at her. "You have to understand. No matter how he feels about you, he won't jeopardize this whole operation. Just a little FYI, you're out of passes, Annie. Really out."

"Thanks, Lou." Annie felt she needed someone in her corner. Maybe Lou would take that position. "Are you mad at me too?"

"Nah, I couldn't get mad at you, Annie." He grinned. Lou had grown fond of this classy woman. She brought some semblance of balance into Tony's life. Annie couldn't know it yet, but she had a great deal of support from Tony's crew. "She has a lot to learn about this family, and Tony is the best teacher, bar none," Lou noted to himself.

Annie pressed her lips together thoughtfully. "I think it's my move, or lack thereof, now."

At Tony's office. Lou opened the door for Annie, then stepped back, leaving them alone behind closed doors. As always, Tony was impeccably dressed. He wore a beautifully made dark navy suit, complete with a vest. A silk kerchief set off the tie. Platinum and diamond cufflinks fastened the cuffs of his white French shirt. Tony was seated at his desk, talking on the phone, and never looked up. Biting her lower lip to stop the sting of his disregard, Annie began to move slowly around the room, looking at the art and photographs scattered about the shelves.

Studying the faded images, Annie felt herself pulled into a past. Tony's past. There were family photos with men and women, surrounded by children, everyone laughing. There were photos of children standing awkwardly, hoping the camera session would be short. Some pictures were of women, all somber. The majority of the photos were of men: working in shops smiling at the camera, sitting around tables ignoring the camera, and standing in groups posing for the camera. There were also maps—maps of countries, cities, and detailed structures. Annie recognized the countries, but none of the buildings. The last wall was filled with photos of churches: beautiful buildings with stunning architecture and windows that took her breath away. When she stepped back from the last photo, she remembered Tony.

Turning around quickly, she found him watching her closely, his expression tender. His anger was gone. His eyes were filled with love. Annie realized they had always been that way, even in his anger. She had been too defensive to notice. She slowly approached him. His eyes followed her. The stillness in the room was thick. Annie had never felt such a mixture of emotions. She hated things not being right between them. Annie walked around the desk, leaned against it, and faced him as he rose up from his chair. She had thought long and hard about what she would tell this man. This demanding, gentle, hot tempered, overpowering mixture of a man.

"I can't change what I've done. In part, it's because I love my family so much. I have to do something; I can't sit idle. You want me to stay out of it; yet my ranch and family are already deeply involved." She paused a moment before she continued quietly. "Honestly, this is because I've tried so hard to run from you. I shouldn't get involved with you. You're a gang . . . a mob . . . you've probably even killed people," she blundered on. Annie stopped herself, frowning as she looked at her hands, horrified she may have offended him.

Quickly, she looked up at him. Tony simply watched her in silence. His face had darkened. She continued, speaking still more softly. "Tony, you've moved in where no other man has been. I'm afraid, Tony, afraid to let go and lose myself. You're so overpowering. I've always stood alone, independent, done what I want, when I want. Now I see independence slipping away, and I'm not certain I even care if it does. That frightens me. I can't even think straight where you're concerned. It's happening so fast. I'm scared to let go." Annie's eyes were filling with tears. She was not aware of them, only that she must somehow make him understand.

Trying desperately not to hurt him, she went on. "Everything in me says I should run away from you, as fast as I can. Heaven knows I've tried. It's no use; I just come back. This is where I feel the safest, most comfortable, the most," she struggled to find the right words, "the most every good thing."

Tony's heart filled with feelings he had long ago decided would never belong to him. As Annie spoke, the cloud lifted. He knew, now, she would love him, in spite of what she believed him to be. Tony knew he was winning. Slowly, gently, he pulled Annie to him. He held her close to his heart. He kissed her head, spoke soothingly into her hair. "You cannot run from me, Annie. Do you really believe I could ever let you leave me? I, too, have spent a lifetime alone, and never cared. You've changed all that. I am what I am, and I make no apologies. Annie, you have to understand; what I am responsible for is more than you and me. It's greater than our story. You must not be afraid of me or of us. You absolutely have to trust me."

Holding her at arm's length, he brushed her hair from her face. "Don't cry, Annie," he whispered. With his kerchief he softly dabbed her face.

"Wherever we're headed will be just where we are meant to go. Annie," he lifted her chin up and looked into the hazel eyes once so full of mischief and now filled with uncertainty, "you can't ever get away from me. My family is not a traditional family the way you think of it. We still follow the old lines. When you're in, you're in. You have to know that. You are mine. I *never* give up what belongs to me. Forget trying to get away from me.

"Besides, in these past few days, I've spent a great deal of time thinking about you and what you can offer this project. Your strength lies in the computer. Information is only as good as its source and timing, and you have skills and possibly resources I can use. With Lynn's help, we could move forward much quicker. Use all that energy on this project." He smiled down at her.

"Annie," he whispered softly, "remember the dance." His lips found hers, and for a long moment, she was swept away. With great reluctance, Tony finally pulled away and called for Lou. Walking her to the door, Tony added, "I'll see you in the morning. Get some rest. We have work to do." He kissed her forehead and turned back to his desk. "I can feel her tremble every time I touch her. She must know this struggle between us is over," he thought confidently.

CHAPTER 24

Annie lay awake long after the lights were off. The silence of the room was broken only by Lynn's gentle, even breathing. Moonlight peeking through the window shot a sliver of light onto the beveled glass of an ornate antique mirror that glanced onto the bed where her sister slept unaware.

Rising, Annie pulled her robe about her and walked to the balcony. She gazed at the garden below. In the moonlight, she could see the stately urns, statues, and benches placed throughout the shrubbery and flower beds. Annie could imagine the inspiration for each statue standing as a silent guardian. The tranquil paths beckoned to her.

Turning, she moved quietly out of the room and down the hall. At the door to Tony's office, she hesitated, listening. Silence. Gently opening the door, she stood in an area lit only by the security lights beyond. Moving noiselessly across the room, she opened the French doors and stepped onto a patio. Beyond the patio was a path that snaked around the grounds and returned to this starting point. Annie stepped onto the path. And as she walked, she kept up a running debate inside her mind.

"He's a gangster, probably a killer; possessive, domineering, and quick tempered. Yet I can't even think straight where he's concerned.

"Allen trusts him. His men are very loyal, at least most of them. He is gentle with me, patient, and . . ." tears began to trickle down her face, "and it's too late. I never wanted to fall in love, but I have."

Tony stood at his bedroom window and watched as Annie's slim figure on the garden pathway faded from view. He knew she was troubled by his life and what he represented, but he would make no apologies for the same. Somehow, she must find peace with their love. He knew in his soul she would never leave his heart. He could never let her go.

* * * *

The next morning found Lou at the door of the sisters' suite, waiting to escort Annie to Tony's office. "This is the last free tour you get. From now on, you and Lynn can find your own way around this place." He winked at her as usual. "Lynn, in a few minutes, I'll come get you. Tony has a plan."

"Fine with me," Lynn thought. "I'd like to add a few things I thought of last night to the diagram Annie and I are working on."

Tony stood when she entered, and smiled, his eyes taking her in tenderly. When the door was closed, he came to her and kissed her, long and slow. "That was good morning," he offered, still amazed at how she affected him.

Flashing a grin up at him, she admitted, "I think I could grow to love good mornings." Striving to regain her composure, she slipped from his arms, walked across the room, and leaned against one of the large over-stuffed chairs facing his desk.

Tony followed and drew up behind her, but he did not speak. He was in no hurry to leave the moment. She nervously began the conversation, eager to get him past the mood she felt him sliding into.

"Am I allowed to ask questions? Because I have lots. To begin with, tell me about the guy with the feds. And Spook. And Angelo. Please tell me just what is going on, Tony. I heard from Allen and know he is alive, but what is going on? Who is he looking for and running from? How is all this connected to Allen, and to you?"

"Lynn is going to join us. I wanted a second alone with you," he said, turning Annie to face him and running his hand along her chin. Again, he kissed her. "Later . . ."

Tony touched the intercom, ordered coffee, and sent for Lynn. "Let's move over here, Annie." He directed her to the far side of the office. They sat around a small table. Answering a knock at the door, Tony had the coffee tray placed on the table and showed Lynn to the third chair. The man bearing the tray gave a friendly nod to the sisters and backed out. Tony was already pouring everyone a cup.

As Tony served them, he began to speak. "Twelve years ago, I was invited by an intermediary to meet with a couple of men reportedly working for the government. The meeting took place in New York, at an eatery of my choice. Old school. And it turns out they *were* old school, as agents go. They both were clean and would stay that way. They weren't so worried about casinos, sports racketeering, et cetera; they were after drug transport and sales. Over the years, we corroborated on several 'projects' so I could test the waters. We concentrated on Asian and Latin gangs involved with drug smuggling. Not by design, we found ourselves in the middle of human smuggling lines. People will do all sorts of things to get into America."

Tony took a few sips from his coffee cup before continuing. "I know what I am, Annie. My family is from the old country, and we have held to those traditions, as much as we can, given the change in times. Then we saw the kids, babies really. Little ones sold for labor or sex in return for drugs or drug money. We made a family decision to join those two agents. Your brother is one of those agents. Over the years, my mother came to know him and considered him family. We are strictly silent partners. As far as their bosses are concerned, we do not exist. I get certain things done, remove certain obstacles and provide cover or protection where I can. As time has gone on, our family has gotten smaller and much more specialized. By doing so, we have also gotten much more effective. We have projects in other countries, with help from the people asking our assistance."

"Please don't tell me Jacko was the other agent with Allen," Annie shuddered.

"No. Sam is the other one. You and Lynn want to help, Annie. I under-stand; but you are not very good at taking orders. In this game, the rules change daily. You *have* to be willing to do what you're asked, when you're asked, without questions. We are nearing the end, we hope, of stopping a huge operation involving several countries. The Gala in New York pro-vided us with a chance to see anyone outside the usual attendees, who came. We know everyone there had an invitation. We're connecting the people there, with the ones most likely to have sent them notice. The raid was Allen's idea. It provided us with a cover of sorts."

Tony leaned back in his chair. After a short pause, he continued. "The arm from Mexico is desperate to get the drug lines set up and front peo-ple in place before the border wall is complete. There is a war going on in Mexico, right under the U.S. government's nose. The Border Patrol, Immigration Customs Enforcement, and other agencies are simply too few and too restrained. That's just part of it. Many of the men coming in are not workers . . . we believe they are terrorists. Their only objective is to kill. They are not concerned about dying themselves. That makes them more deadly for the American enforcement agencies. Someone pays a pretty penny to get guys over here. The drug lords don't care about anyone's cause except their own. They just want the money." He rose from his chair and moved to stand behind it.

"Jacko, we believe, is working for the Columbians. He turned before he ever joined Allen, but Allen felt like it would be easier to keep tabs on him if he were close. Jacko doesn't know Allen's real partner. Lately, men have gone missing without a trace. I'm thinking the steer trick may be our answer. Each time, Allen has been somewhere else and Jacko has been on his own. Unfortunately, although the ranch allows Allen to work quietly, it also provides Jacko with a place to work. At any rate, after we *bury* Allen, Jacko should move on. At least that's what I'm hoping. I want you to ask your friend to get a DNA match on the kid from the steer, if possible. If he is who I think he might be, we have a war on our hands. I think Jacko is in the middle, but I can't prove it.

"Rhino said he would get a DNA match for us, but with everything going on, I haven't called. Surely he has an answer by now. I'll find out."

Annie grimaced. "Tony, we're going to actually bury Allen? That's going to be a little weird."

"Well, you don't usually keep dead people around do you? That is your first assignment. Make arrangements, and keep close tabs on who helps, attends services, and so on. I'll see to it you two are aware of everyone we are working with. You can scratch Spook off your list. You'll have no reason to doubt any of the rest of my men."

"I'm guessing they were new to you?"

"Spook was not new. Lynn, can you give us a minute?" Tony walked Lynn to the door. Annie's heart beat faster, as she watched Tony close the door and return to her. "I'll only say this once, Annie," Tony began, looking directly at her, his eyes locking onto hers, his voice firm, leaving no room for argument. "You don't fly solo anymore. I can't afford to lose even one man because I'm distracted. I'm not willing to chance losing you."

"Tony, I need to know. I need to hear it from you . . ." Annie hesitated. "I have to understand what—"

"You have a right to know as much about me as I can safely share with you."

"Are you and the Tuscano family really a gang?" Annie started.

"Yes."

"Have you actually killed—"

"Yes."

Desperately trying to hold back her tears, Annie turned away from him to look out the windows. Her heart was breaking, her mind was numb. How could someone she loved be what he admitted to being? Yet, if she were honest with herself, she already knew all these things about him.

"Annie, I've never made any pretenses. I said before, I am what I am. I can help in ways no one else can with this war. And that's precisely what it is, a war. This is my country, too, Annie. I make no apologies for any of it."

Finally, Annie turned back to him, her hands clasped tightly in front of her. "I don't know about all this. I only know how I feel inside. How I feel when I'm with you." Her voice was quiet but she spoke with confidence.

"I'm so sorry I hurt you the other night, Tony. I said awful things. I am so, so sorry."

Tony crossed to where Annie was now standing. She waited for him, felt his arms encircle her. Leaning her head on his chest, she closed her eyes. Tony turned her face up. "Look at me." When she opened her eyes to look into his, he continued. "You are so forgiven, Inamorata. You were before I left the room that night. With time, you will see more clearly. Give it time, Annie. I know what I am. I also know what you are." His arms tightened around her and he kissed her once again. Moments passed before Tony walked her to the door, nodded to Lou and Lynn waiting on the other side, and turned back to the office.

Lou walked back to the suite with the sisters. At the door, he grinned, "Welcome to the family, Annie."

"Boy, am I ready for this?" Annie asked, aloud. "I feel like I'm living someone else's life."

"Oh, I think you're ready," Lou answered. "You just have to learn to trust your instinct, Annie. It's that feeling in your gut. The more you use it, the better you will get at reading it. Takes time, but you are ready." As he walked away, he called back to her, "Believe me; you will never have reason to doubt how Tony feels about you." Annie flashed a crooked smile at Lou.

Lynn was already sipping hot tea. Now, she grinned at her sister, "At least we have help, and we will know what is going on. If we can get rid of Jacko, we're sailing."

The sisters spent the rest of the day wandering the grounds and residence. They passed men everywhere. Venturing outside, Annie was surprised to find the path she had taken in the evening was only accessible from Tony's office. The roaming helped both. Evening fell, as they wound their way back into their rooms. Waiting for them, was a note from the kitchen, requesting they call for dinner whenever it was convenient. "Good, I'm starved," Lynn admitted. Calling the included number, she had their dinner sent up. They heard nothing further from Tony or Sam.

CHAPTER 25

Juan Saldivar closed his phone slowly. Seven men sent, only three returned. Diego watched his uncle carefully. "What happens now?" he thought. "The son gone and the patrón aging too rapidly." He shook his head and left the room. Returning shortly thereafter, he brought with him three men. All were members of Saldivar's cartel and trusted. "Tell him what you told me," Diego urged the men.

Saldivar listened patiently and learned that all three had entered the U.S. by way of Camargo, Mexico, into Rio Grande City, Texas, and traveled north. The driver, with three years on Saldivar's crew under his belt, headed toward New Mexico. When one of the men had questioned the driver about the route, he assured them it would be safer; with the increased scrutiny of their usual route, he didn't feel safe flying. It didn't seem to matter, since the final destination was New York, and if a detour meant safe arrival, time could probably be made up elsewhere. Everything seemed to follow the usual pattern until they arrived at Raton, on the northern border of New Mexico. For some reason, Junior felt uneasy. While the driver was relieving himself at a gas station, Junior instructed the men to split up. Two were to get out of sight and wait for his call to rejoin them. He and the other two would stay with the driver. "That call never came, Señor Saldivar."

Word spread quickly; Junior had been taken, but not by the feds. Faustino, one of the men hiding at Junior's order, finally found Junior, his men, and the driver, but he was too late. The driver and some other man had killed Saldivar's son and his two men. Faustino watched from cover as the other man then turned his weapon on the driver. "Who was this man?" asked Saldivar.

Faustino frowned. "I've never seen him before. Gringo . . . speaks Spanish. Looks like a federal man . . . turned maybe. He picked up some other guys to help him. I asked around in Raton and Trinidad; one guy came to me. He's here."

"Bring him."

Diego called through the door, and an older man entered. He was dirty, unshaven, and poorly clothed. Holding his hat in his hand, he stood respectfully before one of the most powerful men in Mexico's underbelly, yet the man was not afraid. He had seen too many things to be frightened any longer. Now, he wanted revenge against the gringo. The men killed by the gringo were innocent of any wrong, and the man wanted to make things right for them and their families. "You know who killed my son?"

"Sí Señor. I know where he took your son."

"Talk."

"The man is called Jacko. He uses my men a lot to dispose of problems. He is a federal man, but works both sides. His partner never knows anything this Jacko is doing. Never with him when he works. The partner has a big ranch in Colorado. The word on the street is Jacko had him killed too."

"Did the partner have anything to do with my son?"

"No. Jacko works alone. He's very bad, Señor."

"Who is this partner?"

"I don't know; we just deal with Jacko. No one has ever seen the partner. Maybe he doesn't really have one, I don't know." He paused. "Let me work with you."

"Why would I need you?"

"You probably don't but to get Jacko. I want him too. After they got rid of your son, all three of my men had an accident. Of course, no one cares about a few illegals found dead in a car accident. I care."

Saldivar nodded, then waved everyone out except Diego. "Put him up in the ranch house." He paced back and forth. "Someone has to be giving orders to Jacko. He's not doing this all on his own—especially if he's had his partner killed. I'll take care of this tomorrow. I need to think."

Saldivar watched as the sun slowly crept away. The money and power he wielded meant little tonight. He couldn't remember things anymore. He felt old and tired. Tired of the game . . . never at ease . . . always on guard . . . and now his son, his only child, his life . . . gone. Maybe it was time he quit . . . let someone else take over.

CHAPTER 26

Annie couldn't believe she had slept for twelve hours. The relief of clearing things between Tony and her was greater than she had imagined. Glancing around, she could see Lynn still snoozing. Moving quietly, Annie freshened up, pulled her hair into a ponytail, and donned her robe. Roaming down the hall, she ran into a housekeeper. "Do you know where I might find Tony? I don't want to bother anyone, but I need to use a phone."

"Certainly; I'll be right back." The woman immediately turned and left the hall.

While waiting, Annie wandered the corridor filled with beautiful original works of art. None were familiar. She was so engrossed in the art she failed to hear Tony walking toward her. He stood in silence and watched her, amused. The black robe swung about her as she wandered along. Her hair caught the light from chandeliers hanging along the hall. Her face was free of makeup, fresh and clean. Her hands were in her pockets as she strode slowly along, studying each piece. Occasionally, she would stand back, and one hand would find its way to her lips. She scrutinized the paintings and their frames, the sculpture and its pedestals, and gently touched each tapestry. On several occasions, she shook her head, ever so slightly, as if disputing the art or presentation.

"Finding some pieces you like, Annie?" he finally spoke.

Startled, Annie jumped. "You shouldn't sneak up on people, you know," she scolded him, laughing. She turned back to the wall of treasures. "I love art. My business is finding art for people with money, as you know." She looked at his collection again.

"You see; there are people who collect art that touches their soul. They care nothing about the prestige of *owning*, they care about the painting that touches them, the statue that speaks to them, or the tapestry that captures their heart. These are my favorite collectors. For them, I would travel anywhere. I think you're like that. These are beautiful, though I've never heard of any of these artists."

"They're little-known Italian artists. Collected from all parts of Italy, mostly smaller villages." He walked closer to study one of the paintings. "You seem to object to the presentation of some of these pieces."

"Well," Annie hesitated, a little embarrassed, "it's not for me to say how you should display your art. I just think you sometimes must take care to be certain the frame does not speak over the object it frames. That's just my own opinion, not especially shared by art collectors and museum curators. There's a tendency to overwhelm the pieces with unbelievable frames. It's a hard balance I suppose, since many pieces almost demand a spectacular frame."

"I think your point is well taken. I shall endeavor to keep that in mind." He smiled affectionately, his eyes kind and warm.

They walked the rest of the length of the great hall in silence. Annie could feel Tony watching her closely. She needed to break the silence. "I'll bet you love Italy and have been there many times. I've been often, but always on business to specific places and always on the run it felt like. I want to go sometime strictly for pleasure, for fun. Maybe one of these days."

"I do love Italy, and go home frequently. My family on both sides still lives there. You would love it too." Tony looked at her, standing there so defenseless. The thought of what was beneath her robe made him smile. "We will be wed in Italy, Annie," he thought to himself.

"Hmmm." Annie turned to him. "On another issue, does it matter what phone I use? I need to call my friend and my brother. Is there a problem with using my personal phone? You asked us not to use them, but I'm afraid neither Rhino nor Earl may answer an unrecognized number."

"You probably should not use your phone from here until we find Jacko, since it's easily traceable. It's not my plan to have him find you first. Has he tried to call you yet?"

"Well, that's another thing I need to use the phone for. I need to check my voice messages. Better get Lynn something to use, too, please. She has a business to run."

"They'll be brought to you. What else can I do for you, Annie?" Tony's voice was soft and suggestive.

Skillfully sidestepping the mood she found him in, Annie moved them both quickly back along the hall, her arm linked in his, gabbing away. "I think that would do just fine for now. Please let me know when you might have lunch; I'd love to join you if you don't have other plans." By now they were at her bedroom door, and she slipped inside. Tony stood for a moment looking at the closed door. "Our time is coming, Annie, slowly but surely," he whispered.

Two phones arrived shortly thereafter. While Lynn brought Earl up to speed, Annie checked her answering machine. Nothing. Calling Rhino was more productive. "Need another favor, guy. I suppose I'm taxing your patience, but is there any chance you have the DNA on that stuff I brought you? I really need a positive ID."

"I'll never begrudge doing you a favor, Annie, and I do have the DNA. I did some research and found out he's a young man named Saldivar. You should know he's the son of the patrón of one of the biggest cartels out of Mexico. I think he was to take over the business soon. Hope you're safe and not mixed up in any of this, because it's going to get mean."

"I'm fine. Thanks, Rhino. Talk to you later."

Annie sat down across from Lynn. "Remember the big guy from Mexico? His face was all over in that stuff from the library."

"Yeah, why?"

"Well, his son is the poor guy in our steer."

Lynn's eyes met Annie's. "I think this doesn't sound too good for us. What do we do now?"

"I have to let Tony know," Annie replied. She found him with several of his men, sitting around a table, deep in discussion. One of the men nodded toward her. Tony got up and walked toward her. His smile was warm. "What can I do for you, Annie?"

"Rhino tells me the man in the steer was the son of a guy named Saldivar, from Mexico. Do you know of him?" she asked.

"I do. I need to let Allen know. Thank you. I'll talk with you later," he said as he brushed her hair back, kissed her forehead, and turned back to the men. The frown on his face was deep.

CHAPTER 27

Night found Annie awake, as was usual lately. And just as usual, Annie found herself on the winding path, again. The night was soft, not hot and muggy. For some reason, the stars seemed brighter. She could hear crickets clamor, and somewhere close by she could hear frogs and nighthawks begin their nightly serenade. It was heavenly peaceful. Annie had grown to love this path.

"You shouldn't be wandering out alone, Inamorata." Tony's voice came to her from the shadows, as he emerged onto the path.

Annie whirled around to see him walking toward her. "*Anthony Tuscano*, you're going to give me a heart attack!"

"Might I remind you, little one, this is *my* path? You should not be out alone, by the way, least of all dressed in your sleeping gown," he gently scolded, smiling at her discomfort. "I've been watching you from my window for several nights now. What brings you outside at such an hour, Annie?" Tony firmly placed her hand on his arm and stepped in time with her.

"I'm safe here, remember? I come here to think."

"Does it help?" he asked with genuine interest, looking down at her.

"Yes, I believe it does. It's quite peaceful here." She walked along not at all averse to having him at her side.

"Then you will love my *real* home." Tony smiled at her. He had already arranged for a winding path with water and landscaping to be added off the villa's master bedroom suite. That phone call had gone out the first morning after he had watched her nocturnal stroll in the garden. They wandered along the path in a comfortable silence.

"Do you walk at the ranch too?"

"Oh, yes. I walk wherever I find myself. I hope you don't mind."

"Not at all. I'm glad you like it."

As they wound their way back, he led her through his office, down the hall, and into a large room. Its windows were covered with subtle green dupioni silk drapes that ended gracefully in soft puddles on the floor. The walls were done in thick rough-surfaced stucco of a copper color. Huge beautiful oils hung strategically about the room; the theme of each painting was the Tuscany countryside in vivid shades of rust, green, yellow, and beige. From the raised ceiling, stained glass lights hung from bronze chains, casting soft colors throughout the area. The wood floor was a deep mahogany polished to a shine. The room was empty except for several burgundy-colored leather overstuffed lounge chairs with matching ottomans. Near them stood a dark cedar accent table with a reading lamp. Crossing the floor, Tony pushed a button, returned to her side, and took her hand as the waltz music she loved so much began to play.

"Tony, I'm in a bathrobe, for heaven's sake," Annie protested softly.

"And the most beautiful nightgown I've ever seen."

"You've seen quite a few, I take it?" Annie teased.

"Possibly. And men, Annie? Have you collected men as well as fine art?" His voice was teasing, but Annie sensed a serious note. She frowned for a few moments as if trying to remember them all. "Well, Annie?"

When she looked into his eyes, she was not surprised to see a shade of jealousy. Wistfully, she sighed. "I've known some wonderful men." She glanced at him again. He saw the twinkle in her eyes, but he did not want to hear there had ever been anyone. "None I've wanted to stay," Annie added softly. Tony smiled slightly. He would be the one to show Annie what the nights could hold. She would want him to stay. Instinctively and with experience, he knew she would be worth his trouble.

"We're going to dance." Tony suddenly announced. "If the robe is cumbersome, take it off."

"You're awfully bossy."

"You're very stubborn."

Slipping out of the robe, Annie laid it across one of the chairs. The nightgown she wore had long, loose sleeves and a high-necked collar encircled with rows of delicate white lace. A soft silk, it draped her body gracefully from a gently gathered empire waist. The dark green color brought out Annie's hazel eyes.

He took her in his arms and moved her onto the floor. "You're the first woman I *ever* wanted to take dancing, Annie." At that, he moved across the floor with Annie in his embrace, following his lead. She could hear him chuckle.

"The music suits you; you do dance very well."

"You, sir, lead very well and make it easy to follow."

As they made a tight turn, he pulled her closer. He could feel her body against him, the desire flushed through his very being. "Then why do you fight me, Annie?" he spoke softly in her ear. She closed her eyes. Still commanding the floor, Tony moved her around it again. He looked down at her, with arched brows, awaiting her answer. Annie looked into his deep brown eyes, her gaze soft.

The music filled her soul and took her beyond her worries. His touch and nearness, however, jumbled her thinking. "I'm not certain. Fear of capture, I suppose," she finally mumbled faintly.

"Let's take that issue off the table. Consider yourself captured. What else?" he countered smoothly.

"That's a little frightening to me," she admitted, looking up at him again. He looked so serious, though not unkind. She had never seen him like this, and she felt awkward. As the *William Tell* "Overture" began, she hesitated, looking at Tony with concern. "We're not going to dance to this, are we?"

As the run began, he commanded quietly, "What I say, when I say."

"Turn," and she did. He twirled her on and on, and when the run changed tempo, he grasped her firmly, turning out with her. So it went.

By the time the dance ended, Annie was moving flawlessly. He laughed out loud as he pulled her close and hugged her. "Not so hard, is it?"

Breathless, Annie noted between gasps for air, "Only the part where you won't let me leave."

Tony looked down on her, smiling tenderly. "Do you really want to leave, Annie?"

"No," she answered softly, "but what if I did?"

"Umm, it's my job to be certain you never want to." With that he kissed her.

Finally ending the kiss, yet holding her close, he whispered, "You'll come to see it is not what you think it is, Annie. Heaven knows I love you. I believe you love me too." Not waiting for an admission or a denial, he picked up her robe, threw it around her shoulders, and walked her to her room.

"You're very romantic," Annie remarked, realizing he hadn't really answered her.

"I'm very Italian," he responded. Lifting her face, he kissed her, long and slow. "Good night, Inamorata," he whispered, reluctant to let her go. Slowly, he walked away. "I don't know how much longer I can wait for her to admit what she obviously feels," he said to himself.

CHAPTER 28

Faustino and Diego listened as Juan Saldivar questioned a man who had come across the U.S. border to see Diego. This man had watched from the shadows the night three of his companions loaded a body into a pickup. He was not a witness to the killing, but had stood in the dark, unnoticed, while Jacko instructed the other men loading the dead man. Saldivar's questioning rambled, "What did Junior say when you left?" he asked for the third time.

"Señor, he couldn't talk. He was dead when I found them."

"Why didn't you follow him?" asked the elder Saldivar, struggling to understand. "Junior should be here by now. Diego, call his number again. Where is Lena?" Saldivar was becoming agitated, looking for the wife who had been dead for thirty years.

The informant turned to Diego, puzzled. Frowning, Diego shook his head sadly. "Tio, we need to rest now. After lunch we can talk again, huh?" Saldivar nodded. Calling to the butler, Diego watched as his uncle was led away.

He excused the outsider and turned to Faustino. "What do we do now? He's no use anymore. I think this has pushed him over. We can't let him continue giving orders."

"Why can't we? No one needs to know it's you, not the Viejito. You are the one the men get orders from anyway. Too much rests on this move, now. Besides," Faustino reminded his friend, "I don't think our 'partners' would believe you if you tried to pull out now. We know what's to happen; let's do it."

"Go back to Trinidad; find Jacko. Bring him here. I'll get rid of the guy outside. He knows Tio has lost his mind. First, we meet with all the people around here. NO ONE is to know what condition he is in. We say he's gone north. If word gets out, I'll make them and their families pay. Round everyone up."

* * * *

When Diego finished speaking to the crowded room, there was silence. The faces looking back at him were tinged with fear. They were told the old man was going north. No one could breathe a word that he was gone from the house. They knew too well what would happen if any word got out. It was always like this, though. The old man was even more violent. Everyone present knew at least one person Saldivar had tortured and then killed for talking. "Do I make myself clear? Even on your deathbed, you breathe no word of any of this." Heads nodded seriously. The room was still. Diego dismissed them with a wave of his hand, turning away as if even looking at them would make him angry.

CHAPTER 29

Early the next morning, with Tony's kiss still on her mind, Annie went looking for him. She found Lou first, sitting on the patio reading the paper. "Is Tony around?" she asked. "I need to talk with him."

"Yeah, he's in his office."

Annie walked toward Tony's office. Knocking gently on the door, she waited. After a short while, two men came out, nodded to her respectfully and continued down the hall, deep in conversation. Anthony Tuscano followed them to the door. His face lit up when he saw her standing there with that grin of hers and a glint in her eyes as if she had just discovered where Santa really lived. Taking her hand, he led her inside his office and closed the door. Standing toe to toe, he gently lifted her face, bent down, and kissed her tenderly, then watched her. Annie stood very still, her eyes still closed.

At last, she opened them, her smile replaced with a serious frown. "Should you be doing that? I should have asked this last night, last week, some time before, but is there a Mrs. Tony someplace?"

"Yes, to the first question, no to the second." He smiled fondly at Annie. "I've won, Annie," he thought with satisfaction.

Slowly, Annie began, "Please Tony, we need to talk."

Tony waited. "Listen—" Annie began. His hand, gentle over her mouth, kept her silent.

She was quiet for a moment then began carefully removing his hand, keeping possession of it, and smiled. "You need to know," she noted, "I'm not the kind to settle down and cook at home, you understand."

"I know." He acknowledged, smiling. "I know you so well, Annie, you would be amazed."

"You know?" Annie laughed a little uncomfortably.

He continued, sure of himself, his voice low, "You are struggling with who I am, but you're letting go, slowly, Annie, slowly…"

"I won't make any promises about staying out of trouble, although I'll try, honestly." Annie interrupted, moving things along.

"Oh, you'll stay out of trouble, one way or another," he promised, his voice full of emotion and authority, his eyes taking her in affectionately. "You *will* stay out of trouble." He could not believe how fortune had chosen to smile upon him, after so many years. This was one to keep, and keep her he would, at all costs. Right now, he had to be certain she understood the danger she might be in.

"I'm not wild about you going back to the ranch, but I've had several men watching for me, since I found out you two were leaving for *Wyoming*," he noted dryly. "They will be staying. If I hear anything to make me believe it unsafe, I'll let you know, or if you're already there, I'll send help and have you moved. With Saldivar's son out of the picture, we're not certain what may happen. I'm more concerned about Jacko for the time being. I have people looking for him, as does Allen. I'll keep you posted." He stopped, and watched Annie's reaction. She had listened quietly.

"No one seems to know what's going to happen next. We have to wait and see," Tony continued. "Allen is guessing they might be gunning for whoever they think is responsible for Junior's demise. I don't think they have that luxury just yet. Personally, I think they are too busy trying to figure a way to move forward without the son. I would feel better if you were able to stay here."

"We'll be fine, Tony," Annie assured him. "I expect to get some kind of government notice about Allen. I'll let you know." She smiled at him.

"Things should get quiet for you after Allen's funeral. No running around, Annie. Am I clear on that?" he asked through narrowed eyes.

"Yes," Annie nodded. "It's going to be strange to arrange a funeral for Allen."

"You realize," Tony added, "if you still haven't heard from Jacko, he either knows Allen is still alive or Jacko is dead too. One can only hope." He brushed her hair back gently. "The day will come when I don't have to let you go; the day when your home is here," he promised himself. He kissed the top of her head then, holding her hand, he walked with her to the patio, where Lou and Lynn sat visiting.

"Lou will be taking you to the airport."

As Sam and Lou loaded what luggage they had, into the car, Tony walked a short distance away with his arm around Annie. "Be very careful, Inamorata. I'll call you later. Keep in touch, every day. I don't like this, but for now . . . don't go anywhere alone, understand?" He took her into his arms again briefly before he walked her to the waiting car.

As the sisters got into the taxi—driven by Sam, of course—Annie turned to Tony, asking anxiously, "Will Sam be okay after everything he did for us? I wouldn't want to have his cover with Allen blown."

He leaned on the window edge. "Yes. Everything is under control. Annie, you and Lynn must be careful. You can't be tied to me as far as Saldivar is concerned. Let me know if you find anything unusual when you get home." Pausing, he touched her cheek, "I don't suppose it would do any good to ask you to stay out of this would it?"

"What, and miss all this fun? You've got to be kidding!" She reached up to give him a quick kiss then she sat back, waving "bye" as Sam pulled out.

Lou and Sam rode in the front, talking quietly. Annie and Lynn did the same in the back. It seemed they had hardly begun before they were at the arrival gate. Paying Sam, Annie and Lynn strode into the airport. When they had passed security, and were seated alone, Lynn noted, "You paid Sam?"

"Of course. He's the cab driver, right?" Annie, a quick study, was learning.

CHAPTER 30

Pulling into the driveway that night, the girls listened for Buster. Annie felt bad that he had been alone for so long. While he used to roam the ranch unnoticed, Buster had become very much a house dog that took care of Annie. She called to him anxiously. He bounded around the house, yipping his "welcome home, Annie." His tail wagged so hard, he could barely run. Kneeling to hug him, Annie shared his enthusiasm at their return. The house was untouched and quiet thanks to Tony's men from Aguilar, who had scoped out the premises.

Despite their exhaustion, Lynn and Annie took Buster for a brief reunion hike a short way up the canyon. The soft breeze whispering through the evergreens and aspens provided background music for every creature: the frogs were out in force, owls hooted back and forth across the canyon, while the excited yapping of coyotes sounded reveille for the night's hunting party. The familiar silhouette of the West Spanish Peak dominated the skyline. The absence of the clamor of civilization that had drummed in their ears in New York provided a quietness that was in harmony with the sounds of the wildlife.

* * * *

A day later, two men in a car with a government license plate pulled up to the house. After introducing themselves and producing ID, they told Annie and Lynn their brother, Allen, had been found dead in Mexico. The DNA matched. The Mexican government had conducted an autopsy. As gently as possible, the men informed the sisters that the head and hands were missing in an apparent effort to slow identifying the body. Stunned, Annie asked, "In Mexico? He was in Denver, the last we heard."

The men looked at each other before one of them spoke. "Honestly, ma'am, we don't know much else. The Mexican government is investigating this death as a homicide, for obvious reasons. Unfortunately, although we can ask, and have, we will not be involved in the investigation going forward."

"Just where do we pick up Allen's body?"

The second man answered. "I realize this is unbelievably hard for you both. There is a morgue at Fort Bliss, in El Paso, Texas. I'll have the body held there if you like. You will need to contact a funeral home near here, and they can coordinate the transfer of Allen for you. Here's my card, with both an office and a home phone number where I can be reached."

Lynn slipped her arm around Annie and said quietly, "We need to notify our other brother. One of us will call you back when we know more."

"We'll wait to hear from you, ma'am. Here are the certificates of death: one from our department and one from the Mexican government. Again, I'm very sorry for your loss. Is there anything else we can do for you?"

Lynn shook her head; both sisters were crying. The men quietly left.

Annie went to the phone straight away to call Tony. When Lou answered, she let him know they had just received Allen's death certificates, and they had the names and phone numbers of two federal agents.

"I'll let him know. Hang in there, Annie," Lou said in an attempt to encourage her.

Ending the phone call, Annie walked to the front porch. She felt none of the awe the view from this vantage point usually inspired. Instead, she felt a sadness in her heart. "When are we ever going to see Allen? How long is all this going to continue?" she whispered to a silent world.

CHAPTER 31

Early on the morning of Allen's funeral, Earl's pickup pulled up to the house. After a subdued visit over a cup of coffee to catch the sisters up on Allen's latest doings, they left for the church.

The funeral mass was at St. Anthony's Catholic Church in Aguilar. It was a small church, built of stone, standing firm against the passing of time. Annie still felt protected sitting inside its walls. Sunlight pouring through the stained glass windows marked the floors with red, blue, gold, and green splotches. The last Kirk family funeral had been the one to put her parents to rest. Today, most of the same people were here again.

Annie hated funerals. As Mass began, she felt the heavy burden of what could be coming. The feeling of impending doom hung on, despite every effort she made to dispel the sense that she was rehearsing for another tragedy soon to come.

Annie was grateful Tony had spoken with the priest. Only those directly involved knew the mass was for the poor person—who, Annie had learned, had died of natural causes—chosen to take Allen's place. Father Jacob prayed for the family of Allen Kirk. Annie heard them gratefully, mindful that her family certainly needed the prayers.

Afterward, a luncheon was held in the church basement. Men came through the receiving line to offer condolences; men Annie doubted could have been friends of Allen's. She tried to place them, filtering them through her memory of all the faces she and Lynn had seen lately, but to no avail.

Later, when all the guests were seated and eating, Lynn and Earl and Annie sat at a table by themselves. "Do you see anyone or anything unusual?" Earl asked his sisters.

Annie shook her head. Earl leaned closer. "Don't look now, Annie, but I wonder if you know the guy who just walked in. He doesn't look like he belongs here at all. He looks like a 'suit' to me."

Annie stood to refill her teacup. Glancing around, she spotted the man Earl must have been speaking about. Her pulse quickened. With a conscious effort, she calmly sat back down. "Lynn, remember the two guys who kept walking around at the Gala looking at everyone? He's one of those bodyguard types, right?"

"He sure is. Did he know Allen, do you think, or does he somehow recognize us? I don't remember either of those bodyguards ever looking us over."

The man's gaze wandered over the crowd, carefully noting everyone at the gathering. But none of the three siblings was surprised when he wandered over to them.

"My condolences to you and your family," he said, directing his words to Annie. He had a thick accent; though it wasn't one she could readily place.

Studying him briefly, she answered, "Thank you. How did you know our brother?"

"What matters is how well *you* knew him. If you think this is over, you're sadly mistaken. You think because he's gone it's finished?" His voice was icy. He looked at each of them individually before turning on his heel and walking away. The three looked at each other. Annie's heart sank. Tony was right. They were far from safe.

Annie rose and found a deserted corner. She hadn't planned on calling Tony from the church, but their visitor's comments troubled her. When Tony came to the phone, he immediately detected the anxious tone in her voice. "We just had a visit from a man I remembered seeing at the Gala.

There were two men roaming through the crowd, looking everyone over. This guy was the smaller one. Thin, real cold. His eyes have no expression. He essentially told us just because Allen was gone didn't mean it was finished. Do you know him? Whatever does he mean?"

"I might know of him. Has a thick accent. If he is who I think he is, he works closely with the man Allen and I have been tracking. I'll follow up." Tony's voice softened. "I must remind you, Annie, this is not a good situation for you and Lynn. I'm glad Earl is there. Be sure someone keeps my men in the loop. I'll call you tonight."

Looking out over the quiet grounds surrounding his estate, he prayed for the first time in his memory. He prayed for his future wife's safety.

* * * *

As the luncheon drew to a close, the siblings made the rounds to thank people for taking time to attend the service. Most difficult was deflecting questions regarding Allen's demise.

Back at the ranch, Lynn put coffee on while Annie checked the answering machine. Nothing from Jacko. "Maybe Tony is right," Annie risked hoping. "Jacko isn't a problem anymore." With coffee in hand, Earl herded them out the back. They began to walk up the hillside, where they'd be able to talk freely. Earl nodded to several men fading away discreetly. Annie found their presence comforting.

"Tony thinks he may know the guy from the reception," Annie told her younger siblings. "He thinks he might be an associate of the man he and Allen are following. Tony's going to call me later tonight. It's getting a little thick," Annie finished. She and Lynn exchanged uncomfortable glances. "Tony is so right, this is not some game. Maybe this time, I've bitten off more than I can chew," Annie admitted to herself.

Earl weighed in. "The one that could help us, of course, is Allen. By the way, you realize, Annie, that it was Tony who came up with the idea of 'hiding' Allen in Mexico and having his 'body' discovered there. It was brilliant. Now everyone wonders who did what. Jacko should be a wreck."

Annie had not realized Tony was responsible for setting up Allen's "demise" in Mexico. His maneuvering may have kept Allen safe a lot longer, and she found herself grateful.

"Mystery man is making threatening comments. He should be encouraged by this funeral. Why couldn't that mean we're off the hook? Saldivar has no way of knowing his son was 'buried' on our ranch, does he? Unless Jacko is talking. I can't imagine that," Lynn noted.

"Jacko is possibly—hopefully—dead," Annie reminded Lynn. "I can't believe I just said that," she added under her breath.

"Earl, how does Tony know where Allen is? We don't even know where he is. Only you know. Tony told me he and Allen have worked together. I know Sam is Allen's partner and—"

"Earl?" Lynn added. Both women had stopped walking and stood waiting for Earl's reply.

Earl stood for a moment looking off into the gathering shadows, thinking, "Maybe this is the time to unload . . . or maybe not." He paused to decide just how much to tell them. Taking a deep breath, he turned back to his sisters. "Allen and I have worked together for quite a while now. Not as long as he and Tony, but nearly. Until recently, I hadn't been as active as they are. I do have a business to run. Lately, it's a tie. Sam was the first person Allen called from Mexico. Everyone has my cell." He watched his sisters' reactions as the news sank in. He also saw tinges of anger begin to fray the edges of their understanding. "Look at it this way, you two have lots of support. Everyone had a vested interest in keeping you alive and well."

"How long were you going to wait before you shared that tidbit with us? That's the question I'd love you to answer," Lynn demanded.

"To be honest, we hoped not to ever have to tell you anything. Then Annie and Tony rocked the boat—in a big way. And Tina, poor thing . . ." He waited, trying to deflect some of Lynn's spark.

"Personally, I think the boat was rocking when Allen showed up here nearly dead," Annie corrected him. "Speaking of Tina, though, what could the lists she kept mean, and of what value are they and to whom?"

"For that answer, we need to go to Allen," Earl informed them.

Wearily, Annie could only shake her head. "I think we all need to get some rest. That's a lot to digest." Without another word, she turned back to the house.

* * * *

After getting ready for bed, Annie was curled under her comforter when Tony called and brought her up to date.

"Saldivar is rumored to be gravely ill. He may have passed the business off to one of his top people. All the increased activity and violence along the border have cut deeply into profits, so whoever gets Saldivar's spot will be a target for competing cartels. The assumption about Tina has always been she worked for Jacko. I've never believed that. It's interesting that both she and Saldivar's son are now dead. If you look at the whole picture, the groups from countries like Pakistan don't belong to any of the South American families, but they do fund some of the operation. We haven't made much of a dent in the weapons issue. I've always believed that's where we'll find the ghost."

"Tony, are Lynn and I still in the thick of this? With Allen gone, these drug lords just move on, right?"

"I wish it were that easy, Annie. We need to know who Tina worked with. I'm certain the other invitees to this party—namely, the Cubans, Venezuelans, Pakistanis, and on and on—will try to get the information she had. That should tell us who needs and is using it." Tony added, thinking out loud, "I'm starting to wonder when the group after Tina's list will put you and Tina together. There were plenty of others working at the clinic. Unfortunately, the driver you identified wouldn't give up his boss."

"So we still aren't sure who had Tina killed? Have you figured out what Tina's list means?" Annie asked.

"Not yet. Maybe we don't have all of it."

"I'll be at the clinic this Wednesday. I can check the computer again."

"Okay, but be careful, Annie." Tony's voice was so soft she could barely hear him. "I love you."

After he hung up, Tony let his anxiety overtake his thoughts. "She has no idea how bad this could turn. Yet if she doesn't resume her work at the clinic, it looks worse. I just need to get her here with me; someplace where I can keep her safe."

Annie closed her eyes. "Oh, Tony, why couldn't you just be an average Joe?" she wondered.

* * * *

The next morning, Lynn and Earl reluctantly packed to leave. They both had businesses that needed attention. "Are you sure you're okay with us leaving this soon?" Lynn asked.

"I'm fine. Tony's guys are here. Call me when you're home safe. You know, it's a real shame we waited until something like this to get together again. Maybe this is a lesson for all of us."

"What a lesson!" Earl rolled his eyes.

CHAPTER 32

Faustino spent two weeks roaming around Raton and Trinidad. He found out nothing about Jacko, but he did find out Jacko's partner had been killed, and his identity had been confirmed by matching DNA.

Faustino attended the service. The relatives who survived their brother seemed lost. He didn't think they knew anything. The people at the service were locals, except for a few of what appeared to be family friends. Nothing unusual. He asked around, but no one could tie the partner to Jacko except for the ranch the partner owned, or at least his family did. None of his information turned up anything to indicate the partner was involved. Faustino decided Jacko must have had him killed.

Faustino checked out of the motel in Aguilar and phoned Diego to report that he was headed for Denver. "The Venezuela guy runs things in Denver. Don't trust him. He's got lots of firepower, so be careful," Diego warned.

Faustino wound up at a bar on the north side of Denver. The place had a reputation for tough bouncers. The kind of place one could go and not draw attention to himself. According to Faustino's sources, Jacko frequented the establishment. No one seemed to know anything about Jacko, or if they did, they weren't sharing. Faustino drank then left. He checked into a cheap motel. His call to Diego was brief. "Look, nobody is talking here. These people don't know Junior. If Jacko is here, he's very careful. Anyway, maybe Jacko didn't get the list when he killed Junior. We know Junior had someone here in the states he worked with. Are you still getting calls from your other partners?"

"Yeah, and they aren't friendly chats," Diego confirmed.

"I think Junior's contact was the woman killed in Aguilar. She had that list somewhere. That's why everyone is looking for it. I'm going to the clinic."

* * * *

The receptionist at the Aguilar health clinic watched the man sign in. Very few new people came to the little town, let alone the clinic. "Can I help you, sir?"

"Sí, I'm sick. Is there a doctor? I can pay a little."

She smiled. "Don't worry about that; of course we'll see you. Fill this out and the nurse will call you back in a moment."

Faustino sat to fill out the information sheet. He signed as Juan Saldivar Jr. No one reacted to the name.

He was called back, complained of abdominal problems, took the free samples the elderly physician gave him (along with the key he slipped off its hook unnoticed), and left. Faustino now knew where the computer was, where Tina had been killed, and who had found her. It seemed to be the only news in town, and the nurse in the back had been eager to share the details. Leaving the clinic, he drove around the area, noting security lights and alleys. He drove back to Denver, to check out of his motel room, and returned to Aguilar.

Because Aguilar was small and out of the way Faustino was certain if he were to be seen, someone would remember him, a stranger. He took back roads into and through the town, passing what might be a soccer or football field as he entered town. He eventually pulled into an alley near several abandoned houses then walked swiftly to the clinic's back yard. He could now hear cheers coming from the direction of the playing field, being carried across the night air. In a little town like this, everyone would probably be at the game. Faustino would need to move fast. When the game was over, the town would be crawling with people.

Moving stealthily, he slid along the falling cinderblock wall next to the office. He slipped the stolen key into the door and entered the clinic quickly. In a few strides he reached the doctor's office, where he started up the computer without turning on the lights. He could find only clinic information, however. After taking time to rummage through the office, he nevertheless left empty-handed. Replacing the key on a hook behind the nurse's station, exactly as he had watched staff do, he left the way he came, unseen.

Driving out of town, Faustino called Diego. "Nothing there. It's just a plain clinic. No one even knew Junior. The computer room is full of patient stuff, and it looks like everyone on staff uses that one computer. I don't think she kept anything there. She probably kept the information wherever she lived. Will keep looking. I need to go back to Denver anyway."

"Not to look for Jacko, you don't. He's dead. Over a woman. Stupid. One less thing for us to worry about, eh? Just find that damn list. I know Junior kept copies of that disk, but Saldivar can't remember his own name, let alone anything else. Pobricito. Bye."

* * * *

Cece's brother, Julio Ramirez, felt good today. He sat eating in a quiet corner of a common fast food restaurant. His first assignment had gone well. Better than anyone could imagine. His homeland, Cuba, had taught him well the value of silence and time. The gringo had died slowly, talking all night, begging toward the end. Now Julio knew about the list this woman Tina had kept. The list would tell of everyone Saldivar dealt with, plus more, like who came into the states and what they could do. Julio just had to find out where the dead woman had kept the information. Jacko believed Tina was giving information to more than one of the groups. He also told Julio about Tina's friendship with the sister of Jacko's partner. The gringo himself didn't know where the list was, Julio was certain. Julio was a clever man. He had already been by the clinic, but it didn't seem like a good place to keep something like that. Somehow, Julio needed to find it before anyone else did. If he could be the one to give it to his boss, he could possibly do something in future operations besides watch. Finally.

CHAPTER 33

"Tony, for the second time in one week, some guy with a thick Spanish accent has checked into the clinic to see the doctor. He wasn't really sick. He's looking for something . . . and that something is probably Tina's list, I think." Annie walked with Buster at her side.

"I don't suppose he was careless enough to sign in with a real name," Tony wondered.

"He signed in as Juan Saldivar. That's the name of the guy in Mexico, right? It didn't mean anything to the staff, though. I'm going into Aguilar again Friday and plan to check the computer. Just who did Tina keep that list for, anyway?"

"I'm not certain, but it looks more and more like she worked for Saldivar." Tony thought about Annie's eyes and smile. His voice softened. "I need to see you. I'll get back on Friday; Lou will pick you up for dinner. Early."

"I'd like that. I miss you too. You have a deal."

* * * *

Early Friday morning, she drove into town. The possibility of inadvertently giving out information and placing someone in danger played with her mind. Slowly making her way up the steps, she passed a young man leaving. He nodded as he passed, and Annie had to stop herself from turning to get a second look. Inside the office, she jotted down every detail she could remember about him on a slip of paper she stuck in her purse. The staff informed her this was the second time the visitor had come, this time for a follow-up visit. At the computer, Annie was not surprised to discover that someone had made several attempts to log on after 11:00 pm, according to the computer warning message.

Tony called to tell her they would drive to Trinidad for dinner, around seven. After saying good-bye, Annie walked out onto the grand porch. "We're going to spend all our time on the road. I think it's time Tony had a picnic."

Calling him back, Annie suggested, "Tony, why can't we have a picnic here on the ranch tonight? I realize that's probably not something you do often, if you have ever done it at all. Let me take care of it; I'll even pack enough for everyone. We'll drive up the canyon from the house. Just think, a quiet dinner beside a creek, beneath the stars . . . couldn't get any better. Come a little earlier, if you can." Tony agreed.

When Tony arrived at the ranch, he was dressed in jeans, a sight Annie never thought she'd see. "Wow, I've got to take a picture! This is like history, right, guys?" She snapped his picture on her phone. After letting him look at it, she hit the delete spot. "Not so good to have your picture out there, although I'm certain there are plenty of them floating around. Now, there's the basket and the cooler, Buster is staying home. I just need to grab some ice from the fridge."

Annie went for the ice while Tony checked the doors to be certain everything was locked up. His eyes followed her. She was happy, laughing, teasing everyone. His smile was filled with tenderness and pride.

Loaded up, they left the house. Annie directed them to a road that led to a small pond fed by a rapidly moving creek. Near the head of the pond, a grove of aspens surrounded a peaceful meadow filled with summer flowers. The early evening light shone through the surrounding trees, skimming the area as if a stadium light had been turned on.

Sam parked the car and Annie jumped out of the vehicle. "We can start a fire here," she instructed Lou. She popped open a table that had four small stools attached. On the table she placed a cloth, lantern, plates, and silverware. From the cooler, Sam removed a bottle of wine. Rummaging through the basket, he found a corkscrew and four wine glasses. In short order, Lou had the fire crackling, and a large foil roll of vegetables were cooking, followed soon by the steaks Annie had marinated. Dinner rolls, butter, and olives finished the menu.

Annie led Tony alongside the pond, pointing out frogs, tadpoles, and different tracks. Tony stooped to snap off an Indian paintbrush and slipped it behind Annie's ear. Hand in hand, they wandered back to the impromptu picnic grounds. Tony was bewitched by the slender treasure laughing and walking with him. Everyone was so relaxed they hardly noticed it was after eleven and time to return to the house.

"I don't know about anyone else, Annie, but thanks for one of the best evenings I have ever spent. Boss, I'd say she's worth all the trouble she causes." Sam grinned, giving Annie an affectionate hug.

Lou agreed. "We should join the Boss every time he comes up here to the ranch, Sam. In fact," he noted seriously, "it would probably be a lot safer not to have dinner in town." Tony nodded in agreement, his heart at peace for the first time in a long while.

CHAPTER 34

Inside the Hummer, Tony pulled Annie close, and kissed her. She laid her head on his shoulder. Tony knew he had won. He also knew Annie didn't quite know it yet, but she would . . . in time she would.

He could easily have spent the night here with her. He *wanted* to spend the night with her. For a split second, he could imagine slipping one of her expensive nightgowns off. But he knew he needed to be patient—still. He opened the back door of her bedroom to let her in after glancing around the patio. As Tony turned to leave, he frowned and wondered aloud what had become of Buster.

"Oh, he's around," Annie assured him. "He likes to scout at night. I'll call him to come inside." Tony kissed her good night. She watched his lights until they were out of sight. "Now to hit the clinic. Tony won't like this, but I need to try one more time. The last time someone tried to access the computer files at night was after hours on the day the guy came into the clinic. He was there today. I don't have to go in, I'll just watch the back," she said to herself as though she needed the pep talk.

In her rush to get to the clinic, Annie forgot all about looking for Buster. She also failed to notice Tony's men weren't anywhere around. Instead, she picked up her purse and pulled the door closed behind her. As she turned, she stepped into Julio, who had hidden on the patio. He brutally grabbed her before she could think about trying to run. She could feel his breath in her face and smell the cigarettes and coffee he lived on as she struggled against his strength. He slapped her hard as he pulled her to him and tried to drag her around the house. Annie fought desperately to pull away. With her free hand, she tried to scratch him. With his fist, he swung at her face. He hit her with such force she fell backward, pulling him with her. Staggering into the wall, she tried to scream, her mouth filling with blood. He hit her again. She tried to yell again. "Yell! No one to hear," he taunted, as he jerked her upright, slapping her again. Blood splattered onto the windows.

"*He* can hear," Annie corrected him, her voice breaking, spittle and blood running down her chin. Julio quickly turned to see Buster lunging toward him. Loosening his grip on Annie he swung his gun up. Annie smashed the gun aside just as he fired. The pain in her hand was intense. She lost her footing and slammed into the corner of the wall, the force snapping her arm. Annie screamed. Julio fell to the ground at Buster's assault. Under the security light, Annie could see them struggle. She began to crawl around, looking frantically for the weapon. Her arm and hand wouldn't work right. She didn't feel the pain—yet. Her only goal was to stop this man. Catching sight of the weapon, snatching it, she stumbled up, not certain what to do next.

Julio was struggling to stand, dragging Buster with him, and for one terrible moment, Annie thought he might get away. She raised the gun and pulled the trigger, not three feet from him. Julio fell. Buster locked onto his throat, emitting a horrible growl from deep within him. Frozen, Annie watched as Julio struggled briefly, while Buster maintained his hold. By now, Julio was gurgling. Eventually, he jerked, then lay still. Buster shook him again, then turned and limped, bleeding and whimpering, to Annie. Collapsing to the ground, Annie began to cry. She swept the ground with her good arm, found her purse, and took out her phone.

Lou answered immediately "Annie? Are you there?" Hearing him, Annie began to shake.

"I think I just killed someone," she whispered.

"Annie, I can't hear you! What's going on?" The phone went dead.

Struggling to catch her breath, Annie sat still a moment. Straining to stand, she looked around anxiously. "What if there are more?" she thought. Urging Buster up, she moved them slowly around to the darker side of the house. The pain in her arm and hand was now unbearable. Hidden from the light, she slid down to hold her wounded dog close. He was bleeding from a wound in his abdomen. She jerked at the flimsy straps on her shell, pulling it off and clumsily bound him, her injured hand nearly useless, her arm hanging loosely, every movement excruciating. Buster lay quietly, his head in her lap, quivering. His leap of protection had saved Annie; she needed to save him. "Please Tony, come quickly," she murmured over and over as a prayer.

* * * *

Tony rounded the house and ran to her. As he reached her, she began to shake again. Tony knelt and pulled her to him. Annie winced and moaned.

Sam stood over the body lying in a pool of blood on Annie's patio. The man's throat had been torn away, and he had a gunshot wound in his chest. The violent struggle was one the man had lost, horribly.

Lou walked around the corner. "There's no one else here, Sam, including our guys. The house is empty. There's a Jeep behind that pine, but it's empty, too, nothing in it. I think the guy was alone. I don't know who he is. There's nothing on him, but we've got the gun he carried." Lou's voice dropped. "Where in the hell were our men? Do you know who was supposed to be here?"

Sam shook his head. "No, but I've already called in help. They should be here pretty soon. They were due to relieve someone now anyway. We need to find our men."

Sam and Lou joined Tony and Annie around the corner. Her teeth chattering, Annie was trying to explain what had happened. "He grabbed me as I was leaving the house. I never saw him until he stepped out onto the patio." Her chest was covered in blood, her hand was oozing, and droplets of blood continued to fall from her mouth and nose. Both her eyes were swelling badly. With Lou's help, Tony pulled her up as gently as they could. When he touched her arm, she moaned, sinking into him.

"Where was Buster?" Tony asked, holding Annie steady. He pulled his jacket off and draped it around her shoulders.

"He came around the side of the house while I was trying to get away. That man tried to shoot Buster, but I hit his arm. After that, things just happened. He was on the ground with Buster, and Buster was making this horrible sound." Annie was crying now. "I found the gun, and when he stood, I shot. He fell, with Buster at his throat. I didn't know how to tell if there was someone else here so I tried to hide. But Buster is bleeding and couldn't go anywhere. Please, we need to get help for Buster. I killed him, Tony. I think I just killed someone!" Now she was sobbing and shaking uncontrollably.

Tony held her closely, gently. "You had to, baby. He left you no choice. We need to get you to a doctor and Buster to the vet's. People will get here soon to clean this all up. It will be like a bad dream." A second vehicle had arrived. Dominic and several other men were talking with Sam and Lou. No one knew her attacker.

Buster was placed into the back of the Hummer. He lay down, whimpering softly. Tony took a couple of towels from Annie's room. With one he wrapped her hand and with the other he wiped her face. He could see by the unnatural bend in her upper arm it was broken. He pulled the throw from her bed around her shoulders. Turning to Lou, his voice deadly calm, he asked, "Where is her protection? Who was on this?"

"I've already called. The relief crew was almost here, and Dominic has a crew right behind them. I don't know what happened, but I will before we get her to town."

Tony nodded. "We need to get you to town, baby. Let's go." Tony slipped his arm under her and half-carried Annie to the Hummer. He slid her gently onto the backseat, as if he feared she would shatter. Annie could hear Buster moaning and she tried to comfort him with soothing words. It all felt like a horrible dream.

Tony spoke briefly to Sam and Dominic before he slid onto the backseat beside Annie and wrapped her in a protective embrace. Annie couldn't stop shaking. She wasn't certain whether it was from the attack or knowledge she may have killed someone. Closing her eyes, she tried to concentrate on Buster. She began to cry quietly, again. Her head and face hurt worse than ever, and she could tell her eyes were swelling. She could barely open her jaw.

For the first time, she could taste the blood. Touching her face, she felt the steady trickle from her nose. Her hand was bleeding and throbbing again. With even the slightest movement, searing pain shot into her arm. She gripped her elbow, holding the arm tight against herself. Using strips of cloth he tore from another towel, Tony bound her arm tightly against her as best he could. She leaned back onto his chest and closed her eyes, small sobs escaping her. "Please tell me I didn't kill someone," Annie whispered. She couldn't tell if Tony heard . . . he simply held her, speaking softly, calming her gently.

"Lou, call Dr. Bolatti and Dr. Grazanti. We'll take her to Aguilar." Lou watched his cousin in the rearview mirror. Tony looked at Lou and nodded. The time was now. He would have to do something now.

CHAPTER 35

"Looks like a bullet just grazed his head. Not anything serious, but he may have been out for a while." Buster lay quietly on the table allowing himself to be treated. The vet eyed Annie sitting nearby; she refused to be looked at or to leave until she knew Buster would be okay. Tony didn't argue with her. The wait would give Dr. Grazanti time to get in.

"Mmm, that explains why he wasn't out as usual when we got back to the house, Annie. I didn't like that at the time, and I should have done something about it." Tony looked down at Annie tenderly, cursing himself for not acting on his instincts. He excused himself and stepped outside the room to use his phone. "So where were our men?" He listened intently as the man on the line described where he found the bodies.

"He'll have an awful headache tomorrow," the vet continued describing Buster's wounds to Annie. "And it looks like the second shot hit his belly. I don't know how it didn't do more damage. He's going to be okay, but he'll feel like heck for quite a while."

He watched Annie curiously. "Funny thing, that boy Tony. Known him all his life. Knew his folks too. We all came here together, you know. Never knew him to worry about any woman except his mother. You must be special," said Dr. Bolatti kindly. "Course, it makes his job a lot harder now." He shook his head, and moved away, humming to himself while dialing the phone.

He returned after speaking with Dr. Grazanti. "Here, I need to X-ray that arm before you leave."

The old man was gentle. Still, every movement was torture to Annie. Eventually, he had one he thought would do. Handing the film to Tony the old vet patted his shoulder. "Thanks, Zio." Tony looked at Annie, worry written on his brow.

"I'll stay here until Dr. Grazanti calls. You'll be back." The vet patted Annie. "The dog will be fine. Tony will take care of *you* now."

Annie's mind was numb. She still couldn't think beyond the knowledge that she may have killed someone. Tony took charge as usual, and for once, Annie gratefully let him. He and Lou helped her into Tony's house and into a small room that was used as an exam room. "I see this isn't the first time someone has been here, probably beaten and shot too," Annie thought as she surveyed the area. The elderly doctor was waiting. Closing the door after Tony, he helped get Annie onto an exam table. Gently, Dr. Grazanti cut her bloodied bra off, stripping her to her waist. Annie was still reeling from the attack and hardly noticed. The doctor immediately began to assess the damages. After carefully examining her, he bound her arm to keep it immobile then cleaned her up, including the abrasions about her face, and finally the gunshot wound on her hand. Annie moaned, nearly fainting, as he rinsed and flushed the hand wound.

Once the injuries were dressed, he wrapped her in a soft blanket, nodding to Tony. "We'll need some help, and I'll need to repeat the X-rays to be certain the bone is in place."

Annie waited, not certain what would come next. Both Lou and Dominic entered. Gently, Tony lifted her, and they all made the trip back to the vet's office.

While they set up, Annie closed her eyes. The exam table was covered with a blanket, and Dr. Bolatti stood by, waiting. Baring her arm and shoulder, Dr. Grazanti looped her torso with a sheet, bringing the ends up over her shoulders and handing them to Lou. Grasping the broken arm just above the elbow, below the break, he spoke gently to Annie. "We need to set this arm, little lady. They'll hold you; I'll pull. We X-ray again. If all goes well, you get a cast or maybe an immobilizer."

Annie looked around uncertainly. "Has anyone had this done before?" she asked, looking at the ring of men around her.

Tony answered quickly, "I have. Dominic has too." She looked at Tony with raised brows. His eyes were kind. "It hurts like hell," he stated.

Annie closed her eyes with dread. "Let's get on with it. I want to go home."

Tony gently slid her to the edge of the table so that her broken right arm swung off the side, supported by Dr. Grazanti. Leaning over her, her face turned into him, Tony grasped her head and chest firmly. Lou tightly held the sheet wrapped over her shoulders, holding them steady. Dominic leaned over her hips and legs, pinning her motionless. The only part of her body free and movable was the injured arm. Dr. Bolatti grasped her arm below the elbow to stabilize it.

On the count of three, an agonizing groan filled the small room. Waves of nausea swept over her. "Breathe, Annie," Tony instructed her. "Take a deep breath. It's over." He expected screaming, crying, something more. Proudly, he studied her anew.

"I'm going to throw up," she said, feebly struggling to sit up. With Dr. Grazanti and Tony supporting her, she vomited. Gently, they laid her back down. X-rays confirmed the bone had been set properly. Annie was shaking with the trauma. Dr. Grazanti quickly put a soft immobilizer on her. He stood to look at the slight, trembling form wrapped once again in the soft blanket. Years of working for Tony and his family had trained him well: he never asked questions; he simply treated every man brought to his exam room. This was a first for Tony, though. Dr. Grazanti had patched up nearly all of Tony's men, including Tony at one time or another, but never a woman. From his bag, he prepared an injection for the nausea, one for pain, and one for possible infection. Dispensing the necessary medications he gave clear instructions she was to rest for the next several days.

"You'll have a real bad headache, and your face will hurt; I don't think anything else is broken. Tony, keep ice on her face. It's going to swell a lot more. Your hand hurts because you took a bullet between your thumb and finger. Bullet went clean through, but that was a dirty wound, what with dog hair, blood, and debris. Keep it elevated. Your arm shouldn't hurt now. You have bruising on your chest and ribs; don't think you've a fracture there. We'll take another look when I see you again in a couple of days, unless something changes. You may have to sleep in a recliner or propped up on pillows until that arm heals. Take the pain pills like they're ordered, please. At least for the next day or so. You *must* stay quiet."

He laid his hand gently on her forehead. "You're in good hands with these gentlemen. Just stay quiet for a while." Dr. Grazanti shook his head. He watched Tony gently lift and carry Annie to the waiting vehicle. He didn't know who she was, but she had taken a severe beating. He knew Tony well. Someone would pay for this; she was obviously Tony's woman.

Back at his mother's house, Tony helped her into one of his shirts with a side draping the injured arm. Tony's first thought was to have her stay with him there, but Annie wasn't comfortable with that arrangement. Eventually he agreed to let her go home—with added protection.

With assistance, Annie climbed into the Hummer. She was much more steady, but still visibly shaken. Closing the door Tony slid in next to her. Annie leaned onto his shoulder. She was miserable, everything hurt, and she was worried about Buster. Recalling the vision of Julio and Buster, tears crept from her closed eyes. Because of her, a man was dead. She could hardly believe what this night had given her.

At the ranch, Tony tenderly removed Annie's clothes, helped her into a gown and got her settled in spite of her feeble protests. Propped up on pillows, her arm and hand well supported, he smiled at her. "As much as I would love to stay, I need to take care of some things tonight. Keep ice on that eye and cheek. Keep a pillow under your hand. I'll bring the doctor tomorrow. You'll have more company, but they're with me. I'm proud of you, Annie. You did well." He bent to gently kiss the swelling face.

"I can't have someone following me around. That means . . ." Annie began to protest.

"Annie," Tony's stern, authoritative voice left no room for discussion, "I meant what I said. You are not to do anything without letting me know first. Tonight was just a taste. You don't want the rest. These people mean business. They don't care if you're a woman or not; you're fair game if you're involved. Do you hear me? If I think for a moment you are not following my request, you will find yourself on a long vacation someplace else, until this blows over. Period."

He paused to let his words sink in. "By the way," he added, "why were you leaving the house tonight?" He stood with his hands on his hips, frowning at her. Annie moaned and looked away. Turning back to him, she was not surprised to see he stood still, awaiting her reply. He had blood smeared over his shirt and jeans. With the scowl on his brow, he looked formidable.

"I had this crazy idea I could tell who has been trying to get into the clinic to check Tina's records. The computer shows that two times, around eleven at night, someone tried to log on. I didn't intend to go into the clinic, only to watch the door. Please don't say it; I know it was a stupid idea." Annie closed her eyes.

"Not just stupid, Annie, dangerous. No more. You will not run around like a loose cannon. You have to let me know what you're doing and where you'll be. This is getting heated. I have other things going on, and I can't worry about you and everything else. Do you understand me?" he asked.

Annie did understand, after tonight, only too clearly. She nodded in agreement. He sat back down on the bed, watching her, tenderly brushing her hair back from her face. She finally began to doze off. Tony brushed her cheek with his hand and softly kissed her. When he was certain she was asleep, he left. What he hadn't told Annie was that a lone shadow lurked near the clinic, well hidden in the overgrown brush. If someone intended to enter the clinic, Tony would get a call. He chose not to tell her about the bodies of his men, found when the area was searched following the assault on her.

* * * *

Tossing fitfully, repeatedly awakened by nightmares, Annie finally raised herself up on the mountain of pillows to check on Buster. He was awake, but instinctively understood he was to lie still beside her. Soothingly she patted his head and leaned over to kiss him and moaned. Still so edgy after her ordeal, she felt the need to secure the house again. Forgetting she had company, she struggled from the bed and walked unsteadily into the living room. Startled, she froze. Two men were sitting on opposite sides of the room, silently watching her.

"My . . . my name is Annie," she began carefully, pulling the robe draped about her shoulders tighter. Recognizing Sam, she smiled halfheartedly. "What a night." The other man looked familiar, but Annie couldn't think of his name. The medication was on board, and she was fuzzy.

"We know."

Both men stood and Sam formally introduced his partner, Dominic. Not certain how to treat the visitors, Annie offered them both coffee, grateful when they declined. "Thank you for helping me. I don't hurt so much now, though my hand still does. What am I saying? Really, everything hurts like hell," Annie babbled. "So, what happens now? I mean, you two will be here all the time? I have extra bedrooms . . ." She paused, holding her head. "This is a little awkward for me. Truthfully, I'm *very* uncomfortable with all of this."

"Don't worry, Annie, you'll not even notice we're around. One of us will sleep while the other watches at night. At least one of us will be awake and in the house with you, always. There are more men outside, but you won't even notice them. Don't go anywhere without letting us know," Dominic instructed her. "Lou and I are brothers, and Sam is our cousin, so we all feel like we know you. You look bushed, just go on back to bed."

Sam . . . she felt safe with him around after getting to know him a little at their picnic. If the other guy was Lou's brother, she knew she was in good hands. Annie admitted to herself she *was* tired, and everything really *did* hurt. Her head pounded, and her eyes watered. Her injured hand had a heartbeat of its own. She rose slowly, unsteadily, until Sam grabbed her arm. After walking her down the hall and helping her up onto the bed, he propped the pillows around her arm. Stepping out quietly, he closed the door behind him. It felt good to lie back again. Buster moved closer to her, and she relaxed. Lying in the dark, Annie went over and over the attack. Alone and frightened, she cried. The pills took over and she drifted into a deep sleep.

The next morning, Annie struggled to sit up and was instantly reminded of her condition. One eye was swollen shut, and the other would open only slightly. Her cheek was swollen and bruised, her jaw was stiff and ached, and her upper lip was split and puffed-up. A knot had come up on the back of her head, and she could barely lift her good arm. The restraint held the injured arm still. "At least *that* doesn't hurt," Annie said with a wry smile. She was unable to take a deep breath. The pain in her hand blended in rhythmically with throbbing everywhere else. After attempting to stand, then sinking back upon the bed, reluctantly she realized she needed help—a *female* companion who wasn't packing a gun— and Lynn was the only person Annie wanted.

* * * *

Lynn answered the phone hesitantly after several rings. "Annie? Oh, thank goodness. I got the weirdest phone call last night. This guy called asking for you. At least I think he was asking for you; with his accent it was hard to tell. When he could tell I didn't know what he was talking about, he hung up. Are you at home? What's going on?"

"I'll call you right back, I'm fine but I'll call you back," Annie said abruptly and hung up. Talking was difficult and Annie winced with pain. Lynn's announcement reminded her someone might tap the house phone. She sat still trying to think.

Pulling a robe over her shoulders, she slowly walked into the great room. "Good morning, Sunshine," Sam smiled. "You look like a fighter, girl. I'm thinking the other guy must look worse."

"Please don't remind me," Annie struggled to speak clearly. "Could someone have tapped my house phone without me knowing it?"

"Yes, your phone could be compromised. Didn't Tony give you a phone? You really should just use that one. We can talk to him about the house phone when he calls." Sam watched her move carefully toward the nearest chair.

"He's trying to figure out who the kid from last night was," he continued.

"Kid! I killed a kid?" Annie's heart lurched. "He sure didn't feel like a kid."

"Well, I'm using the term a little loosely, but he was a younger guy. We're not certain who he is . . . or, rather, was. By the way, it's hard to tell just who killed him, you or Buster. I'm going with a tie."

"Hmm. I'm not certain that was a joke, but I can't think without coffee." Annie shuffled toward the kitchen.

"Got you covered." Sam smiled. "Dominic made himself at home. You're just in time for some of his homemade biscuits and gravy. He LIKES to cook . . . go figure."

Annie felt better with strong coffee and a little food, although she couldn't chew well. Buster was barely moving about, though his belly wound was dry and he was eating a little. Unable to stay up any longer, Annie limped back to bed with Sam's help. She tried, unsuccessfully, to dial Lynn's number. Sam watched for a second then took the phone from her. "What's the number? I'll dial for you," he gently instructed her. Annie forgot about Sam when Lynn answered.

"Lynn, can you come? Some guy jumped me last night. I'm going to be fine, but . . ." her voice broke. "Everyone has been super, but I need you."

Lynn agreed immediately. Annie ended the call, set her phone down, and to her surprise, she slept again.

Sam hit redial and filled Lynn in on the prior evening's events. "Don't start out just yet. I'm thinking Tony is going to move her. She's asleep now. I'll let you know as soon as we know where she's going." The conversation ended after he promised her he would see to it that Annie was safe.

* * * *

Early afternoon, Annie's cell phone rang. Fighting the fog in her mind, she answered. Tony let her know he would come to pick her up around eight. She interrupted him, not allowing him to finish, "Not to be ugly, but I am—ugly, I mean. I feel worse than I look, if that's possible. Maybe if I sleep a little more . . . I can't go anywhere like this." She fell back into the pillows, closing her eyes. "I don't think I like this business one little bit, Tony."

"I'm sorry, but you have to come. I'd feel better about you not being at the ranch just now. We think one of Saldivar's men may be headed your way. The young man who attacked you last night was not with them, so I'd say it's safe to assume you're on several radars now. I can't cover you on that ranch. Too much area. Go ahead and sleep for a little while, and I'll have Sam and Dominic get you up when I'm ready."

As usual, his order was definitive. This time she didn't care. "I'm sorry, Inamorata, but it's too late to decide you don't like this business." Annie didn't even say good-bye; she just touched the "end" symbol on the phone screen.

* * * *

Hours later Annie struggled awake as she heard Dominic knocking at the bedroom door. Trying to sit up, she answered groggily, "Come in. What's going on?"

Poking his head in the door Dominic said, "Tony says you're to pack enough things for several weeks. If I were you, I'd pack everything I could think of, just in case. And not to worry; Buster gets to go along on your date too."

"Now? Okay, but I'll need to call Lynn and Earl to let them know what's going on."

"Don't worry, Annie. We'll let them know. I think Tony has already sent for Lynn."

"All right. How long do I have to get ready? My face and head are killing me. My hand hurts too."

"Truthfully, we need to leave here in about twenty minutes."

"What!?" She could tell by the look on Dominic's face she might as well not ask any more questions. "I'll be ready." She sat up as he closed the door behind him. After a struggle, she was finally dressed in a long, loose caftan. Opening the door again, she called, "Can someone help me? I don't think I can pack my things very fast."

Both men came to her assistance. She pointed and they stuffed her bags. Twenty minutes later she was ready to go. Slowly, Annie trudged to the great room. Hesitating, she remembered the briefcase. At her direction, Sam found and retrieved the case and keys. Buster was still subdued, and it took extra urging to get him to limp along.

Annie stood on the porch while the men hauled things out to the black Escalade. She looked beyond the creek to the hay field and took in the pasture just below the house. Closing her eye, she listened to the sounds of the bluebirds, robins, magpies, and songbirds. Taking a deep breath, she smelled the lilacs, roses, and sweet williams in full bloom. Floating beneath their fragrance, fresh pine added just a touch of spark. Shaking her head sadly, she took the hand Sam offered her and began the walk down the stairs to the vehicle waiting to take her away. Annie was surprised at how unsteady she was.

Dominic stood patiently, watching her take her leave. Sam helped her into the backseat, placing a pillow under her injured arm. He gently patted her shoulder. Annie smiled back at him, too depressed for tears. Dominic leaned into the opposite side, handing her an armful of lilac blossoms. "Thank you," she whispered teary-eyed, burying her face in the sweet smelling flowers.

The dust flew up behind the Escalade as it slowly made its way toward the county road. Absently, Annie thought how badly the ranch needed rain. She watched the house grow smaller and wondered if she might not see it again. The hum of the road and the music softly playing put her to sleep. Dominic looked into his rearview mirror, and his brown eyes filled with sympathy as he watched Annie move fitfully around. Often she would start awake with a slight cry and then sit looking into space toward the window. He could imagine what images were filling her thoughts. He fought nightmares every night.

CHAPTER 36

Faustino watched the house. Lights went on and off, doors were opened, and people wandered in and out. Someone obviously lived there. Who? He knew the sister was still living at the ranch, but these were all men, five or six of them.

Just then a woman stepped out onto the front porch. She stood a long time looking out over the grounds and the driveway. Faustino had never seen the sister, but this woman looked to be about the same age Diego had told him she was, and by all accounts, she was easy to look at. "Maybe the gringos have a different idea of 'easy to look at,'" he muttered after studying her through his binoculars.

Later, when the lights were all out, he placed the binoculars in their case and left his post. He decided to return to the house early the next morning.

Pulling the wig off amid jeers and laughter, the "woman" closed and locked Annie's front door. "This better work, or I'll never hear the end of it from you goons. The things we do for the boss."

* * * *

Morning found Faustino slipping into an empty house, only minutes after the woman and her escorts drove off. He began a systematic search. He spent a little more time in the rooms on the lower level, where he found the framed photographs of that dog Jacko, and the partner, though. His search didn't take long, however. It was obvious Tina's list was not to be found. Stuffing pictures into his backpack, he slipped out the back door and immediately punched in Diego's number on his phone.

CHAPTER 37

Landing added a sense of foreboding. She looked out the window, but with the onslaught of rain, could see nothing. Dominic helped her unload, but never spoke.

Annie was hustled under an umbrella to a Suburban. She was burning up. Dr. Grazanti had warned her about the problems with the dirty wound. It appeared his fear was well founded. She couldn't remember when she had last taken her medicine nor what she might have taken. Her head throbbed, her closed eye watered, and her jaw ached. She could scarcely move her hand without severe pain. Neither Sam nor Dominic was inside the vehicle yet, and she had a brief moment of hesitation. Grateful Buster was with her, she slid inside. The warmth was welcome, as was the blanket Dominic soon tucked around her. Without further conversation, the party took off. The rain hammered the Suburban relentlessly, the wipers beating their own rhythm. Annie tried in vain to calm her aching head. The dreary weather made her feel worse.

Arriving at their destination, she was too ill to care where they might be. Standing inside shivering, she waited while Dominic gathered her luggage. He walked with her upstairs and opened the door. After quickly looking around, he turned to leave. "Oh no you don't. Where am I and why am I here?" Annie's voice was tired and weak. She peered at Dominic through the slit of one eye.

"Because I sent for you," Tony answered from the living area. Crossing to her side, he instructed Dominic to notify Dr. Grazanti Annie had arrived. He held her closely, kissing her bruised face. He could feel the heat. Moving her under brighter lights, Tony examined her closely. His eyes were filled with concern. He wasn't prepared to see Annie this way. Carefully, he moved his hands over her face and arm. Leading her to the couch, he sat her down. "I needed to keep you someplace safe," He left her sitting while he took her luggage into the bedroom. Returning, he sat beside her, his arm around her.

* * * *

"Where are we?" Annie asked weakly. "Is Lynn coming too? If you 'kidnapped' her, you'll have hell to pay."

Tony nodded, smiling. He had sent Sam after Lynn, as soon as Annie was with him. Now he was picturing Sam bustling Lynn around. "Yes, Lynn is on her way. Let's just say you're in a safe place, near Denver. I've found out some interesting things about your friend Tina. I thought we could get into her computer first. However, she had unusual living arrangements and kept odd company. The house is paid up and still in use." While he talked with her, he studied her battered face.

Frowning, Annie turned her swollen slit of sight toward him. "Tony, why are we in Denver?"

"What do you mean?" He brushed her hair back. Closing her eyes, she leaned into him. She couldn't remember ever feeling this bad. "Maybe I'm going to die." Annie thought to herself. She was still for a long moment. Tony watched her, wondering if he should just get her to bed.

"For starters, she lived in Pueblo," Annie finally replied, her eyes still closed. "I'm certain, because I visited her there. Besides, what else could anyone find? I can't imagine that everyone hasn't been there already." Annie's head felt like it would explode any minute.

"Pueblo? All the information we have on her gives an address in Denver," he said, more to himself than Annie. Her condition concerned him

far more than the location of Tina's condo. However, sitting around in
the wrong location would result in their losing valuable time; time that
would be tight as it was, given the circumstances.

"Like I said, I'm certain I went to Pueblo. I probably still have her
information on my phone. You transferred my contacts. I can look."

"Not now," he corrected her decisively. He had intended to move
quickly, but Annie was worse than he thought. He would not jeopardize
her health. "After Lynn gets here, maybe tomorrow or the next day. Let's
see how you feel." He helped her up and led her to the bedroom. "You
are to rest, Annie," he ordered firmly as he sat her on the bed. He closed
the door behind them. Unhurriedly he turned the bed back. Carefully he
began to remove her immobilizer. Horrified, Annie realized he was going
to undress her.

"I can do this, honestly." She protested, halfheartedly pushing his
hand aside.

Tony countered quietly, "Annie, I've already done this twice. While I
would much rather the circumstances were different, this is not the time
for you to become modest." With that he had her caftan off, her nightgown on and her feverish body propped up on pillows, tucked into bed
before she could think how to stop him. Sitting on the bed, he looked
at her, his dark eyes filled with love and concern. Loath to leave her, he
got up and returned with her medications. Sitting back on the bed, he
handed her water and the pills Sam brought from her house.

"What are these for?" Annie asked.

"One is a mild sedative, Annie. The other two are antibiotics. You have
a fever, your hand is red and swollen." He smiled at her affectionately.
"You really can't go anywhere. You might as well give in and behave for a
change. Let someone take care of you. That someone is me. Dr. Grazanti
is on his way."

Annie sank down into the pillows. "I'm glad you're here, Tony," she
whispered.

Tony stayed until he was certain she was asleep. Leaving her door ajar,
he began meeting with his men in the suite. When Dr. Grazanti arrived,
Tony led him to Annie. She barely remembered him coming. She was
racked with fever and haunted with nightmares. The hand was grossly

swollen, reddened and hot. The large bruises on her chest, side, and back were all clean. The doctor changed her dressings and administered a stronger antibiotic for the infection. "I'll be back this evening. I think she's septic; her hand was really dirty and now she's got a roaring infection. Keep an eye on her. If she gets worse or you're not comfortable, just call, Tony. I'm close. We have to stay on top of this."

Tony nodded. He watched Annie sleeping. "If anything happens to her . . ." he murmured.

Tony stayed nearby. It seemed Annie's fever was not getting any better. He called Dr. Grazanti. This time Grazanti stayed. All the next day and into the night, Annie lay on the bed tossing and burning with fever. The doctor started intravenous antibiotics. Tony changed the cool towels he had covered Annie with in an attempt to cut the fever. Improvement came slowly. Her fever broke during the second night, which left her weak. When Dr. Grazanti finally left, she was cool and resting easier. Tony stepped out to speak with his men.

"Where is the computer man? He could have walked here by now." Tony was pacing in the sitting room. At any other time, he would have used Sam. Sam was still trying to get Lynn. Weather had them socked in. "That's a problem. We're getting spread too thin," Tony admitted.

Unaware of the past two days, Annie awoke on the afternoon of the third day feeling washed out and filthy. Her hair was matted and she could still smell the blood that had splattered over her. It seemed she could still smell that horrible man's breath. Her room was empty, though she could hear the hum of voices from the next room. With great effort, she struggled out of bed, wobbled slowly to the bathroom, pulled off her gown, and turned on the shower. Buster padded along beside her. The stiffness, made worse by swelling, caused even the simplest of actions to be painful. Pausing to catch her breath, she stepped into the stream of steaming water. The heat made her dizzy, and she fell against the wall. A moan escaped her lips as her wounded body connected with the tile. Just then, the shower door flew open.

"What the hell do you think you're doing!" Tony reprimanded angrily as he leaned in to turn off the shower and steady Annie.

"Please, I feel just awful. I need to clean up, Tony." Annie's plea touched

Tony's heart, and his manner softened. Annie knew she needed help, but hated that the help would come from Tony. Again. "Is there no end to my complete humiliation?" she asked herself.

Undaunted, he took action. Removing his suit coat and tie, rolling his sleeves up, and grabbing a washcloth, he helped Annie sit down on the portable stool that stood in the corner of the shower stall, careful to protect her injured arm and hand. Sighing, she leaned back with closed eyes. "I think you've done this many times." Annie teased him in a soft voice, her eyes still closed. Tony smiled. "Actually, this is a first for me."

* * * *

Later, her hair washed and combed, and her battered body dressed in a fresh nightgown and robe, Annie felt more like herself again. She even felt well enough to sit out on the balcony in the late afternoon sun. Tony ordered a tray with fruit and tea be delivered to Annie's room and the bed linens be changed while she was resting there.

"I'm sorry you have to bathe me, Tony," Annie murmured, blushing.

"Don't be," he said. To ease Annie's embarrassment he brought up the subject of Tina once more. "I'm curious about Tina's living arrangements. Why would she keep this place up and live somewhere else? Why would she have a publicly listed phone number? Maybe she had more than two careers."

"Two?" asked Annie.

"She was a physician's assistant, correct? We know she had extracurricular activities, but what else went on with her? Now I'm not so certain I want anyone in her condo here. There's a rough bunch using that condo. I'm not positive, but I have an idea why she never let it go. I think it's in her name for convenience. I doubt she herself ever spent time there." Tony stood to lean on the balcony railing.

"Because someone else uses it? It certainly was not ever her. Do we know for sure just who she was working with or for?" Annie began to feel human again. The sun shone warm upon her. She leaned back in the chair, closed her eyes, letting the warmth begin to heal her. Buster lay at her feet, dozing.

"Not yet, but we're getting there. It can't be Saldivar or Jacko. Jacko had her killed, but the hit was a mess, since no one got the information. Jacko worked with the feds, so they don't have the information or he would have gotten it from them. I don't think the group from here knew so much about her. She was good at keeping her cover it seems. That leaves Cuba and Columbia. Jacko also worked with the Columbians, so they don't have the information, either. Cuba didn't know, since the kid who attacked you is from the Cuba group. He seemed to go between groups, but still wouldn't have gone after you if the list were with the Cuban or Venezuelan group in Denver."

"How could he go between groups? Where is the group in Denver from?" Annie's eyes were still closed, but now a frown marred her expression. While they talked, Tony's eyes took in her bruised and swollen face.

"He was the little brother of one of the families from Cuba, but when he came here, the rest were stuck in South America. Suddenly, he had nowhere to go. His brother called in a card, and he wound up with the bunch from Venezuela in Denver. Only one family or cartel from each area is in on this. The big dream of Saldivar was to unite them all, controlling a lot more than the drug running," Tony continued. He wanted to hold Annie closely.

Annie opened her eyes to look at Tony. One eye was nearly normal. The more injured eye was twice its usual size, but nevertheless she could open it. "And your family, Tony? How do they fit into this?"

Tony studied Annie. Finally he spoke. "We don't. We're not interested in getting into any of this for reasons that I can't discuss with you. We are interested in seeing this plan fail on a grand scale."

He walked beside the railing, thinking, then returned to Annie. Squatting in front of her, he held her hand, looking deep into her eyes. "Annie, don't ask questions. You have to trust me, a decision your brother was comfortable with."

Annie sighed. "I know," she answered softly. "The immediate issue is what do we do in Denver, or do we need to go to Pueblo?"

Both were silent for a moment. "It seems we would waste less time if we go to Pueblo. Lynn is on her way, finally. I could reroute her plane." Tony finally spoke. He looked at Annie's tired face. "Maybe not. We'll wait here for her. Better for you, anyway." He knew Annie was too weak to do anything yet.

* * * *

Dr. Grazanti brought drops for Annie's eye and more antibiotics. He was thorough and fast with an easy touch. This time, he sat on the side of her bed for a long while. "You look better, Miss Annie. How do you feel? Are you eating? Moving around a little? You've had quite a round, I say."

"I feel much better. Tony has me sitting outside and pushes food at me like my grandmother used to do. Thank you for being so kind to me." He smiled at the slight form lying in the bed. Not many people thanked him besides Tony.

Dr. Grazanti stood at the door speaking in a low tone to Tony for several minutes. From Tony's reaction to the aging man, Annie could tell they knew each other well. Closing the door after the doctor left, Tony returned to her side. He sat on the edge of the bed, watching her doze as the tablets took effect. Looking at her, he shook his head. The anger inside was almost more than he could conceal from her. The man that beat her was gone, apparently a rogue. Still, she had become a target until the information contained on Tina's computer was secured. He knew this was but the tip. Her identity and where she lived were out. He needed the list and he needed it soon. "Just what the hell is on that list?" he wondered. "Probably nothing, but like the Emperor's clothes . . ."

Sam brought Lynn by, late in the afternoon of the fourth day. Annie was ecstatic to see her sister; Lynn was horrified to see Annie. "Oh Annie!" she gasped, her voice filled with alarm.

"I'm feeling some better, and it *is* easier to rest away from the ranch."

"You two catch up; I'll see you in the morning. This time, the men at your door will stay put. Get to bed early," Tony ordered gently. He kissed the top of Annie's head, brushed her hair from her face, and left the sisters to visit in private. Annie filled Lynn in on all the details.

"It was awful, Lynn. I've never before thought I was going to die, but I did then. I can't remember thinking what I was going to do, I just did it." A tear slipped out of her good eye. "I killed someone, Lynn." Now a flood of tears came.

"That's called self-defense." In her down-to-earth way, she brought Annie back again. She hugged her protectively.

Lynn made certain Annie ate something before she took her evening medicine. Slowly, Annie drifted off to sleep. Lynn lay awake staring at the ceiling. Her heart was heavy with worry. She watched the numbers change on the small clock near the bed. Sleep came reluctantly.

* * * *

When they arrived in Pueblo, it was quietly settling down for the evening. Lynn sighed. "I don't suppose it would do me any good to object to this whole operation, would it?"

"Really, Lynn, I'm sorry you were dragged here, though I am glad you're with me. Tony has some crazy idea that there is another list. We might have better luck, since most people think she lived in Denver." Annie shrugged her shoulders casually, glancing sideways at her sister.

"Except you, of course," Lynn commented dryly. "You would be the one to have stumbled onto her *real* living arrangements."

"Well, sort of. I do have her address. I don't think she kept everything on her computer. She talked a lot about where to keep personal papers. I didn't think about it until just now, but I have an idea where they might be. Let's find Tony and get this show on the road." Carefully, Annie stood up. Her body still ached.

Wandering the house, they heard his voice behind closed doors. He was angry, and other voices blended in, indicating a heated discussion was taking place. The sisters waited for a few minutes. Annie hesitated before suggesting, "Let's just cruise by the house. I can tell you if it's the same one. There have to be others who know she lived in Pueblo. I don't think we have much time. Let' s find someone with a vehicle we can borrow."

Lynn shook her head in disbelief, "I don't think that's a good idea at all. Every vehicle I've seen this bunch in looks like an official government car. You'd stick out like a sore thumb." Still, she could tell they were going, one way or another. "Maybe we could take a taxi or something. Better yet, maybe we shouldn't go at all. Now *there's* a novel idea."

"Not a taxi, too easy to follow or check up on. Let's see if Sam is around, or Lou, or anyone we would know." Annie ignored Lynn's suggestion to let it go.

After searching the house, they ventured outside. On a secluded veranda sat several of Tony's men, including Sam and Lou. They stood when the sisters approached, but sat down again at Annie's request. "We need a plain car. Not something anyone would notice if it drove down your street. Nothing sinister or big or expensive. Can anyone help?"

Lou groaned. "Annie, you're going to get us all in trouble, you know. We can't let you wander around. Don't ask, please. You realize it's not just you he gets mad at, don't you? After your last scrape he'll be madder than hell. Give us a break, girl."

"I'm sure Tony said I was not to be left alone, right? I'm reasonably certain he would not consider Lynn a proper escort. So here's the deal. We're going. Allowing us to leave unescorted would be awful. Either walking or riding, we're going." With that, the sisters turned and headed for the front drive. It was already late, and would soon be dark.

"To think, all these years I thought you were meek and mild!" Lynn murmured.

"Okay, Okay," Lou called. He spoke briefly to Sam. Sam smiled and caught up to them.

"That was ballsy, Annie. Come on, I know just the car."

Annie and Lynn were soon slipping in and out of traffic in an older nondescript PT Cruiser. It was faded blue with no unusual marks or dents. "How appropriate, looks like a Mafia car from the '40s," Lynn laughed. Sam grinned happily. Plainly, he wasn't worried about Tony and was delighted to haul Lynn anywhere.

Annie gave the address to Sam. They entered an area with upscale garden homes. "This is it, I'm certain. I remember the park and lake." Annie looked around at the familiar landmarks.

Driving by Tina's house, it looked like all the others, neat and occupied. The outside was well tended. Annie had Sam pull in the drive; she got out, casually checked the mail as if she belonged there, and headed for the front door. Lynn and Sam followed. Holding her breath, Annie punched in the code from her phone. The door unlocked. They stepped into the entry hall. "I'm going to need help. I'll point, you two reach" she ordered.

Moving through the house to the back, Annie quickly found the computer. Taking a chance, she logged on, using Tina's condo entry code before letting Sam take over. Sam copied every file, deleted several programs, and took every disk or flash drive they could find. Annie next led them into the kitchen. Annie removed a container from the freezer. It was in a special sealed wrap, protected from temperature extremes and moisture. Her last stop was in Tina's master suite. Hidden beneath a loosened tile, beneath clothing and old pictures, was a flat mailer with flash drives and discs. She started to leave, but Sam headed back to the office and removed the external hard drive. He returned with a dog food bag containing the external hard drive and the computer main drive. Thus loaded they left the same way they'd entered. As they pulled away, Annie sighed with relief. "By the time someone figures out she doesn't live in Denver, we'll be long gone. Thanks, Sam."

When they returned, Sam led them to Tony's office, where both Tony and Lou were waiting. Lou was subdued. Tony was livid. Before he could speak, Annie blurted out angrily, "I don't think it was necessary for Lou to insist Sam be with us. This place is in an exclusive area. We would be just fine! He won't talk to us, won't do what we ask, and I'm not at all happy he dragged us back so soon. Tony, you told me to get the computer. That is *exactly* what I did." She stood glaring at Lou, who was standing behind Tony.

Tony started to speak to Sam. Instead he just closed his eyes and shook his head. Sam and Lou slipped away. Then Tony turned to Annie and Lynn. His face was dark with anger. "After what you've just been through, you pull this? I told you Annie, one more time and you're both out of here. You don't follow orders and you put my men at risk. I'm finished trying to get through to you." By this time, his voice was cold and unyielding. "You're gone! I'm sending you both away. Maybe then you will learn to take orders!"

"Just make sure wherever you send us has computers, so we can get the list everyone wants before someone else gets it." Annie answered calmly as she began to slowly unload the material they had taken onto Tony's desk. Tony stopped speaking and walked over to the desk. He stood quietly for a moment, then turned toward Lynn and said, "Can you give us a moment?"

Tony stood in front of Annie, his hands in his pockets. "How difficult would it have been to let me know you were leaving? You just nearly got killed, and still you do this? How many chances do you think you get, Annie? No more. Since you cannot bring yourself to come to me, I'll have to make it harder for you to leave." He was still angry, but always with her, his anger dissipated quickly. He looked at her, noting the fire in her eyes. "Eventually, girl, I'm going to rein you in," he thought to himself.

"I tried to tell you, but when I came to your office, you were having a rather heated discussion I didn't want to interrupt. I'm concerned about how much time we have to get this figured out. I promise you, Tony, I'll always find some way to let you know from this moment on. I should be just a step away from you if we are to work wherever you plant us." Tony smiled down at her. He knew well where she would be and how difficult it would be for her to slip away again. Of that he would make certain.

"No, Annie," he corrected with authority, "you won't just let me know, you'll *ask* before you move from now on. Do you understand me? You'll *ask*." He paused. His expression was set. "You can't always know what else is going on. I won't let you put yourself, my men, your sister, or anyone in danger because you are too headstrong to take direction." Annie knew he was scolding her. Deservedly so, perhaps. He tipped her face up, "Nice move to keep Lou and Sam out of trouble." His voice was low but firm.

"I'm sorry, Tony." She looked up at him with a contrite expression.

He held her close and noted, ever so quietly, "I'm guessing you think it's easier to get forgiveness than it is to get permission. You will find that is not always the case, my love." He smiled to himself when he heard Annie's little gasp. "Now," he continued, "I'm expecting a call from Earl, and you two have work to do." Without another word, he left the room.

CHAPTER 38

In Denver, with rain pelting his face, Faustino stepped out of Welby's Bar and Grill to call Diego. Diego was in a foul mood.

"The patrón is useless now. Can't even feed himself. You need to get those files, damn it! Everything is dangling. New York won't move until we have the information. They're going to sell the merchandise to someone else if we don't help them unload it soon. I need answers by tomorrow evening."

"You'll have them," Faustino curtly replied, hanging up. He spent good time at the bar. Liquor made men talk. Faustino had what he wanted.

Sitting across the street from Tina's house, he watched as people wandered in and out of the place. None looked like junkies, but they weren't clean-cut citizens, either. He decided to wander in himself.

Diego waited for the call from Faustino. Evening had long passed. Still nothing. An uneasy feeling kept gnawing at him. He tried calling again. The call went immediately to voice mail. Calling off and on during the night, Diego knew his friend was gone. That left him. He gathered a few men he trusted, into the office. "Get ready. We're going north. Meet in Denver. If we don't deliver the list, it's war. I don't think we can win."

CHAPTER 39

The hours ticked by. Annie and Lynn struggled to understand what they were reading, trying to piece together information. More than once, they found themselves locked out of certain programs on Tina's computer. Taking what information they had, they wrote copious notes. Slowly, a picture of drug and human smuggling emerged. A picture with decades of activity. Together the sisters made lists of names and drew diagrams of who was linked to whom and noted when someone was eliminated. Many of the surnames sounded Asian, not Mexican. The monies involved were huge, and they wondered why anyone would pay that much for people. They concluded it had to be the drugs.

By midnight, the sisters were beginning to make mistakes and have trouble remembering what they had just read. For safekeeping, they made copies of everything and then ventured outside the room. Annie asked the man keeping watch, "Is it possible to lock this room?"

The man nodded to Annie and left. He returned shortly thereafter with Lou. "Wow, you both look bushed. Here is the key. Make sure the door to the patio is locked."

He stood by while Annie secured the room then led her and Lynn next door to their room. "Is Tony around?" Annie asked.

"No, he's gone already. I think you two are supposed to leave day after tomorrow." Bidding them good night, Lou left.

Annie wandered onto the veranda. She caught sight of an army green Suburban rounding the curve toward the gate, followed by several similar vehicles. As they sped up the long drive, Annie caught sight of some type of gun out one window. She ran inside, yelling, "Lynn, move it, we are so out of here!" She ran next door to retrieve their paperwork and Tina's computer. Using her one good arm, she began to clumsily stuff everything into satchels and knapsacks. Lynn joined her. When Sam ran down the hall, he saw the sisters leaving the room lugging their bags, with Buster on their heels. Sam grabbed the bags and motioned to them to follow him.

They ran down dark halls, through an old exit, and onto a ramp that turned out to be a wooden boat pier. Silently, a Boston Whaler moved up against the pier and Sam, Annie, and Lynn boarded as fast as they could. The boat moved along the heavily wooded embankment to another dock. From there, everyone climbed onto the pier and ran toward a black Hummer that was parked on the side of the road in anticipation of their arrival.

Once they were situated in the escape vehicle, Annie turned to Sam and asked sarcastically, "I don't suppose you know what that was all about, do you?"

"We always expect to get raided. Remember, Tony runs a family business, so to speak. There are those few in Homeland Security that resent the leeway he has. I'd bet a month's pay this had nothing to do with what we're working on. This was a fishing expedition just to see what they could scare up. Tony doesn't scare, though, so they'll go home empty. He's not in the habit of leaving anything lying around. They made their point; he is under increased surveillance."

Sam paused, checking behind them. "We do need to get this computer stuff someplace secure quickly, just in case we get pulled over. If, by chance, these guys were to get their hands on it you would never get it back.

"What happens now?"

"Tony has a friend near here. We're going to drop in for tonight, and Tony will get with me."

Annie smiled slightly. "I have a better idea, but I'll need a plain car that won't funk out on us."

"What are you thinking, Annie?" asked Lynn suspiciously. "We can't go back to the ranch and we can't go to my house. Just where does that leave us?"

"Don't worry. Trust me. Sam, we're going to leave you. I'm not telling you where we're headed, so you won't have to lie to Tony. I'll talk with him this time. I'm certain he'll be mad—again. Just get me the car."

Sam pulled into a secluded park. He spoke briefly on his phone then turned to his passengers. "Perfect."

True to his word, Sam had arranged for someone to rendezvous with them in the park. The car he drove was an older model Jeep that was clean, had a GPS and full tank of gas. As the sisters changed vehicles and settled Buster in, Annie gave Sam a quick hug. "Take care of yourself, Sam, and Allen and Tony too."

Sam just smiled. Before he stepped away, he gave Lynn a long hug, which she returned with a quick kiss. "Stay safe," he whispered into her hair. Lynn turned back toward him to wave as she opened the passenger door.

Once they were on the road, Lynn asked, "Okay, just where *are* we headed?"

"You're going to meet my friend Rhino. No one here knows him, but as you know, he's an expert at computers and has plenty of room. And . . . I don't think he's ever been raided!"

CHAPTER 40

Tony was so angry Annie could hardly understand him. Eventually, her calm voice won out, and he settled down.

He finally agreed she probably was safer away from him just now. She promised she would keep in touch but avoided telling him where she would be. Annie suggested he could put her on the back burner and not think about her. "That will never happen," he said to himself as he ended Annie's call.

Immediately, Tony called Sam, who reported, "I dropped a tracking device in Lynn's purse. There's one in the Jeep too. Will keep you posted." When Sam called back in the early predawn hours, he gave Tony a measure of comfort. Perhaps she *would* be safer in Las Cruces. He knew Rhino well.

* * * *

Buster's grumbling reminded Annie he might need a pit stop, so she pulled over at the next rest stop. Lynn insisted she should drive for a while and let Annie rest.

"We're headed toward Las Cruces. When we get to Albuquerque, let's stop for the night." Annie yawned. "My hand and head are killing me." Going without sleep for so long was taking its toll.

"If it's all the same to you, let's try to make it without stopping. You go ahead and sleep."

* * * *

The sisters arrived at Rhino's place exhausted. Safely in his guest room, they slept for the next twenty-four hours. When they were up and moving around, he fixed breakfast while they brought him up to date. Their story ended, he kept his own counsel for a few minutes until they had begun to eat. Then he brought up a subject Annie hadn't even thought about.

"So, thus far, at least six people are known dead and one is assumed dead . . . a government agent no less. My sweet, this is not as simple as moving merchandise for The Blue Dawn, you know. I can't see how you'll ever be safe as long as any one of the groups is left and knows your identity. I'm amazed that so few know it so far." The room was silent except for the hum of the fan.

"Well, let's look at what you've brought and see what we can match or make sense of. I'm thinking we'll start by identifying a provenance. I'll put the coffee on, but when I say we quit, we quit. Agreed? If by chance we need to hibernate, so to speak, we do so, immediately, without question. Agreed? I'll take your blank stares as a resounding yes!"

"What is a provenance?" Lynn asked as she rose from the table.

"A provenance is a record of origination usually applied to valuable works of art. That's how Annie uses it. In this case, we'll identify where each item we're finding—person, firearm, drug load, or exchange of monies—starts. Then we try to follow where it goes. We'll keep track of how many we tie one to the other."

Rhino designed a spreadsheet on which they were able to plot similar transactions and connections. He spent time teaching both Annie and Lynn what programs he used and how to use them. Eventually, a pattern emerged from the current versus older closed transactions they were tracking.

"We're looking at something ugly," Lynn observed. "This makes me a little more than uncomfortable."

"I would say you're dealing with human smuggling here, but not for labor. I think you've got a terrorist camp buildup going on. This isn't going to be pleasant," Rhino noted as a matter of fact.

"This is huge. Are you certain?" Annie looked from Rhino to Lynn in disbelief. "I mean, it looks like they are scattered all over the country. Can we find a way to tell if they are headed to the same place, ultimately?"

Rhino thought for a moment. "I'm not sure, but I would think someone on your side might have some idea. This information leads me to think they all head to New York and then go to wherever."

"Guys, someone has to be directing all this activity. Does any name jump out? And look, some of the names—like this guy Rhamidid—don't seem to belong to any group. Do you think they have some kind of authority?" Lynn asked.

Annie, who had been walking around the room as she listened, said, "I think we need to call Tony tonight."

When Annie placed that call, Tony came to the phone immediately. He listened intently to her before Annie introduced him to Rhino. Neither Rhino nor Tony indicated they knew each other. Instead Tony began, "We have a little problem. The one who could really help now is Allen. He's unavailable for at least a week. I hate to be the one to tell Annie, but he's back at work. I *can* tell you he is expecting some guy who is very important to whatever he is working on. Anyway, I'll have him call you whenever he gets in touch with me again. Ask Annie to call me later."

CHAPTER 41

Diego and his friend Rudy checked into a cheap motel on the outskirts of Denver. They would roam the areas where he knew Faustino had been. Diego knew Faustino must have stumbled on to something. He felt in his bones, Faustino was dead. Already he could hear the thinly veiled threats in every call received from other groups eager to move forward. If he couldn't produce the information soon, all hell would break loose.

Rudy snuffed his cigarette out on his boot heel. Diego was good, but he wasn't Saldivar, at least not to the men they would be dealing with.

Diego watched his lieutenant stirring cold coffee. "What is it, compadre? Do you need to tell me anything?"

Rudy shook his head. "Just get tired sometimes. Don't you?"

"Never. Lately every day has been a blast." Diego replied sarcastically. "Of course I get tired, but never enough to stop. You're not going soft are you?"

"No, just frustrated. People are disappearing and we can't find anything. It's like they left the planet. We're missing something right under our noses; something simple."

Diego agreed. In this business, no one ever quit, at least not willingly and not while they were alive. "I found out Jacko is dead. I don't think he even had time to get at that list. Tina didn't give it to Junior, so it has to be at her house. I've watched that place for days. The people there all look like terrorists. Something doesn't smell right."

Rudy laughed without humor. "Nothing has smelled right since Junior got it. Let's wander into that house and see what's goin' on."

The two took up position across the street from the house and took turns watching the apartment through a pair of binoculars. After an hour or so of no activity Diego suddenly stiffened. "Rudy, one of those guys is wearin' Faustino's jacket; I'd know that piece of rags anywhere. He wouldn't give that up for nothin'."

"Are you sure?"

"Look at it: it's got one red sleeve, one black sleeve, the front is blue, but the back is green—with the number 23 on it. Am I right?"

Rudy studied the jacket while Diego described it. "I guess that's his, all right. Why isn't he wearin' it?"

"We need to get closer."

Recrossing the dark street, they slipped alongside the house. Unable to resist, Rudy slowly raised up on his toes to look into a ground-floor window. Instantly he dropped back down and, grabbing Diego's arm, nearly dragged him away. He nodded urgently toward the block where they'd parked their car. Moving swiftly and silently, the two hustled back to it and dove inside. Rudy drove away as fast as he could without drawing attention. Neither spoke until they were out of the subdivision.

Diego had never known Rudy to be frightened, but he could tell Rudy was beyond that now. "What . . . what's the matter with you?"

"Faustino was there. They *took his head off*, Diego! His head is sitting in there! Place is full of guns and computers, shit like that. Those guys aren't running drugs, man. They're going to cause some serious damage somewhere. I don't think they knew the girl. I don't think Junior knew them. We need to get out of here! We'll go down with them if we're still around here!"

* * * *

While Rudy paced and smoked—his hands still shaking—Diego struggled to make sense of everything. He knew Junior would never have Tina killed; it had to be Jacko. But Jacko didn't have the damn list when he was killed. Tina, Junior, Jacko, and now Faustino. The information must have been *with* her, but where. Suddenly, Diego remembered. Pueblo, she lived in Pueblo.

Rudy was still in a fear-induced daze when he and Diego pulled into Pueblo the next morning. Diego, called his uncle. It was a game of hit or miss with the old guy now, but he needed the girl's last name. Diego prayed Saldivar would know . . . and remember Tina's name. When the caretaker finally called back, Diego had the name he needed.

The men entered Tina's condo. But for an answering machine that sat in the middle of the floor, it was empty. Minutes later, Diego sank into the driver's seat. He was beaten. No list, no boss, and few men left. What now?

CHAPTER 42

Working the computer with Rhino took longer than either sister imagined. The information he was able to recover was massive. Allen wanted it. Tony wanted it. Everyone wanted it.

"Who do we give these results to, Rhino? I want out of this mess, and I want my whole family out. What's my next step?" Annie pushed.

"My move would be to give all this stuff to Allen and Tony," Lynn suggested. "That way, both bases are covered and we should be through with all this, right?"

Rhino shook his head slowly. "I don't think it's going to be that easy. This isn't just about drugs or illegals. It's a lot bigger, now. Seems Tina was working both sides."

Annie and Lynn exchanged moans. "So you think she worked for the feds *and* the cartels. How did you figure that out?"

"No, I think she worked with that Saldivar guy and a cell in Denver. Not one of the drug cartels, but a cell building up."

"What cell? What are you talking about? I thought the Venezuela group was in Denver."

"Remember the weird names we keep seeing? I think they're all part of a cell that's operating in the U.S. Look at the way these names are plugged into the list. They're getting ready for something. I think every-thing else was just a way to get their people into the States. It's getting crowded, you know? Just read. Remember, the information is coded. I think they want the guns. I wonder if that means someone like Rhami-did wants them . . . he can't bring them in, that would be real risky . . . if he gets busted with the weapons, the whole show stops." Rhino paused, thinking.

"This list tells us who does what, who is here and who is still on the way. Several are simply no show, which I suppose means they never made it. If we take out the unusual names and look at the ones left, it's the cartels. They need that list to know who owes for what and what items have made it across. Reverse the name deletion, and you can see the cell, or whatever you call them. They need to know who among their people made it across and what each one's specialty is. You have a real hot potato here, Annie, and you need to dump it quickly, before any of these people decide you may be connected with Tina somehow. You need to talk with Tony soon."

Annie sat on the bed in the guest room to call Tony. When he came to the phone, she filled him in on Rhino's suspicions and how the data supported his thinking.

Tony was listening without comment, but suddenly he broke in, "I want you to come back, Annie. I want you and Lynn to leave first thing in the morning. Just come back here. Things are quieter now. Talk with Rhino and see if he has a secure line to transmit information. Call me in the morning . . . and when you're on the road. Be careful, Inamorata." Annie didn't protest, and as soon as she bid him good night, Tony placed a call to Sam. They would need to find and follow Rhamidid.

The trip back to Denver was uneventful. Annie was steadily getting better. Her bruises now had a green cast to them. She could open both eyes, chew, and move her arm a little. Her hand still ached, but not as bad. She had given up trying to cover all the marks with makeup. She and Lynn talked the entire trip back. Lynn was slowly warming to Tony. Annie knew it was because her sister was getting closer to Sam.

Back at Tony's estate, Annie found Tony in his office. His face lit up when she walked in. Rounding his desk, he met her by folding her into his arms and kissing her. "I hate the times you're gone. If Rhino has some way secure to exchange information, you're not leaving anymore." He held her for a moment longer, then turned to business.

"Okay, lady, tell me again everything you can." When Annie was finished, he walked around the room and stood at the window a long time before he finally spoke. "We've been reasonably certain this was building, but we still can't tell where they plan to hit." He turned back to Annie. "By the way, Jacko won't be bothering you or anyone else again. And Sam is leaving tonight to take all this to Allen.

Annie watched him, smiling.

"Are you wishing you had become a teacher, a plumber, or something less challenging?"

He crossed the room to her side shaking his head. "Would you change your life, Annie?" he asked softly, his eyes tenderly watching her.

"Heavens no! I love my life. Of course, it's a lot easier than yours, my friend."

"Friend? I'm your friend?" He furrowed his brow.

"Of course, my best friend." Annie stood on her tiptoes and kissed him. She would have gone, but Tony wanted more. He took it. "Do friends kiss like that?" Tony smiled to himself.

Annie was trying to catch her breath as he walked from the room.

CHAPTER 43

Rhamidid slammed the stick shift forward in frustration. The traffic was unbearable, and he was lost again. "There are too many people involved. Too many not of our faith. No one has control over them. Always fighting among themselves. Never again will I let anyone talk me into taking on others for a job so precious. Never!"

He careened in and out of traffic, eventually turning off onto a frontage road, and soon found himself slipping into a quieter area. Strip malls banked both sides of the street, and the pace slowed considerably. Pulling over, he took out the city map again. He couldn't tell if he was headed north or south. The thick layer of gray clouds covered the sun and rumbling from them spoke of rain. Think . . . he had to think. Now was the time to be certain of each detail. Soon he would join the others martyred for the only cause that held the promise. Rhamidid looked around him with disgust. Viewed through his eyes, the vulgar window displays were only a small part of the decadence of the country. "The Americans are an abomination," he thought, "doomed by their own corruption. I bring jihad to them."

He missed his own household, but pride filled him when he thought of how they would forever speak of him after he made the ultimate sacrifice for Allah.

Eventually, Rhamidid figured out where he was and where he needed to be. Taking to the streets again, he cautiously increased speed until he found the *on* ramp for the freeway. His run to Tina's house had proved fruitless. Her computers had all disappeared. She had done a good job for him at one time, but had gotten careless. No matter, he didn't need her anymore. He already knew how much the Venezuelans wanted for the arms. One more haul, and he would pay off the ammunition and weapons they would use. Almost there.

He had always followed orders, not given them. He wasn't asked for an opinion, but had anyone asked, he would never have suggested their next target. This was not a game for gangs and cartels to play. This was a time to hit his sworn enemy where it would hurt the most. The target he was to hit wouldn't really hurt the Americans at all. Maybe there was more to the plan than he knew.

After thirty minutes on the freeway, he saw the sign for his exit. Following the map, he found the condo. Denver was much bigger than Pueblo, but he knew just were he was headed this time. He parked several blocks away from the address and walked there.

Opening the door, he was hit with the odor of death and decay. No one was at the condo, just the remnants of those using the place temporarily. Trash was everywhere. Rhamidid followed the smell and found the rotting head of a man. Rummaging through the mess, he could find no clue as to who the man was.

Cautiously he left the building. Glancing around, he walked slowly to his car and left. This development had put him in a bad position. Anyone could have seen him coming and going. Again, anger filled him. "Stupid, stupid people!" he yelled once inside the car, his fist smashing against the steering wheel. "Never, never leave anything behind that someone can use against us! Especially not now. We're too close."

Snapping his cell phone closed, Rhamidid shook his head. The commander was unaware of any change in plans. He had no idea who the head belonged to, nor did he know where their people were.

Rhamidid headed for an all-night diner. Having bought several newspapers, he sat down and. He scanned the papers for any news about any local killings. Nothing. "Of course not," he realized, "no one knows about this yet, or the head wouldn't be there. Who would have left the head? The Mexicans like leaving heads around. But my men would never have allowed Mexicans into the house. Perhaps the head was brought by one of my men. Surely, they wouldn't have done this. We cannot afford to have anyone know we are here. Why haven't I been called?" he fretted.

He could feel the pressure coming down the chain of command to him regarding these unexpected developments. He had to find the men, get the money to the gunrunners, and move the weapons. Rhamidid determined he would meet the runners as planned. At least he could get the guns. Glancing at his watch, he paid hastily and headed out.

CHAPTER 44

Diego had taken a huge chance calling on the gang in Denver. They were run by José Hernandez, a man Diego's old boss had never trusted. Using the most carefully chosen words, Diego gave them all the information. He prayed this would provide him badly needed manpower. In the end, Hernandez had called his boss in Venezuela. His orders were to cut the middleman. Hernandez had already called in a crew to help with his plan. Diego would soon be out.

Unaware of any such order, Diego led them to the condo. Hernandez offered him an envelope after they returned. "What's this for?" Diego asked, refusing to take the money.

"You provided us with valuable information. I trust you are still interested in our bargain. This is just a little retainer." Hernandez shrugged in an effort to disarm Diego.

"I don't take retainers," growled Diego. "Stop worrying about me and find that list."

Rudy and Diego found a spot from which to watch unnoticed. The Venezuelan men were spread around the condo perimeter, patiently waiting. The doors closed at nine, like always. Hernandez's men moved silently toward the target. At a word from Hernandez, the fire started. As men attempted to flee the scene, they were shot down. Explosives were thrown into the building. Everything was over in what seemed like an instant. As of yet, not one neighbor had ventured onto the street, nor had one car driven by the blazing condo. Now distant sirens could be heard, coming closer. Pulling at Diego's arm, Rudy headed for their vehicle, parked farther down the street.

For the second time in days, Diego felt uneasy. He had hated using José Hernandez, but it bought him valuable time. The terrorists would have to regroup. Diego unlocked the car doors. After he and Rudy were inside, he glanced behind him. As he turned the key, he saw the men from Denver running for cover.

* * * *

Safe in his office behind the bar, José Hernandez leaned back in his chair. The men at the condo were the ones ordering the guns; he knew that much. Now their precious jihad would have to wait. Men would need to be replaced and maybe he could get them to use his men. José had never been able to find out who to talk with or what exactly was supposed to happen, but with the guns, it was something big. He felt certain someone would contact him. He would be ready.

CHAPTER 45

Lynn and Annie were glued to the computer screen. For two days, they had done little but load Rhino's programs and disks onto the computer in Tony's office. Just now, they decided to take a break and catch up on the news. Clicking on CNN's online coverage, they pulled up images of a vicious shoot-out in Denver that had been followed by a deadly car bomb. The deceased were scattered all over the place. Police had not released any names. The FBI was now involved.

Tony and several of his men were sitting around a table on the patio just outside. With Annie and Lynn busy on his computer, he had moved outside for the day. Tony looked up at the sound of the French door opening. "What is it?" he asked after one look at Annie's face.

"Come see what we pulled up on the news." She stepped aside as he entered the room. Tony read the screen and scrolled to look at the few captured images. Lou read over Tony's shoulder.

Annie stared at the screen. "Who would be big enough to take out a terrorist group?"

"We don't know they were terrorists, Annie. Maybe it was a really, really bad drug deal," Lynn suggested hopefully.

"I think Annie is right. At any rate, someone is shrinking the playing field," Lou noted.

Tony concurred. "They've already lost Saldivar's son. The Venezuelans, Cubans, and Columbians are still in the running, although Allen and Earl think they act only as suppliers."

"Somebody will probably hit whoever they think blew up the condo, and that should cut even more players out. This might hold everything up for a while," suggested Lou.

Tony shook his head in disagreement. "Now is when the big boys will come out to play."

"Maybe while everyone's fighting everyone else, we can decipher more of this information," Annie offered.

"Annie, you and Lynn are to stay close. You are not to leave without escorts under any circumstances." Tony looked from one sister to the other.

"Okay," Annie promised. She would keep her word . . . this time.

CHAPTER 46

Adeeb, Allen, and Sara were tucked in a back corner of a tiny eatery. Allen watched his old friend closely. Adeeb, born and raised in Pakistan, was concerned with the latest news. Without some kind of control, the groups were imploding.

"The chance is greater that one of the groups will strike out alone or each will try to outplay the other. With Rhamidid's party crashed, he will have to regroup. That should give us more time. Sam, how soon can you find out who the guys in the car were? Doesn't seem likely they were with Rhamidid. The car exploded after all the shooting had stopped. According to what the papers say, the police arrived as the explosion took place," Allen thought aloud.

"I'll let you know when I know anything, but I'd say it will be several days . . . unless they both have dental records. That's not likely. They may never be ID'd in time to help us. Odd how nobody called the police until they couldn't hear any more gunfire," Sam noted.

"Not so odd," countered Adeeb. "Would you call the police on a group like that? I'll bet everyone was so scared of them, they were *hoping* they would get hit."

Allen grinned. "You're probably right. Poor James, all his playground pals are getting killed. Wonder when his number is up. Not soon enough for me. Was Rhamidid with them? Maybe he's gone too. That would be just too easy."

"He wasn't with them; he's already called to find out what happened. Unfortunately for him, even his commander didn't know about it. I'm thinking it was not planned. Seems more likely someone got mad, real mad," Adeeb mused.

The three men watched the sun move slowly beyond the horizon as day closed. Each man had his own loyalties, yet they were intensely devoted to each other. They had worked together for nearly twenty-five years and understood each other very well.

"Who would have thought I would spend all these years helping the likes of you two," Sam shook his head, "Covert counterterrorist from the Middle East, a military undercover sort of CIA guy, and the mob. What a combo!"

"This has been one hell of an adventure. Best years of our lives," Allen added, laughing softly. "This one may be our last, though. We're all getting too old for this stuff. We need to let the younger guys take it now, don't you think?"

"No," Adeeb said flatly. "The younger ones wouldn't work like we do. Nor would they have the drive you two have had. My people—in Iraq, Afghanistan, Arabia, or wherever—are accustomed to fighting, and picking sides. The Americans and you, Sam, like to keep things on a . . . what do you say? . . . even keel."

"Maybe you're right, but at least we don't switch sides like the wind," Sam commented behind closed eyes.

"Ah, you're correct. Let's see, Jacko and James are the most recent. Should I go on? The difference is this: my people move openly, telling the whole world they have found a new reason to fight, then another newer one, and on and on. Your people just slip behind lines whenever it suits them. It's all about their personal gain."

"Sadly," Allen answered, "I'd have to agree. We have a hard time finding serious men committed to the country and not to the party, whatever it happens to be at the time. When did America first have men like us, scurrying around behind the scenes, doing all the dirty work, under cover, operating independently outside accepted practices?"

"The first known undercover men were in France in the early 1800s, but I believe the practice has changed somewhat. Whoever is in office in this country decides how the agencies move. Unfortunately, your country doesn't have the stomach for the real deal. They want rules on things like interrogations, but still want protection. They have yet to understand that the organizations they fight with have no such rules, expect no mercy, and will never divulge information without encouragement. Without such information, you place your country at great risk. This is not a time to be the nice guys. This is a time to win," Adeeb finished in a firm voice.

Sam and Allen felt the weight of truth in Adeeb's words. They were fighting an enemy unencumbered by rules and regulations that impeded the flow of information and safety, both for the country at large and the agencies. Sam felt strongly there were too many bosses, few of whom understood the stakes or players. Allen's association with Tony had shown how organization could be a very effective deterrent when coupled with a drive similar to the enemy's.

"This enemy is not a military enemy, it's a religious enemy. Much more driven and dangerous." Adeeb noted ominously after a brief silence. "Much more dedicated; willing to risk everything."

Allen's thoughts drifted. Poor Annie; he had never intended to drag her into this mess. He was grateful to Tony and his family; at least someone was around to try to watch over his sisters. The last step was to identify just where the intended hit would be and when it would come. The latest episode at Denver should slow things down. The top priority now was to identify just who was directing Rhamidid and keep Rhamidid under close surveillance.

"We need to get some answers soon," Adeeb said, giving voice to Allen's thoughts. "I want to know how Rhamidid and Saldivar got together, along with other groups, like from Venezuela. Just what is the connection? Sam, how long can you stay?" Adeeb looked at his friend.

"Not too long; don't want to be missed. Are you coming over this time? You haven't been in the good ole USA for a while."

"Yes, I would like to talk with Annie about Tina. Do you think that's possible?"

"I don't see why not."

CHAPTER 47

Tony stood at the window again. For a moment, he let his mind wander to the problem with the captivating hazel eyes and smile. What would life be like if he could just walk away with Annie? No, too many people depended on him. People with families. His family too. He turned back to the men in the room with him. Sam was reporting in. It wasn't good. After Sam finished, Tony stood silently, his mind racing.

"I'm still trying to get hold of Allen or Earl. They hit so fast, it was over nearly before it began. When they killed Adeeb, everyone faded back and left. He was definitely their target. Anyone else was collateral damage." Sam held out his hand and dropped the contents into Tony's hand. "Adeeb had this on him. He was to give it to the sisters, so they would know he was with Allen." Sam walked to the bar and poured himself a drink.

"I'm sorry, Sam. I know you and he were friends. Keep trying Allen's phone. Lou, call Annie and Lynn; ask them to come down. Meanwhile, gentlemen, what does this say about the issue we're dealing with, if anything?" The fact that Adeeb could have been with Annie when this happened made Tony sick to his stomach.

When the sisters entered, they found a room of subdued men.

Something had happened. Praying it didn't involve Allen or Earl, they stepped inside. Lynn followed, but had eyes only for Sam. His back was to the room. He stood with one hand on the door frame; the other held a now-empty glass. His eyes were fixed on an unseen object in the distance.

Gently, Lynn touched his arm. "Sam, what is it?"

He started as if awakened suddenly. Turning to see Lynn, he opened the door and left with her.

Annie watched her sister and Sam. "What's going on?" she asked aloud, walking toward Tony.

"A man that works with Allen and Sam, a close friend, was on his way to talk with you. We don't exactly know what he wanted, but he's dead. From what little we know at this point, it looks like a Rhamidid hit. He had this in his pocket. It was for you or Lynn."

Tony met her, turned her hand palm up, and dropped the packet. Annie opened it. Her face immediately registered recognition and anxiety. "This belonged to my mother. She never took it off. When she died, we gave it to Allen, as the oldest. Is Allen—"

"No," Tony interrupted, "Sam says he gave it to Adeeb to give to you so you would know Adeeb was with Allen." Tony tipped her face upward. "Annie, you and Lynn are to stay inside the house until we come for you. I have increased security. Gather your things. We'll probably leave later this evening. I have something I need to do right now, so I'll come by later." He kissed her forehead and left.

Annie clasped the medal with the blessed virgin on it tightly then glanced around. The men were talking among themselves. No one noticed as she left for her room.

* * * *

Tony had little pity for the two men sitting in front of him. He had lost several good men and nearly lost his cousin. He worked hard to remain calm. Closing his eyes briefly, he heard his mother's voice. "Remember, answers come from unlikely places and at unlikely times. Protect this family, and listen, son, always listen."

"You're going to die. How you die is of no consequence to me, but it probably is to you. I know you are not of the faith of the men you hired to 'protect' that house, so I know you have no visions of what your life after death will be. You should have many visions of what your life will be like for the short time you have left. Of course, short is a relative term. Tell my men everything you know, including names. Make no mistake; I mean exactly what I say." With that, Tony nodded to the men standing behind the chairs and left the room.

CHAPTER 48

José Hernandez leaned back in the chair. He hated the food, and the heat was getting to him. He had no respect for the man sitting across from him. That man, Rhamidid, was consumed with his mission to destroy America or at least as many of its citizens as he could. Hernandez didn't care about any "causes" other than his own. His country was run by a dictator with little regard for human life, and he subscribed to that theory. His interest was power and money. He craved both, and like any other good addict, would do whatever it took to get what he wanted.

This latest news had come as a shock to his companion, he could tell. And Hernandez was right. Rhamidid was agitated and angry the list was still missing, angry his cell was imploding, and angry he could only sit by and take orders. He didn't trust the Venezuelan and was certain Hernandez didn't trust him. No matter. He still had a job to do, and for now, he needed the group from Venezuela.

Staring at his water glass, Rhamidid tried to think. Hernandez waited. Finally, standing, Rhamidid tossed loose change onto the table. "I'll call you in three days."

Hernandez watched him leave. Three days. What could Rhamidid possibly do in three days? Most of his men were gone now. And he would need more arms as well as men. Hernandez could supply the arms, but Rhamidid couldn't pay. Rhamidid was in a bind, and the Venezuelan enjoyed it. He began to think seriously about whether he could unload the arms to any other interested party. True, much of the cache was gone, but he still had a good amount stashed. The Columbians and Mexicans were out, and while substitutes from both countries could be found, those relationships would take time to develop.

As in times past, Hernandez wondered just what it was, exactly, that Rhamidid planned on doing with all the arms. America was going through a transition. Elections were coming up and everyone had taken sides. Campaigns were heating up. Security along the border was tighter and the wall was moving faster than anticipated. It would be an interesting fall and winter.

* * * *

Rhamidid stalked out of the restaurant. He was increasingly anxious. Time was slipping away, and he still needed men, arms, and the final plans from the commander. He made a fateful decision. With resolve, he jammed the car into first gear and headed away. His first call to the head of his cell went unanswered. Trying again, he left a terse message: "I'm going ahead. Get me the plans or I'll get them someplace else. We waste too much time."

Rhamidid brooded over the silence from his commander. He refused to stop now. The plan must go through. This was the perfect time. The more he thought about it, the more he believed the target was the best one. Everyone together. He needed more explosives. Those he could get. He needed the plans to the building. That would be more difficult.

He wasn't certain how these things worked in this country. He needed a safe place to stay. No, maybe he should move around. The fool from Venezuela had made his last bad move. Rhamidid simply would not use him any longer. He had always insisted on contacting the others, never being contacted by them. He knew well what he was doing. Pulling over to the shoulder, he pulled out a map and studied it. No, he needed to look at cities. Big cities. Places where he could move about unnoticed. For that he needed light and his laptop. He finally wound up in an out-of-the-way coffeehouse where he could do his research in peace.

* * * *

José Hernandez waited for several days then grew impatient. He had no idea how to contact Rhamidid, nor did his boss in Venezuela. No matter, things were on hold until Hernandez gave them the firepower. He could wait. It would take time for Rhamidid to get another team and the money together.

At this point, Hernandez didn't even care about the list. It wouldn't matter soon anyway. Soon. He smiled to himself He enjoyed the good life in the United States: opportunities were limitless here. Still, he had to have the appearance of acting within the laws. Let the rest get caught, not him. He had worked too long and done too much. Payday. Soon. Then he would be the only patrón.

CHAPTER 49

"Are you okay, Annie?" Tony asked, when Annie answered his knock at her bedroom door. He hadn't found her when he returned to the study and surmised she had retreated to the privacy of her room.

Tony took her nod as a sign to offer her a bit of consoling news. "We're nearing the end, I think. Sam has filled in a lot. He, Allen, and Adeeb were together last week. He believes Adeeb wanted to talk with you about Tina." Tony paused. "With Adeeb gone now, Allen has lost his contact to track the movements of the cell. But everything is quiet. Right now, Allen and Sam are running through all the current names to see if anyone comes to the top. Word on the street in Mexico is the Saldivar holdings are trying to regroup under a different cartel. I don't think they know anything about all this. For now, we sit quiet and keep watch, but go back to life as usual."

"Do you think Allen can come home yet?"

"He probably can't ever come home . . . at least for a long while. Remember, you had a funeral. Everyone that was anyone was there. Wait until all this is over."

Tony walked with Annie down the hall. "I'll feel better with you and Lynn hid away yet close at hand." He turned her to face him. "We're leaving here in an hour. Lou will bring Buster." As he brushed her hair from her face, he asked, "Are you tired?"

"Maybe a little. Lynn and I will be ready, though. Just call." She kissed the hand stroking her cheek then turned to go back inside her room.

CHAPTER 50

José Hernandez waited beside his phone. He should be getting a call any moment. What a stroke of luck to have one of his men working in the very hangar temporarily rented by Tuscano. It was easy to damage the fuel line. Tuscano would be forced to land, and Hernandez's men would be waiting.

For the past three years, every time Hernandez had tried to move the guns, Tuscano's men turned up. He couldn't find out how they knew, but they knew. With Tuscano out of the way, the guns would go to the big payers.

"It's time someone took Tuscano down anyway. We'll see what the Italian and his woman are made of." José Hernandez smiled the smile of sweet victory. About now, his men should be boarding the plane.

* * * *

Tony and the other passengers had been in the air only an hour when the pilot called him up to the cockpit. They were losing fuel and would be forced to land. Sam, himself a seasoned pilot with plenty of hours, offered, "I don't think this is accidental, Tony. We'll definitely have to land to get this fixed."

Tony waited while the pilot called looking for a place to put the plane down. Per Tony's orders, the pilot never filed a flight plan. If they crashed, only witness phone calls would bring help. The only landing strip with fuel was about ten minutes away. They would make it that far, but no farther.

Tony agreed this malfunction had been planned. "Sam, find a second place to land, the same distance we've just flown. We'll make an emergency landing. Have one of our planes—a larger one—land at the second spot. We're not going to repair this one; we'll refuel just to get us to the rendezvous spot. I want extra men when we change planes, just in case. Whatever is going to happen, will happen when we land to refuel. Now, let's get ready for the show. Everybody move." He tapped the pilot on the shoulder; "You've got this under control?"

The pilot gave one confident nod by way of reply.

Calmly, Tony returned to the cabin and announced, "Ladies and gentlemen, we are being forced to land because we're leaking fuel. Listen carefully. We may be boarded, or fired on. Annie, you and Lynn hit the floor if shooting starts. If we're boarded, we act as if we have no idea what is happening. Everyone be certain your weapons are concealed. You know the drill, gentlemen. Questions?"

Annie and Lynn were too stunned to think of any. Annie looked around her. Tony's men were coolly checking their weapons and settling back. Tony sat next to her. "You do exactly what I tell you: no more, no less. You can handle this." He sqeezed her hand and stood up.

Annie smiled crookedly at Tony. She looked at Lynn, who was listening to Tony too. Taking a deep breath, Annie prayed Tony was right.

* * * *

When the plane landed, seven men carrying weapons demanded they be allowed to board. The Tuscano entourage would have to let them on; they needed the fuel. Sam opened the door and the stairs dropped, allowing the rough-looking lot on board. One of the men immediately demanded, in Spanish, that the passengers surrender any weapons. No one moved, but the people seated in the plane did look from one to another in confusion. Annie snuck a look out the window and saw a fuel truck pull up to the underbelly of the plane. The man yelled again; still the passengers sat, looking around as if trying to decide just what he might want.

Frustrated, the leader made a fatal decision. Assuming these well-dressed frightened-looking men and women were unarmed, he backed up to the cockpit. Before he could react, Tony stepped out behind him from inside a storage closet where he had hidden. There was no mistaking the feel of steel against the base of the leader's skull. In perfect Spanish, Tony ordered the men to drop their weapons and move away.

Meanwhile, Sam closed and sealed the side door. While Tony and Lou bound the men, Sam made his way to the cockpit to assist the pilot. Soon thereafter, the plane started up and took off. Tony had begun to question the men, but all of them refused to talk. Without turning, he instructed Annie and Lynn to move to the suite in the back of the plane. "Close the door. Stay put until I come for you," he ordered.

The sisters grabbed Buster and moved quickly into the compartment, closing the door behind them. The voices from within the fuselage became louder then died down only to rise again. And so it went, until the plane began to descend. Sam informed Tony that the second plane would not be able to meet them for another hour. He and the pilot had already set the next landing point.

A knock at the door startled them. "Let me in, ladies," Tony commanded. They quickly obliged. "We're stopping for fuel. We'll have to stop again in another hour to refuel. Everything is under control, but we'll need to go through these landings and takeoffs before we rendezvous with a secure plane."

Annie and Lynn were too frightened to ask questions. They sat down on the small bed with Buster between them. The voices they heard were low. They could hear people outside calling and working with the plane. Eventually, they could feel the engine start up for takeoff. They each moved to the floor in order to lean against a wall as the plane lifted off the runway.

* * * *

"What do you mean they took off? Are you telling me seven men couldn't overtake four men and two women? Whoever arranged for these men to handle the skyjacking will answer to me." José Fernandez's voice became shrill like a crone's. He knocked over the small table before him, sending dishes and drinks flying. As the realization of the failure settled into his brain, his rage evaporated into despair. "I'm done . . . it's over!"

"Patrón, it's not over. This is just a setback. We still have more time. The foreigner can't move alone and will need more men. We can still do it. You'll find a way."

Heaving a sigh and moan, Hernandez sank into his chair. "Do you think we really can move forward now? Do you think the Italian will not find out who gave the men their orders? It's over for us now. I have to leave here, quickly, and hide. I'd rather die!"

"We still have the guns, patrón. Someone will have to contact us sometime. If they don't, we simply hold the guns and sell to the highest bidder later."

Hernandez turned to his lieutenant, "Can you think at all? Who would want these kinds of weapons, and who could take them without having them traced back to us. Huh? Who? No one! Our only hope is to somehow find the people who wanted the guns and, meanwhile, hide from the Italian. Hide, like an insect."

He slumped, brooding. Left alone in the room, he tried to clear his head. His only points of contact had been the woman killed at the clinic and the Saldivars. He really knew little about who else they dealt with. He couldn't even contact Rhamidid. "A big mistake," he chided himself. "Next time, I will know everyone involved, or not deal at all. Next time, if there is ever a next time," he thought grimly. He stood and poured himself a glass of whiskey. Staring out the window, he felt his world begin to crack. He threw the glass through the window, cursing.

* * * *

Annie and Lynn stayed in the small room. They spoke little, and both prayed. Annie's fear of heights rendered her helpless if she allowed herself to think of having to jump or going down in a crashing aircraft. Tony was in control. That brought a great deal of comfort to her.

When Tony opened the door, he found the sisters still leaning against the wall, and each other. Asleep. Stepping to the two women, he gently shook Annie awake. "We've landed. We're changing planes. We need to move quickly." He helped her stand after she jostled Lynn awake. They stumbled down the aisle, with Buster in tow, and deplaned.

Everyone hustled onto the Citation, where five more of Tony's men sat waiting for their boss. There was no sign of the gunmen who had forced their way onto the first plane. The second plane immediately took off from a small well-isolated private airstrip.

"I hate to bother you, Tony," Annie began, "but where are we? We're not in Mexico are we?"

"No." Tony smiled. "We're headed home."

"Wherever home is," Annie thought. Buster made himself comfortable in the back. The rest of the flight was relatively quiet, each person lost in his or her own thoughts. Tony called someone and requested dinner for everyone and a car; Lou dosed. After they landed at another private airstrip, the sisters were bundled into one of two waiting limos. Tony was still busy on the phone, Lou and Sam talked, and Lynn and Annie listened.

Arriving at a guarded gate, the chauffeur stopped to identify his passengers and was allowed entrance. Moving slowly, the vehicle wound its way through well-kept grounds. The residence was enclosed within a twenty-five-foot wall and heavy gate, also guarded. Yellow lights flooded the area with a welcoming glow, contradicting the heightened security. When the limo stopped, men immediately stepped up to the doors and let everyone out, unloading baggage and leading people into the house. Annie held her breath. The entry to the house proper spoke to a time long past. Additional heavy wood doors swung open, and Annie stepped into an authentic Italian villa. "Tony, this is *beautiful!* Where are we?"

He smiled, watching Annie take in the residence. "Welcome to New York."

CHAPTER 51

Settled into their rooms, Annie and Lynn had only a short time before they were called to the dining room. The oversized room was filled with a long table, surrounded by men, most of whom the sisters knew. After Annie and Lynn sat down, taking the only empty chairs, everyone else followed suit. Food arrived, the wine was poured, and the buzz of talking filled the room.

Dinner was wonderful, and Annie could feel the wine warming her. Finally, when everyone had eaten their fill, Tony suggested he and Annie go for a walk. She was delighted. Several men followed a few paces behind them. "Are they really necessary?"

Tony simply nodded and kept walking. He took possession of her hand, placing it firmly on his arm. Neither spoke as they wandered about the courtyard and behind the house. The grounds were manicured, with paths running about broken by small ponds, arched bridges crossing streams, and statues set in the middle of gurgling fountains. Benches sat randomly around the grounds. The air was heavy with the perfume of roses, lilacs, and other flowers she couldn't see. Annie relaxed completely and became lost in happy thoughts. Finally, Tony turned to her and asked, "When did you start loving me, Annie?"

"So, you think I love you?" she teased.

He smiled at her. "No, I *know* you love me," he answered affectionately.

Annie walked on in silence before she answered. "You *do* seem to know
an awful lot," she admitted. "The first time you puffed up like a toad at
me—maybe even sooner. I tried very hard not to love you, you know. It's
going to cramp my style something awful."

"For me, it was your bubble bath," he said, smiling, choosing to ignore
her reference to her independence. "Sometimes it feels like I've loved
you forever, Inamorata," he said tenderly. Gently, he bent to kiss her
head. Annie moved closer to him.

Upon returning to the villa, they went to the study. The double doors
were swung open, and several men were already there, talking. She could
tell by the sound of their voices, this was business. The room went silent
when Tony entered. He made no move to dismiss either sister. Once he
was seated behind his desk, the talk resumed.

At another brief lull in the conversation, Annie asked hesitantly,
"Whatever happened to the guys on the plane, by the way? The ones
with the guns."

No one answered at first. Finally Sam offered, "It's really too bad none
of them had parachutes. Would have come in handy."

"Tony, you didn't dump them, that's horrible!" The room was still
silent as Annie turned anxious eyes toward him. He could see that to her
this was incomprehensible. To him, this was part of the business of war.

"What they had planned for you and Lynn would have been incomprehensible, Annie. Don't think of them as people; more like animals.
Just be thankful Sam could help fly a wounded plane." Lou interjected.

Tony moved the conversation along, ignoring Annie's protest. "Does
anyone have any ideas about what you'd like to see happen next? We can't
give anyone time to regroup.

When Annie looked back at Tony, she marveled that he could just go
on. Looking around the room, however, she realized this room of men
could be the only thing standing between whatever might happen and
the innocent people she knew would likely be entangled unwillingly. Her
thoughts turned to Allen and his narrow escape. The faces of the people
she and Lynn had been studying crossed her mind. The body in the dead

steer, the man who jumped her—all of it came home, hard. Images of people fleeing burning buildings, planes, and bombed cars swept before her eyes.

As the men talked, Annie struggled with herself. Never in her mind could she have imagined she would be mixed up in something like all this. Could she deal with this? Just how much did she love Tony? She closed her eyes for a split second. When she looked at him, he was watching her. His eyes were serious, yet kind and supportive. She knew he knew what she was thinking. He always did.

Annie made a decision. She stood up quietly, moving between the chairs toward Tony's desk. He stopped speaking, his brows up, "Annie? Do you need something?"

"I'd like to try something, with your permission. I've been listening to you all brainstorm, and sometimes when everyone jumps in like this, ideas begin to take shape." She picked up a pen from his desk.

"We need ideas now," Tony acknowledged. From the back of the room, someone handed forward a large flip chart. One of the men placed it atop the credenza and leaned it at a slight angle against the wall behind the spot where Tony stood. Annie began to jot down what she could remember.

"Let's see what we have," she finished, standing back to look it over. "You've already known Tina was working with the Saldivar cartel," Annie continued. "The Venezuela bunch didn't know her. You all knew of her, but not what she did. Do we know about the two other parties involved—Cuba and Rhamidid's people?"

"You can take Saldivar and Cuba out," noted Sam.

"That leaves Venezuela and whoever Adeeb was working with," Annie finished.

"You can take Venezuela out, after the past few days," Tony corrected her.

"We know Mexico supplied the drugs and maybe some men. It's reasonable to think the drugs will be slowed down—for a while anyway."

"What about the money?" someone asked.

"I'd say they may not need any more drugs if they were using them to generate funds," Lou noted. "We should assume they have all the funds needed."

"From the list Tina kept, Saldivar got a lot of money. I'm thinking perhaps that's all the Saldivars did," Sam suggested. "Maybe that was their whole part in all of this. But who paid them, and—"

"No," Tony interrupted, "they could have sold drugs to anyone. Why these people? If you remember, the list shows people moving weapons into the country, but we're not sure with whom—"

"Or *to* whom," Sam added. "From our standpoint, we've never felt like this was about drugs or people. It's more . . . much more."

Tony added, "I can tell you Tina worked for one group, but was involved with another through one man . . . Juan Saldivar's son. Since we can be reasonably certain he didn't have her killed, and neither Venezuela nor Cuba knew her, that leaves the people who are getting all the weapons together. That, of course, would be the people Adeeb followed. Someone must have tipped them off since the raid in Denver took out our only inside source—namely, Adeeb."

"Jacko? How did he fit in?" Annie asked.

"We can forget about him. We think he was running activity and information to whomever paid the most. Not because of any loyalties, or even business. We think he wanted to be the big kahuna," Sam answered.

"We've known for a long time the fight would be on our turf. We just can't tell what or where." Tony was pacing around the room. "We do know they have to regroup, since nearly everyone killed in Denver was with the same group.

"You know, truthfully, Tina's list was just a laundry list," Tony continued, "It really didn't tell much except who was coming in and what they could do. I guarantee Saldivar knew exactly how much anyone who owed him money, owed. I don't think the cell, or whatever you call them, had anything to gain by killing Tina. She was incidental. Whoever had her killed—and I'm almost 100 percent certain it must have been Jacko—made a major mistake. He was after information but killed her too soon, or at least without getting what he was after." Tony finished.

Annie moved to the window, running through a list of questions in her mind. "What could be the tie between Tina and this mess, besides the list? What would have gotten her killed, if not her information? Who of the people involved would kill for the information most already had, though they didn't seem to realize it?"

Annie suddenly turned to the room and blurted, "The girl, Lynn, Tina was the girl!"

"What girl? What are you talking about?" Lynn asked, puzzled.

"Remember the article we read about the guy who got into the U.S. because someone had kidnapped his sister or cousin or something? He was able to come over because of something, or *someone* I should say, at the State Department. He was also the one we saw at the Gala. The guy that stayed with the waiter, remember?"

"I remember the guy. How is Tina connected to him?" Lynn was trying to follow Annie.

"Maybe she's not, but I'm certain he used her to get into the U.S. The article said the 'kidnapped' woman was never found. If you look at her picture, it's Tina, I'm sure of it. I don't know how I missed it before. Someone at the State Department knows this guy and let him in. *And* someone knew Tina, I'll bet. Don't know who, but someone did."

"I think you're right, Annie," Tony agreed, as he turned to his computer. "Can you find the article again?"

"Certainly." Annie sat at the computer and began typing. It wasn't long before she had what she was searching for. "It says here, the girl was allegedly kidnapped but was never located, and the man, who was supposedly allowed to come look for her because of some gray political reasons, got lost in an unexplained shuffle at the State Department. When you look at this girl's picture, you're looking at Tina. It doesn't show a picture of the official who let the guy in, but the slant of the article is that the guy shouldn't have let the other man in to look for the girl. The man they let in was—or still is, I suppose—on one of those lists of people who are not allowed to come into the country because of association with terrorists. Although there's no proof offered of his activities."

"The guy in the State Department was Jacko," Sam said bitterly. "He insisted on this terrorist guy getting in, years ago. Like eight years or so. I remember it caused a real split in his group. That's how Allen and I wound up with Jacko, sort of. Homeland Security wanted him watched."

"I know Tina was seeing someone, but I don't believe it was Jacko," Annie offered. "I remember that when I first told Allen and Jacko about Tina getting killed, Allen was shocked, but Jacko didn't react. He didn't say so, but I'm positive he already knew."

"Pull up that picture of the guy again. The one you say you saw at the Gala. I think I may know him, or at least know of him," Sam said as he leaned over Annie's shoulder to study the picture. "I do know him. His name is Rhamidid, and he has ties to several terrorist groups. I remember that mess. We've been trying to find him for at least five years now. Jacko swore he left the country years ago, soon after it was determined the kidnap was a lie. Allen never believed him, though, and we've followed up on leads. We're still trying to locate him."

"I doubt you would have been able to, given that Jacko knew what you were doing," Tony observed. "You used Adeeb; Jacko must have known that and fingered him to Rhamidid."

"Jacko was killed long before Adeeb was shot," Annie reminded Tony.

"Yes, but each group—or in Jacko's and Rhamidid's case, person—operates individually, although they are working together. That Jacko was out of the picture meant nothing to Rhamidid's people. The plan to get Adeeb went on. When the opportunity presented itself, action was taken. If we are correct, and the other players are out at this time, we must concentrate on finding Rhamidid. I have every reason to believe he and whomever he works with will move forward. We have to find out what they have planned. Sam, do you or Allen have anyone else to help you? Someone to replace Adeeb, I mean?"

"No, we don't. We think since this year is an election year, it would be unlikely anyone would do anything until after the election. History's shown a surge in activity *after* each president takes office. I'm guessing sometime after January, next year. That gives us time to try to stop whatever is planned."

"Can Lynn and I go back to the ranch for a while?" Annie suddenly asked, looking at Tony.

Tony looked over the people gathered in his study. "Leave us." He stood and waited until the room was empty. Rounding the great desk, he took Annie into his arms. "I would keep you with me always, but I don't think that's to be just yet." Touching her face gently, he brushed her hair back; something he had grown to love doing. "I believe it might be safe for you to go home. I'll send men with you, of course. You two are never to go anywhere without an escort. I still reserve the right to send for you, whenever I think I need to. Agreed?" He smiled slowly. His hold was possessive, his voice thick with emotion.

Annie kissed his smile. "Agreed." She wrapped her arms around his neck, and the familiar tremor passed through her as he held her tightly.

* * * *

When she heard the news from Annie a while later, Lynn was ecstatic. "We actually get to go home? Yay!!!! I am so ready to get back to life as usual."

Annie smiled, but her heart was troubled. Yet Tony was lodged securely in her heart. She had but to close her eyes to see his face, to hear his voice, to feel his touch.

His Learjet 85 took them home.

CHAPTER 52

Rhamidid paced. He had assumed a very nondescript life. By day, he appeared to leave for work. He nodded to the few people he saw on his way to the bus station. By night, he kept to himself. He spent hours scouring the Internet. Every scrap of news about the political activities, candidates, and government's decisions filled his head. It was beyond him why such time and effort were taken to decide who could fill the role of leader. All the while, time crept by at a snail's pace. He had done his job well; of this he was certain. No one would even notice him until it was much too late. Then, who would care?

He had gone over and over in his mind what to take, how to act, who to target, but the answer to where was as yet not given. He had long since stopped responding to the rest of his cell. He didn't care where they were or what they would do. He had taken great pains to be certain he would be difficult for them to find. He knew just how they worked; was it not he who taught them? Now they would know the hand of a real master. Once he had opened up the floodgates, nothing could stop the final defeat of the foolish Americans. Them and their careless disregard for the *real way*. This gave him the only peace he knew. In the deep hours of the night, he allowed his mind to wander. There, he could see his land, his family, and his people.

Strange, he had never believed he would miss them. Not while he was in the service for his beliefs. But he did. He missed everything. The food, the people, the men, his family, the sounds—everything. Especially the woman. She had been like an addiction to him. She almost made him want to give up his life's work. When they split, the break was violent. She refusing to stay quietly in the background, he refusing to allow her equal status. How could he? It was simply not possible. At one time she would have understood this, but not after living here so long. Another mark against this doomed country.

Shaking his head, he refused to give in to the longing. No, this is the way it should be. He would show them all. Exactly as planned. It would be just that way. Always, he watched the news. Surely soon he would know. He still had contacts. So far, every bit of information he had received was accurate. He knew what the different political camps decided before the media filled screens with the latest events. The men he would use now were not from his country; they were Americans by birth, but not by belief. They were so eager to latch on to something grand they had been easy to dupe. Now, they hardly took a breath without consulting him. In return, he filled their heads with stories and garbage. How could they know? When he was done, they would be also. The great irony: they wouldn't even know it in time. Fools.

CHAPTER 53

Annie and Lynn spent long hours riding the ranch. In between times, they cleaned, painted, and refurbished the house. Tony and Sam called every day, at various times. It was apparent they were still involved in something, but volunteered nothing. The sisters didn't ask questions. They had experienced enough intrigue for a lifetime.

However hard she tried, Annie couldn't rid herself of a nagging worry. Something was wrong, somewhere. This evening, Annie sank deep into the soft, thick leather chair, which felt cool. Leaning back, she watched the shadows move across the ceiling. "I just can't do this much longer. I listen for the phone, watch the news, and check my email. This is ridiculous and I'm too old. Besides, I miss Allen. I hate the idea he can't come home. I don't believe he really doesn't mind. You know he does. Why can't we go see him?"

Lynn was lying on the sofa. Nearly asleep, she could only make out certain words. She made a halfhearted effort to sit up, but quickly decided against it and sank back, giving in to sleep.

Annie watched her. "So much for this conversation. Maybe I'll just call him." Annie tried several times to reach Allen. Unable to reach Earl either, she finally gave up. Rousing Lynn, Annie suggested they take a walk together. Buster was all ears.

Tony's men had been discreet at the ranch: they followed, scouted, and kept careful tabs on the sisters without interfering. For their part, the ladies made certain food was always available. Other than that, they paid the bodyguards little mind.

This evening, Annie and Lynn walked farther up the canyon and were gone longer than usual. Coming back, Buster ran ahead to the house. With his tail nearly wagging him, he began to bark. "What on earth?" Annie said in a puzzled voice as she and Lynn rounded the house, following him.

Tony stood on the great porch, hands in his pockets, smiling. He watched the two women climb the stairs and remembered how good it always felt to see Annie. Sam stepped through the front door out onto the porch, strode up to Lynn, and lifted and swung her round. "You're sure some gardener. The place looks great!"

"Another three months and the roads will be done. Just what have you two been doing?" Lynn answered a tad sarcastically.

Tony met Annie at the top of the stairs. He walked her to the far end of the porch, his arms encircling her. He leaned against the rail, facing her, and pulled her toward him. Annie let him lift her face gently and kiss her lips. She started to speak, but his finger pressed to her lips stopped her. "I'm first. I missed you. Terribly. I don't like this and think we should work out something better I guess you just have to marry me." He looked deep into her eyes.

Annie gasped. Stunned, she stood up straight, trying to think what to say. "I . . . I never planned to get married." The words slipped out of her mouth. Tony smiled slowly, but his face looked pained.

"You never planned to get married, or you never planned to marry someone like me?" The hurt and anger were plainly visible on his face.

"Tony," Annie countered quietly. "Look at me. You don't know—"

"I know everything about you."

She leaned her forehead on his chest. He always made the world seem right again. He made everything seem possible. Standing still, he waited for her to continue. "Then you must know the answer is yes," she answered softly.

Tony lifted her chin to look at her face, holding her close. "You're sure, Annie?" he asked quietly. His face cleared, his eyes were bright with anticipation.

"Yes." She smiled up at him.

With that, he gently kissed her lips, her eyes, and lips again.

"Tonight. I'm staying tonight," he promised himself.

Annie pulled away enough to look and smile at him. "Let's go on inside, love."

Once inside, the men mixed drinks. When everyone was comfortable, Tony announced, "We're going to have a wedding when all this is over." He turned to smile at Annie. Annie acknowledged the announcement with a nod; her face shone with the contentment she felt. When things had quieted down some, Tony continued. "Can you hook your computer and Internet up to this big screen?"

"I'm certain you can; Allen did it several times. I have no idea how to do it."

"If you bring everything to me, I'll hook us up," Sam instructed.

After the equipment was up and running, Sam inserted a disk. Activity exploded on the screen. Fires, people screaming, smoke, and crumbled buildings. "What is this?" asked Lynn.

"Haven't you been watching the news?" Sam looked at them incredulously.

"There's our boy, again. See the guy on the Jeep? He's the one linked to several bombings in India. He also leads the group in France. England is becoming a hotbed, as is the Netherlands."

"Now I remember where I *first* saw him," Annie interjected enthusiastically. "Tina had a picture of him in her apartment. She said he was a cousin, or something. She looked a little sad when she talked about him. Sad, and a bit angry, as I recall. She was reluctant to say much about him, and she even turned the frame around. I'm certain he's the same guy. I remember thinking at the time there must be a story behind that picture. Tell us about him. You knew him before, Sam?" Annie asked intently.

"Yes. Remember, his name is Rhamidid? He's a known terrorist. He was the key ingredient for several attacks on embassies around the world. Seems his big role has been in teaching the upcoming guys how it's done. He's good at explosives and firearms. He's apparently not much of a planner, though, since as near as we can tell, he only follows orders. Like who to bring on, where to go, et cetera. The FBI hasn't finished with everything taken from that house blown up in Denver, but so far it would seem this guy was not one of the thugs left inside."

"We believe," continued Tony, "he was slowed by recent events, but not stopped. He hasn't left the country, but we can't find him. He has to be waiting for further direction."

"The condo in Denver had a lot of firepower. They were with Rhamidid. He had to buy from someone else. He could never have gotten that much firepower into the states without help. It seems logical, he bought from a supplier here." Sam paused here and waited for Tony.

"He bought from the Venezuela bunch. When Rhamidid's men sold the drugs on our streets, the profit went for guns from Venezuela. We're watching to see if they're bringing in more, or if they meet with anyone. So far, it's dead." Tony stood with his hands in his pockets. He turned and walked to the window. "He was in Denver until last night. He's gone. Drove south about five this morning." He shook his head. "We have no idea just where he's headed. It's safe to say he's not given up and indeed may be on the move again." The room was quiet, as Sam put his equipment away.

Sam and Lynn wandered out onto the porch with Tony and Annie close behind. Tony followed Annie down the steps. Hand in hand, he led her to the creek winding its way past the house. The night was warm, the creek sang as it moved, and Annie wished they were in another time. The evening was still and as usual, they could hear the frogs croaking. In the distance, an owl hooted. She closed her eyes and leaned on Tony's shoulder. He kissed her head. "I don't think I'm leaving tonight," he whispered.

Annie smiled at him, her eyes shining. "Please do stay," she asked softly.

In silence, they walked back to the house. Annie's heart was pounding, the thought that she would spend this night with him filling her with anticipation. An anticipation unlike anything she had ever experienced.

As she opened the front door, however, she could hear the phone ringing. "I hope it's Allen," she thought as she picked up the receiver. Rhino's voice came over the line. His speech was soft, sort of muffled. Annie had to listen intently to understand what he was saying. Color drained from her face; she could hardly breathe. Turning toward the room, she began to cry softly. "Oh no, please no . . ." The room became a blur as tears filled her eyes.

"Annie, what is it?" Tony moved quickly to her side. She dropped the phone and sank to the floor.

Tony picked up the phone, but the line was dead. "Annie, what is it?" he asked again, wrapping her in his arms, helping her stand.

"Rhino. How . . .?" She began to weep uncontrollably.

Tony helped Annie to the couch. She began to rock side to side. "I brought them to Rhino. I brought them to him," she looked at Tony with pain-filled eyes. "And now they've . . ." She could not bear the thought that her actions had put Rhino on someone's radar. Now he was dead.

Tony talked to various people long into the night. The news reporter for the TV channel had little information, but the images were clear. Rhino was gone and had taken everything with him. Tony knew Rhino had worked with many people long before Annie ever brought anything to him.

Sam told Annie about how Rhino had assisted Allen and him, before they ever worked with Tony. "Rhino knew the risks in what he did. With his expertise, he was the one guy every clandestine government team looked to for answers, Annie," he assured her.

While Annie was shocked at how little it seemed she knew about her friend, she could not shake her sense of overwhelming guilt and responsibility. He had never been in any danger that she could tell, until she pulled him into her mess. Tony finally got Annie settled down with the help of a sleeping pill. This was not the way either one had intended to spend the night together.

* * * *

Rhino's murder was confirmation to Tony that Rhamidid was on the move, and now it looked as though he was moving dangerously close to Annie. "Rhamidid took Rhino out. I have to assume he might know about Annie. If he does, she'll be on his list to murder too," Tony confided in a low voice to Sam. "Call Allen and tell him what happened, then get Dominic and Lou up here. I also want the plane someplace close by. I want to be out of here by the day after tomorrow. That should give Allen time to get here. Bring every other man we can spare from mother's house here."

"Maybe we should set up a reception for any visitors," Sam suggested. "The more we eliminate, the longer it will take Rhamidid to build his crew up again."

"You're suggesting using Annie as bait?" Tony asked, his eyes flashing in anger.

"If no one comes, we haven't lost anything. You want everyone here anyway. If they do come, we take them off the table."

"I won't use her as some draw for Rhamidid's men," Tony replied, his mouth set.

"We're set up to take care of her and Lynn here tonight, but tomorrow, they're out of here," Sam urged. "You can take better care of things here on the ranch, than in Aguilar. We can't get a plane here tonight; there aren't that many places to land in daylight. None in the dark."

"Call in everyone we can spare. Close out Denver. Completely." Tony's mind reviewed every possibility. His mother was still in Aguilar. He wouldn't move her as long as possible. Tony walked through the great room to stand out on the porch. Darkness could be one's friend or enemy. Tonight, it would be his friend.

Sam was quiet. He knew his cousin well. His men would follow him anywhere. He was Mafia, through and through. His ties and relations had come to the aide of Sam and Allen so many times they quit counting. Sam was raised with them; he knew it all. Without Tony's kind of expertise and life outside the confines of conventional covert operations, this whole venture, as so many before, would have never gone as far, nor been as successful.

Tonight, as usual, Tony worked as the Boss. Sam was uncomfortable with the way the current administration viewed departments like Allen's, the CIA, ICE, and even Homeland Security. Maybe their best shot at safety would be for Allen's team to completely join Tony. It made more sense. He needed to talk to Allen.

CHAPTER 54

Two men arrived at Rhino's place as darkness was falling. When the Jeep pulled into his drive, Rhino had a sick feeling. He was not expecting any company; besides, no one ever came to visit him. The men were with Rhamidid. Rhino shouldn't know that, but he did. Both men were young, excited and brash. Rhino always expected this might happen. He still was not prepared. Somehow they had found him too soon. He looked around helplessly. There would be no one. He couldn't remember why he had come outside. Then, he knew. He felt them come. His ride was over.

Rhino turned and slowly limped back to the house. He thought about running, but knew he would never make it. He also knew his death would not be quick or easy. For years now he had avoided these people. He always acknowledged someone would eventually catch up with him. These thugs were American want-to-be terrorists. Following Rhino into the house, they began punching him and pushing him around. He was easy prey, crippled and defenseless. They talked about Rhamidid and his plan, unaware of Rhino's linguistic abilities. He had to think of something that would make them want to keep him alive. Barring that, he needed to demonstrate in a big way trouble was coming to the people he worked for and with. Annie crossed his mind. She was his only family. When a cell phone rang, one of the men stepped outside to answer.

"That gate has never been closed, has it? You take me for a fool?" Using his gun, the man struck Rhino across the face, smashing his nose and breaking teeth. Blood spattered. Rhino sank to the floor. He was pulled up again. The man dragged him across the floor and bound him, shoving him down against a wall. The man outside called to the sadistic gunman; he started to hit Rhino again, hesitated, then answered his companion. Grabbing his keys, he gave Rhino a vicious kick for good measure, and left. They would pick up one more from the airport, then return. They were eager to get at Rhino. He had all the information they would need, of that Rhamidid was certain. And they would make him talk.

Rhino listened for the sound of the car leaving on the gravel road. He could tell the car headed west toward the airport. Good. He would have time. Rhino knew he would die before the night was out. "If I'm going, I'm going my way." It took all his strength to sit up. After struggling, falling several times, and starting again, he finally was able to stand. He rocked and slid along the wall to the door switch. Flipping it on with his shoulder, he struggled to a small wet bar. The minutes raced. He fumbled around in the drawer, his hands bound behind him making it difficult. Finally, Rhino found a knife. He had difficulty with the blade, but eventually cut the ropes around his hands. With great effort, Rhino at last freed his feet. He slowly retreated back in time. A former Navy SEAL, he could do this.

Taking the rope with him, he stumbled down the stairs to his lair. Closing and sealing the door above, he calmly set about readying the area. Many times he had practiced this very scenario, usually to eat up some of the time he spent alone. *Poetic justice!* When he was satisfied that everything was ready, he limped to the sitting room. He swallowed all the pills, washing them down with bourbon, and set the timer.

Sitting back in the recliner, he dialed Annie's number. He smiled at the sound of her voice. It was hard to talk clearly as the pills took effect. "Be sure you watch the news this evening, Annie. I'm done. I'm taking

everything with me. Tell Tony it was Rhamidid's boys, but they're ama-
teurs. You know I've always loved you, Annie. You were more than my
friend, to me. Tony will take good care of you." He could hear her gasp
and start to cry. Then he hung up the phone.

"Bye Annie." Rhino closed his eyes, at peace at last.

* * * *

A while later the three men started the drive back to the compound.
They were all eager to have a turn at interrogating—torturing—the weak
cripple inside. This would be their first test. So far, it was going exactly as
planned. Ignoring orders to move quickly, they collectively decided they
would "play" with the man first. They could get information from him
for certain. They would even take all of his equipment, wherever it was.
They spoke about how they could leave him for someone to find, and
how everyone would be afraid. No one would know who had done such a
thing. This would send a message to the others. Jihad was coming! They
were not to be taken lightly.

They finally arrived at the compound and parked in Rhino's front
yard. Each man had his own thoughts as the three stepped into the house.
Fate's gift to Rhino was the timer. The men walked into the room where
they had left him and realized he was not there. Moments later, Rhino's one last message for them was delivered. Explosions shook the area.
Series of blasts continued moving through the tunnels, destroying everything inside and anything above. Rhino's compound was obliterated. Fire
and smoke filled the night sky. Sirens soon began to wail as emergency
responders rushed to the scene. Power lines were down for the area, giving the burning den a bonfire glow seen for miles.

News reports noted that whatever caused the explosion was massive.
Nothing was left. It was assumed there may have been people in the
house, although even vehicles were totally destroyed. The blast dug deep
into the earth, moving out like fingers from a central area. It would be
months before the investigators realized the area destroyed by the blast
was actually an underground maze. All gone now.

CHAPTER 55

The doors to Tony's Hummer opened. Five men stepped out and headed for the porch. "Lynn! Look, it's Allen! I can't believe it, it's Allen. And Earl!" Annie was running across the front porch toward the men. She could hardly believe Allen was home. He spent several minutes just holding his sisters. He walked with them into their family home, and Earl followed close behind. The siblings talked for several hours.

When things had settled down a bit, Dominic volunteered to fix dinner and pulled Lou with him to the kitchen. Everyone else sat around in the great room visiting.

Tony knew Annie still ached over Rhino. He took her hand and walked with her up behind the house. "Are you okay, baby?" He gently put his hand on the nape of her neck and turned her head toward him.

Smiling weakly, Annie nodded. "Thank you." It felt good to have him close again.

"For what?" he asked softly.

"For being who you are, Tony, for being exactly who you are." Kissing him quickly, she headed back to the house. Tony's heart went out to her. This had been harder on Annie than he had ever imagined. "When this is over . . . " he thought.

After a leisurely dinner and time to visit, Allen and Tony brought the rest of them up to date.

"So you see, Rhino worked for us, except he also kept his old ties in place," Allen explained.

Annie nodded. "That explains how he was able to get the DNA. How long have you known him?"

"We've only known him for the last fifteen years or so. He came up on the radar screen because of you," Allen said, turning toward Annie. "During a routine security check, we saw evidence you and he were very good friends. Research told us lots about him, including his renegade activities with several colleges and police units, like NYPD. After visiting with him, we decided he was just what our operation needed. He was great. The best, I'd say, with forensics, and plain old 'follow the logic' kind of stuff. Over time, he also became expert at people watching. Computers and phones? He could fix almost anything. Made them do what he wanted. He could tell you where anyone was, at any time. Unfortunately, someone picked up on *his* location."

"We have no reason to believe his attackers knew who they were dealing with other than his cover, which was an arms dealer," Tony continued. "Rhino wouldn't have gone out without a real, real good reason. We know the guys he killed were with Rhamidid, although Rhamidid was not at their party. We have to find that guy."

"So what do we do from here?" Lynn asked.

"*We* don't do anything. You two are out of it now. You sit tight and wait," Tony answered. "I don't intend to give this guy anything to work with. We need to find him and find him fast. I plan to take you two back to New York with us."

"I agree," Allen commented. "Things are going to get uglier."

"*I'm* thinking that's okay with me," answered Lynn. "I'm more than happy to putter someplace with Annie, but couldn't we be of use some other way?"

"This is our feature of the evening, people," Lou interrupted. "Watch carefully. We'll discuss it after the film is finished. I want to see who you recognize. Maybe we can find some clue to what he's supposed to do."

For the next forty-five minutes, the room was silent. The figures moved in and out of scenes. Annie sat taking notes furiously. When the images stopped, Lou flipped the computer off. "Well? Anyone see anything?"

As usual, Tony sat quietly, watching. Sam and Allen began to discuss where the pictures had come from. Lou listened as he put his equipment away. "Is the material credible? Yes. Our people got the videos."

"Then you should be able to tell us where they were taken, right?" Allen asked.

"Unfortunately, no. The two men we had on him are now dead. One was found floating in a canal, near Denver. The second was found in a boxcar, after it stopped in Chicago. Neither had any equipment on them, and we have no way of knowing if Rhamidid also has the same information we have, but we must assume he may."

"I'd say we should assume he *does*," corrected Earl. "If they have the same information, all they have to do is change locations. Right?"

"Personally," Dominic began, "I would say they do not have this information. We don't keep stuff from the field. Once it has been sent somewhere, whatever we had is destroyed. And I do mean *destroyed*. These guys were caught, obviously, but they were not caught with any of this on them. What we don't know is what they were working on when they were caught. They would have had *unfinished* material on hand. Which could be worse, because it was unseen."

Tony stood up. "Gentlemen, at this point, they know we're on to them, we can follow them, and we're relatively current. What they don't know is who we are. They could assume we're government intelligence and assume we're bound by those regulations. We are neither. I think that's enough for tonight. I need to think a little. We assume we've been compromised. We're leaving early in the morning. Everyone get some rest." He stood and waited at the hall for Annie.

"I would have liked to spend our first night together in Italy, New York . . . someplace romantic. But the way things have gone lately . . ." Tony had closed the door behind him and now stood before Annie, his hand slowly tracing her face, her lips, and moving down her neck. Annie stood, eyes closed, feeling the warmth of his touch spread through her, like water on to sand.

For the first time in her memory, Annie felt she was where she belonged. She drifted to sleep with the peace left in one's being after passion has been expressed and answered by the one you love.

* * * *

A soft knock at the door awakened Tony. He tiptoed to the door and whispered, "Yes?"

"Someone is driving in. Do you want us to take them out?" Sam's voice was also soft, calm.

"Eventually. I want to know what they know first. Let's get the sisters out of the house right away." Tony crossed the room quickly and shook Annie gently.

She rolled over, immediately alarmed. In the room, lit only by the moon, she could see Tony getting dressed and arming himself. "What—"

"Hurry, love. You and Lynn need to get out. We have company." His lips brushed hers as he stepped past her to the door.

Annie threw clothes on and followed him out silently. Lynn was just leaving her room. Pulling Annie against the wall to avoid the moonlight, Tony pointed out the kitchen window. Annie could see a vehicle slowly moving down the road toward the first bridge. The guard light near the bridge provided only a silhouette, but that was enough. The car's headlights were off.

Tony shoved a gun into Annie's hand and pushed her toward a side door on the side of the house opposite from the main road. The sisters and Buster scrambled out the door and up the canyon swell directly behind the house, taking care to stay within the brush thickets. After several minutes they stopped to catch their breath.

With the illumination from the guard lights, they were able to follow the SUV as it advanced toward the big house. When it came to a halt below the barn, at least five men got out of the vehicle. The men all carried large, long weapons. They scattered immediately and were lost from view.

Annie caught sight of one man sneaking around to the back, approaching the kitchen door. Having tried the door and finding it locked, he turned to leave and was joined by another. Stealthily they circled the entire house, trying the latch at each door. They went to the kitchen door again, this time trying to pick the lock. They were finally able to gain entrance to the house, using the same door Annie and Lynn had just exited. As of yet, neither Annie nor Lynn could see any of Tony's men.

Seeing the intruders enter the house, Annie and Lynn began to move even further up the mountainside. Hoping to get a better view of the grounds below, they climbed to a large mass of sand rocks. When they looked back, every light in the house was on. They watched as the men went from room to room, searching. The trio on the mountainside sat still and watched. There was still no sign of Tony or his men.

After a long period, one of the men came out of the master bedroom and onto the patio. He had a flashlight, and began to scour the ground. "Oh no, they're going to track us. Where in the hell is our side?" Lynn whispered urgently. Standing, she watched the men as they searched for her and Annie.

The night visitors quit looking for tracks. Apparently waiting for a rapidly approaching daybreak, they continued to search inside and around the house. They moved in and out of view through the windows. As dawn shed the first signs of daylight, the intruders came out of the house, and again began to look for tracks. Because Allen and the men had wandered around the grounds the evening before, there were tracks everywhere. Eventually, the men honed in on the side door. Looking upward, surveying the mountainside, they began to climb.

"Please do something, Tony," Annie whispered.

Buster sensed Annie's fear, and he began to growl. Annie put her hand over his muzzle. She looked at the gun in her hand. "How close do they have to be before I can hit one? Tony, where are you?" Annie worried.

The men were sweeping back and forth, in wide swaths, moving slowly toward Annie and Lynn. Just then, Annie caught sight of several of Tony's men. The intruders below her were so intent on the job at hand, they failed to notice Tony's men moving around them. Daylight began to send its rays washing down the mountainside, near the sisters. The rocks behind them cast a long shadow overhead.

Below them, several of Tony's men were moving away from the house.

Signaling to each other, they began to fan out, surrounding the uninvited men. Suddenly the silence of the early morning was shattered as shots rang out. Annie could see the puffs of dirt flying up when bullets hit the ground near the men climbing toward her and Lynn. The men immediately returned fire, and the sounds of gunshots echoed through the valley. The noise was deafening. Both sides were armed with much more than Annie's little pistol. Annie and Lynn crouched behind the rocks, covering their ears, praying the right side would win.

Lou climbed up the mountainside to Annie, "Okay, you two. Now let's get you out of here, and someplace safe. Don't talk; we're taking you around the barn. They may not even know what you look like, so we're going to try to get you ladies out without them seeing or hearing you. Keep Buster close to you."

Lou spoke briefly into his phone. Turning to Annie, he told her, "Everything is set. You three head out; move fast, I can't give you a long time. Get in the last vehicle. Stay down until we tell you otherwise. Got it?" Annie nodded. Lou continued, "We'll be right there. Get going."

The sisters scrambled off the hillside, around the barn, through corrals, and toward the waiting Hummer. Eventually, Lou returned with Dominic. They loaded all the computer equipment and everything else they could find. Sam and Tony got in and the Hummer turned around and moved out.

"Are you two okay?" Tony asked. Assured the sisters were fine, he spoke to someone on the phone.

"Who *are* those guys?" Annie asked.

"We don't know now, but we will know soon. I'm taking you to the plane. You and Lynn are headed to New York. At least I can keep you safer there."

"What about Allen and Earl? Are they all right?" Annie asked.

"They're fine. They stayed to help with the information gathering going on at the house now." Tony replied. He watched as what he said registered with Annie. She looked a little sad, but made no comment.

The ride to the plane was quiet. The four men talked about how these men could know Annie was there or if they were fishing. Annie listened, but kept her opinions to herself. Par for the course, the Hummer took them up a canyon road and stopped. Sitting ahead on a long stretch of dirt road, an airplane waited for takeoff.

"What do you think will happen to those men at the house?" Lynn asked quietly.

"I don't want to know, but I would like to know if they are the same people who got to Rhino." Annie suddenly touched Tony's arm. "Which reminds me, with all this excitement, I almost forgot something I found out last night. While you guys were visiting and putting things away, I hit the computer. Using street signs and landmarks I located the people we saw on the video. Rhamidid is with the same guy nearly every time he goes out. I'm sure who he is. His name is Riyadzi. I remember him. When we set down, I'll show you."

Tony's brows shot up. "Really? Good for you. Sam, what do you know about a Riyadzi?" Tony stood up and led the way to the back of the plane. The four men sat deep in discussion.

Safely settled into their old rooms in Tony's estate, New York felt like a welcome respite. "Maybe Tony is right. Maybe it's time we let them do their thing. The problem is, now that I know what I know, I want to keep up with all the activity. What do you think?" Annie asked Lynn.

"I really like the idea of staying in one place. One safe place." Lynn noted.

After dinner, the sisters and Buster wandered. The grounds were now familiar, with their marble statues gracing expanses of manicured lawn, picturesque bubbling fountains and numerous flowerbeds exploding with colors and heady scents. Trees were everywhere. "This is so peaceful." Lynn noted dreamily.

Wandering around the corner, they sauntered down a tiled pathway, new to both. Turning around a bend of heavy vegetation, they halted. The area was alive with activity. Lights flooded every corner. Men were coming and going. As they stood astounded by the activity so well hidden, a man approached them. "Excuse me, ladies. I will escort you back to the house. You are not allowed in this area." He indicated they were to precede him back the way they had come. Although the man was not threatening, it was clear they *would* leave the area. He followed them back to the large patio area. "I'll leave you here. Have a pleasant evening." Bowing slightly, he backed away and was gone.

Sitting down, Annie noted ruefully, "This would be Tony's idea of a deserted island."

"Not really," his voice came to them from the darkness. Both women jumped. He stepped out into the light. "I would prefer no phones, no people, and no guns." He walked to Annie and bent to kiss her. Kissing Lynn on the cheek, he returned to Annie's chair. Squatting next to her, he studied her. "I'm sorry about your interrupted stay at the ranch. It would seem Rhamidid is going about business as usual, eliminating anyone he deems a threat. They made a mistake with Rhino, though. Rhino would have been a well of information. Come with me. I have something to show you." He stood and waited for the sisters to pass. Entering the study, Annie sighed. She loved this room. Tony pulled up two more chairs. When they were seated, he turned the computer on. Annie recognized the white rhino. When the site opened, she read:

"Tony, Rhamidid still going. Using local talent. Not good. Knows Sam and Allen. Knows about Annie, not her face. Was Tina's lover. Were extremely close at one time. She still worked for him. He never approved of Saldivar. Tina did. Watch the elections. Very important. Taking all info with me. I've always loved Annie. Take care of her."

Annie's hand went to her mouth. *And I loved him, in my own way.* She reread the message, "He knew the people after him. How does Rhamidid know about me?"

"If I were a guessing man, I'd say from Tina. She still worked for him, Annie. He's put two and two together. You have to stay off the radar." Tony walked to the bar, setting three glasses up, he poured Crown over ice. "Things are going to move quicker. I may not always be here. I've asked Dominic to keep an eye on you. He'll have several men with him. He can get me if he needs to. You can always use the cell I gave you. You still have it, right?" he glanced at Annie. "Lynn, you can have Dom call Sam, but he won't be in the country. He just left with Allen and Earl. You two get some sleep."

Lynn left the study for their room. Holding Annie, Tony brushed her hair from her face, as always, kissed her, and smiled affectionately. "I do not expect to see you running around everywhere anymore," he warned. "Men will be in and out. You two have to stay put. And Annie," he held her closer, "last night was the first for the rest of our lives. You're going to be my wife." He looked deep into her eyes. "I have to go to work; good night Inamorata," He touched her face briefly, then turned to leave, not allowing a response, paused and came back to her. Taking her into his arms, he kissed her long and passionately, leaving Annie trying to breathe normally.

Annie entered the suite she shared with Lynn with thoughts of Rhino. She never suspected he might have had another life. Clearly, while his unusual living arrangements and other activities had not mattered to her, it had to others. To her, he was a dear friend, to others, a library housed in a horribly misshapen body. "In the morning, I want to share my project for Rhino, with you. We'll need computers, though." Impulsively, Annie added, "I'm glad you're here, Lynn."

"I'm glad too . . . I think." Lynn replied. "Allen and Earl have taken off again, so now it's just you and me, babe!"

Sleep came in short fits. Dawn found Annie and Buster sitting on the balcony, watching as Tony loaded up. He glanced up and stood watching her look at him. She stepped to the retaining wall and sent him a gentle kiss. Life was precarious and not permanent. Annie watched his car, until she could no longer see the taillights.

CHAPTER 56

By the time Lynn awoke, Annie was downstairs fixing a light breakfast for them. Taking a tray up to Lynn, she joined her on the balcony. "Today, we work on the file Tony left for us. We can add to the spreadsheet Rhino gave us." Annie stopped speaking, her thoughts on Rhino again. "Oh, Lynn, I can never go back to whatever I once was . . . not after knowing these people are in our midst. Especially not after losing someone like Rhino to them. I remembered something Rhino told me one of the times I was with him. I may have information, and lots of it. After we eat and get going, I'll show you where. How did you sleep?"

"Okay, I guess." Lynn shook her head. "You're going a little fast for me, but I'll catch up. Have you seen Tony this morning? Is he already gone?"

"He's gone, but I did get to see him." Annie smiled.

Annie and Lynn took over the study Tony had assigned to them. Rhino had given Annie five 16 GB flash drives along with two external hard drives, each 70 GB. Enormous amounts of information were contained on the drives. Each flash drive followed the setup Annie and Lynn adopted. Two hard drives contained a similar setup, but with past activities, rather than people, listed. On one flash drive they found an index. Annie and Lynn worked from that index, compiling information from Tony's folder.

That evening, the sisters found themselves watching news on every channel they could find: BBC, the Mexican station, and any other stations available.

As the project grew, it became clear they would need more equipment. Dominic had the additional hard drives and computer brought in, as well as four more televisions, all mounted in a group. To one side, the Global Incident Map was left displayed, with auto refresh programmed. Standing with Dominic as he adjusted the biggest screen, Annie asked him, "Just what is it you do for Tony?" At first she didn't think he heard.

Then he smiled slowly and replied, "Let's just say I'm a much better shot than any of the others and much more inventive. I finish a lot of projects for Tony. I can take very good care of you two." Without further comment he continued to work. Annie remembered Lou asking once if it was time to bring Dominic in. Involuntarily, Annie shuddered.

After working for several days, they had every bit of information moved to separate external drives, each holding 2 TBs of information. The final step was to order and set up two new computers, with as much storage as they could buy. Everything was labeled. In one conversation with Tony, Annie found out there was a wall safe in their room. All the information was duplicated and stored. By the time Tony came back, Annie and Lynn had massive amounts of information available.

Sam spent two weeks setting up a program that would match pictures, key bits of information or similarities to an individual, then notify them what group, country, or individual was matched. It ran somewhat like a DNA bank for law enforcement, but with different parameters. The men set about learning the system. When they needed to know something about an incident, man, group, or country, Annie or Lynn gave them printouts.

Every step was taken to keep the sisters, their location, and activity secret. With Tony's help, Annie began to determine just who she could rely on for additional information. Slowly, leads began to come to them from covert sources. These sources were from other countries and agencies. Just as slowly, requests came to them for assistance. Late summer ran full sprint into fall as Annie stepped quietly into Tony's world, bringing Lynn with her.

CHAPTER 57

T he breeze was crisp. There was a hint of fall in the air and leaves were beginning to change colors. Tony, Lou, and Sam were in New York City on business. In a moment of madness, Annie decided to go visit Tony in the Big Apple. "Are you sure you want to do that?" Lynn worried. "What if he doesn't want to be surprised?"

"I suppose he'll have to deal with it," Annie laughed. "Come with me. It'll be fun. If they don't want to visit, we can play for a day or so."

Annie called the hotel where he stayed. He had checked in, but he was presently out of his room. Unable to convince Lynn to join her, Annie took the SUV and drove into the city on her own. She checked into a room in the hotel and left to find her man.

Annie frequently came to the hotel with Tony, so the staff knew her well. As she crossed the lobby, the concierge called to her, "Hey, Miss Annie. Haven't seen you in a while. Been too busy to play?"

"Yes, but not this weekend. I'm here for the art exhibit in Central Park!" As a rule, Tony had lunch at one of several restaurants near the hotel. If Annie didn't find him, she would give him a call. Familiar with the places he typically ate lunch, she started off down the sidewalk.

Since coming with him to New York, she saw the city in a different light. She delighted in the bustle, noise, and sheer life that enveloped her on every trip. At the fourth restaurant she peeked into, Annie saw him.

Smiling in anticipation, she stepped down the stairs. Then she saw his companion. The woman was dressed casually, blonde hair hung about her face, which was heavily made up. Her hand held Tony's in a familiar gesture. She was leaning in toward him, smiling seductively as she spoke. Annie was stunned. She walked up to the couple.

"Tony?" Annie's voice was soft, its tone incredulous. Her heart was beating so hard it hurt. Her chest tightened; she felt like she might choke. Fighting to maintain control, she looked from one to the other. "So I'm not the only one. How humiliating," Annie thought.

"Oh, I see he hasn't told you about us. What a pity. And you are?" The woman's voice was husky and oozed sensuality.

Turning to leave before she made a fool of herself, Annie left quickly. Tony called after her, but she kept moving. Desperate to remove herself, she practically stepped out in front of a cab pulling up. "Take me away from here, please!" she begged the driver.

He had seen that look before. "Jump in, let's go." He moved into the traffic with ease. The taxi smelled of cigars and perfume. It was older and had seen better days. The seats were worn and stained. The driver, normally a happy talkative fellow, watched her in silence. Annie sat shaking, thoughts tumbling through her head. "What do I do now? I can't go home. Where can I go?"

Ultimately, Annie knew she needed to get away from Tony. She gave the cabbie her hotel address, and when she reached the hotel, she had regained some composure. Quietly she told the cabbie, "I'll pay you very well to wait for me. I'll only be a few moments." The cabbie looked at Annie. He had no clue what her story was, but she looked like she would be good for the fare. Why not?

"No problem, lady."

True to her word, she came back down in ten minutes—with her bag and a plan. "Can you take me to JFK now?" she asked as she slid into the cab. Forty-five minutes later, as the cabbie maneuvered his way to the departure area for the airline Annie had specified, she asked, "Is it possible for you to wait while I make certain I can get a flight?"

"Yeah, I'll be right here, in the taxi lane." Annie handed him four hundred dollars.

"Please don't leave. I'll hurry." When she came out, she had a ticket in hand. "I have one more favor, sir. I know that eventually you will have to tell someone who will ask about me that you took me somewhere. Would you just drive around before returning to the city, and give me three hours? After that, it won't matter."

What harm could it do? "Sure thing. I'm headed to lunch anyway. I have another pickup on the other side of town after lunch. Are you going to be okay, lady?"

Annie didn't answer. She tried to give him another hundred-dollar bill, but he refused. As he drove away, he called out, "Good luck!"

Annie ran back into the airport, held her breath through security, rode the escalators, found her gate, and sat. She couldn't look around for fear he would be there. She had to get on the plane before he found her. Her flight would leave in thirty minutes. "Just give me thirty minutes," she prayed silently.

When Annie boarded, she finally relaxed. The scene she had just witnessed at the restaurant and the woman's taunting words were plastered in her mind. Silently, she argued with herself. "How could he *do* something like that? How *long* has he been doing that? I feel so ashamed and stupid." One lone tear trickled down her cheek.

Grateful for the distance between seats in first class, she stared out the window. With her business she had made this flight at least four times a year. It had always been a time of anxious anticipation. Now it was desperation that drove her. She had to be someplace where Tony couldn't find her. Her initial hurt was matched with anger. "I wish I had never met him. How could I have fallen for him? I'll bet he's got dozens of women just like that cheap-looking tart. Lynn was right. Poor Lynn. Now she's involved with Sam. This is just impossible." Her mind kept her awake for the entire flight.

Nine hours later, the plane landed. She had no idea what she would do next. She only knew where she would go. With one small bag and her tote, Annie stepped into the night. At the car rental, she was immediately provided with the only vehicle left. The manager knew her well. He was surprised she came this time without calling first. No matter. Her company paid him very well. He never asked questions, simply took care of her. He handed her keys to a red BMW sports car.

Maneuvering the familiar streets, she slowly drove out of town. On the road alone, her tears fell. Twice she pulled over until she could regain control and drive. By the time she reached the quaint typical Italian villa that had been converted to a bed and breakfast, it was late morning. The sleeping rooms were upstairs, opening to the courtyard. The courtyard had tables, chairs, and a smaller area set back where a band played daily. A fountain at one end bubbled continually. Flowers of every description filled large pots placed everywhere. Annie's home away from home. When the old proprietor saw Annie, he yelled to his wife and ran to meet his guest. Trying not to fall apart, she asked apologetically, "Do you have any room? I'm sorry I didn't call ahead."

In his thick accent, the old man scolded her. "Always, Annie. We always have room for you. Don't ask. Here, let me take your bags, come with me." His wife followed, armed with extra blankets and Annie's usual pot of coffee, as they led her up the stairs. The band below was beginning to fill the courtyard with the sounds of romantic Italian love songs, one after another. Annie groaned inwardly. Certain she was settled in her room, the gracious couple stayed just a short while. Neither asked her any questions. "We see you in a little while. If you need anything, call. Mama or I will be right here. You gonna be okay, Annie?" She nodded. The couple kissed her and left her, the old man shaking his head.

She was in the corner room. The bedding was elegant Italian linens, the colors muted rusts, browns, and yellows. The balcony from her room looked out on the distant vineyards and hills. "My favorite room, how ironic," she thought.

After she locked the door, Annie sat on the bed. The music filtered through the windows, filling her with a painful ache. Slowly, the tears came again. This time, she lay down, hugging the pillow. Her body was racked with the waves of sadness, betrayal, and anger that washed over her. The image of the woman, her hand on Tony's, how she leaned in to him, it was all so awful. Annie trusted him, fell in love with him. He had taken care of her, seen her in the worst of conditions. Humiliated, she wept. She couldn't gain control. The crying wouldn't stop. As morning slowly crept into her room, even the sun hesitated to disturb her. After hours of weeping, she finally slept.

CHAPTER 58

As Tony sat waiting for his last appointment before he, Lou, and Sam returned to the estate, he had Annie on his mind, as usual. She drove him crazy without knowing it. They needed to get married—soon. He smiled to himself as he pictured her dancing with him, her gown soft to his touch, her body moving in time with his. He loved her laugh, her eyes, her . . . Startled, he turned toward someone calling his name. Letty slipped around tables toward him, hips swaying and mouth smiling enticingly. "Why, if it isn't the elusive Anthony. Such a welcome surprise. May I sit?"

Ignoring his irritated *no*, she sat down and seductively grasped his hand, leaning toward him. Just then, she caught sight of the woman headed their way. This was not Tony's usual woman. This one had class; the kind of woman a man would love. Instantly recognizing why he never called on her anymore, Letty purred, addressing the woman now staring at the two of them. Tony was shocked to see Annie and even more shocked to hear Letty address her. Jerking his hand from beneath hers, he called to Annie, but lost her in the crowd. "What the hell are you doing, Letty? There is no 'us' and you know it. There never was."

Letty shrugged. "Oh, I know, but I used to have you sometimes. Now? Never."

"You never had me, Letty," Tony corrected her coldly. At that moment, his lunch companion, an elderly man, appeared.

"Am I interrupting?"

"Certainly not. She's leaving. Please, sit," Tony stood. The gentleman and Tony eventually concluded their business. Excusing himself to make another appointment, the gentleman left. Tony paid, cursing the delay. He angrily strode out of the eatery. Lou and Sam were pulling up, as Tony stepped out onto the sidewalk.

"Boy, he must have had an awful lunch!" observed Lou. "He looks like someone slipped him liver and onions."

Sam chuckled. Sliding into the backseat and slamming the door, Tony barked, "How long have you two been here?"

"Five seconds, maybe." Lou answered. Sam shrugged his shoulders.

Briefly, Tony described his lunch. His cousins exchanged glances. After a moment, Lou asked, "What do you want to do?"

"Find her, of course. Sam, call Lynn and see what she knows. It goes without saying this is not to be discussed. Lou, get me to the hotel." Tony's voice was more controlled.

Sam spoke briefly with Lynn. "Annie wanted to surprise you. Lynn thinks she checked into the hotel several hours ago."

"She certainly surprised me." Tony muttered. He called the hotel. "She's already checked out. At least they think she did; she just tossed the key at them on her way out. I'm sure she won't go back to the house. Get me to the hotel. She had the Lexus, no telling where she's headed," he said, his voice now heavy with a sense of urgency.

Lou whipped in and out of traffic, while Sam took a call from the hotel. "She left the Lexus at the hotel, Tony."

"Call whoever you use. Find out what cab picked her up. I want to know where she is." Tony shook his head again. Lou pulled the car under the porte cochere. Before it stopped completely, Tony was out and storming through the lobby.

For two hours, Tony paced in his hotel room. "I didn't even have a chance to say anything. Damn it! Where could she be? It's been four hours at least."

Sam finally reported in. "The taxi took her to JFK over three hours ago. Cabbie didn't know what flight or anything else. Just dropped her off and left. She only had one bag."

Lou was already on the phone to Tony's contact. Again, Tony played the waiting game. By turns, he worried about Annie and became angry at himself for allowing any woman to affect him like this.

When the contact finally called back, Lou shook his head. "You're not going to believe this. She went to Italy." Lou groaned inwardly.

"Italy! She went to Italy? You've got to be kidding me!" Tony raged. "Why the hell would she go to Italy? Are they sure? What's in Italy? You're positive?"

"She went to Italy. I've got her one-way ticket confirmation and flight number to Rome. You're not thinking of going there, are you? You can't be thinking of going to Italy, Tony. Not now. We have no idea how long this might take," Lou spoke quietly. He knew his cousin. It was useless to say anything, but he had to try.

"Yes, Lou, I am well aware of how long this might take. We go now. Sam, you go back to headquarters. Cover things; I'll be in contact. Keep Lynn out of this as long as you can. Lou, get two tickets there. We leave here immediately. Give us a day or so to find her, then book us for three back. Damn it!" In anger, he smashed his phone on the tile floor.

"Tony, what if she doesn't want to come back? Also, I think you might want to take Dominic with us. He's spent more time in Italy than you and I combined." Lou quietly suggested.

"I'm not *asking* her. She's *coming* back," Tony answered through clenched teeth. "Fine! Get Dominic. Three there, four back."

Tony paced while Lou worked on the tickets. Thoughts spilled through his mind. "Who could track her for me in Italy? Why Italy? Who does she know that well in Italy? Damn that temper of hers. If she had only let me talk."

"The annual inspection is just starting on your plane. If we leave before next week, we fly commercial. We've got the first available seats out, day after tomorrow at ten in the morning. I've tried every airline." Lou waited for an explosion.

Tony's voice was now low and controlled. "Day after tomorrow, Lou? That's the earliest? Do you know how much of a head start that gives her?" Tony's anger began to boil, again. "Who is she running to in Italy?" he asked himself. "Sam, talk with Lynn, see if Annie has checked in with her yet."

Sam nodded his head. "We're already on it boss. Lynn said Annie goes to Italy pretty frequently for her art dealership. Has a passport, so it must have been easy to buy the ticket and go. Dominic is on his way here. He thinks he knows what rental agency she might use if she rents a car there."

"The real question is how did I let this happen?" moaned Tony. "I had a perfectly normal life before this. For some unknown reason, I fall for someone with track shoes on, always running away." Tony shook his head, trying to keep his temper in check.

"I'd say your life has never been *normal*. Dominic says you'd have done far worse if you had found Annie like that, with another man," Lou commented casually.

"He would say that," Tony returned, as he continued his pacing. "Of course, he says that to you, not to me."

CHAPTER 59

When Annie finally woke up, it was early afternoon. She rose slowly, aching from the long night spent fighting herself. After a shower, she dressed in the same outfit she had worn the day before and tried to look a little less like someone who had cried for hours. Swollen eyes and a puffy red nose didn't leave much to the imagination. Just trying to think was burdensome. She trudged downstairs, dreading the possibility of meeting anyone. Luckily, the little courtyard was empty. Mama came at once, sat her down, and poured coffee for her. "Tell me why it is you cry, Annie? Who hurt you?"

"I'll just start crying again. I'm so . . . I don't know if I'm angry or hurt. Whatever it is, it feels awful." She sat with her head in her hand. She had never felt so crushed.

"You're both, and I think it was a man. You finally have a man, and he hurts you. You can't give up, Annie. You just get up and keep going." The old woman patted her shoulder, kissed the top of her head. "You're not the first," she said then walked away to assist another guest, giving Annie her privacy. "I couldn't agree more." Annie thought sarcastically.

She finally forced coffee and dry toast down. She donned her sunglasses and left the courtyard behind her. The sun was warm on her face. The sounds of children playing in the street and women yelling to each other provided distraction from the painful tape repeating over and over in her mind. She took the path behind the villa, leading away from the little village. It wound its way through a lightly wooded area, along fields of grape vines, and past an orchard of olive trees. This path was like a dear companion to Annie. The few homes scattered about the hillside housed friends she had made over the years. She knew every family in and around the village. The familiar smells of the countryside in Italy wrapped around her. Many times she had wandered the trail, ending up on the far side of the hamlet, to wander back to the villa using the main street, visiting with everyone. Today, she craved solitude.

She knew she should call Lynn. Finally getting herself together, she dialed the number. Lynn answered after the first ring. "Where are you?"

"Please don't say anything. I came where I can feel protected; where he can't find me. I'm just letting you know I'm fine. I finished the last download we needed. You should be current. If someone needs something you are uncertain about, get Sam to help. He knows as much as we do. I'm sorry, Lynn. Love you."

"Annie, wait, don't hang up. I'm glad you're there. Stay as long as you need. Just tell me what happened. Sam keeps calling to see if you are here or if I know where you might be. Of course, I say 'no' to both, but what's going on?"

"It's a long story. I was so stupid. Should have kept my heart under cover. I'll call later. Love you." Annie hit the end icon on her phone. She hated hanging up on her sister, but couldn't bear to say anything more. She walked until dark, trying to think her way out of the problem. No matter where her logic took her, the image of the woman with her hand holding Tony's and her sultry voice pushed logic aside. In her heart, Annie recognized that the woman knew Tony well—very well. All these years Annie had refused to allow herself to care for any man. "Oh, why did it have to be Tony?" she cried inwardly. She was consumed by anger and sadness.

When she got back to the villa, the courtyard was alive with locals. She tried to work her way through the crowd unnoticed, but to no avail. More than one person stopped her to visit. She wound up sitting down with several couples and having wine.

The wine on an empty stomach made it impossible to stay in the conversation. She gave up. "I really need to get to bed. I love seeing you all again." Smiling, she slipped back to her room.

Inside with the lights off, she crawled under the covers without undressing and cried herself to sleep again. Her work, her sister, her brothers . . . everything was tied to that man. She had to think of some way to get away from Tony.

So it went, the next day and the next. She ate little. She cried less. She walked and walked more. The old couple began to worry about her. Soon the whole little village rallied around their friend. People came by to visit, refusing to be put off. They even sent the children. Annie gave it her best effort, but each day was a struggle she couldn't win. She could not imagine being with Tony again. Sadly, she could not imagine being without him either. She felt like she was in quicksand, sinking slowly. She also felt responsible for Lynn and for the work they'd done on behalf of Allen and Rhino. "Oh, how I hate him! I hate how messed up I am because of him!" she said to herself.

CHAPTER 60

Tony had made the flight from New York to Rome so many times before he lost count. Today it was like flying in a single-engine 1940's vintage aircraft. The hours crawled. By the time they landed, he was no longer sorry, he was only angry. Lou and Dominic got busy.

"I need to check on something," Dominic told Lou under his breath as he walked away.

Lou and Tony sat in a small bistro near the airport waiting for Dominic and the driver Tony used whenever he was in Rome.

"Here is the company name and the car model. They're tracking her," Dominic said calmly as he slid into the booth next to Tony, handing him a scribbled paper.

"Who? Who is tracking her? And why?" Tony demanded, his eyes narrowed.

"The car company. I had a hunch about Rhino. He set this up years ago. Apparently, Annie comes here a lot on business. Rhino arranged for her to use the same rental company each time, had them place a tracking device in whatever car she used and paid a special driver. Rhino told the company it would be well worth their while to not lose her. He was good for his word. This time she refused the driver. Rhino paid them very well to keep her safe. They hadn't heard from Rhino, but still set the device. I didn't tell them about Rhino."

Tony's car pulled up. Dominic gave quick directions. In an hour, they were parked at the high-end car rental agency Annie always used. Dominic routed out the manager. Though anxious to assist the three ominous-looking gentlemen, he initially refused to give information out about one of his best clients. It took Dominic very little time to persuade him to provide the information. Tony asked the questions; the man looked from Tony to Dominic. He took them to the office in the back. The technician gave Dominic the details. "It's still there?" Tony asked suspiciously. "She's staying with someone; she has to be. Who?" he said to himself.

"Hasn't moved since she first parked. Not one time. It's the same town she always visits," the manager checking the screen assured him. Dominic picked up a map.

Lou called ahead and eventually found out where she was staying; he booked two rooms. Their driver tried to take a shortcut, only to be held up by construction and garbage trucks. Tony's fury was near boiling. "This will absolutely be the last time she ever runs from me. So much is going on, and I'm in Rome, trying to find Annie. If she had only waited five minutes!" he muttered under his breath.

When at last they were out of the city, the driver hit the gas. No one spoke. Looking around at the small piazza as they entered the village, Tony could see why Annie would like it here. It was her kind of place: quiet, clean, full of life and beauty. As he checked into the villa, Tony asked to speak to the owner. The manager came to the front desk. "The owner is not here just now. He usually leaves early for his lunch and a nap. He is very old. Would it be possible for you to speak with him in the morning?" His tone was pleasant, but he refused to disturb the proprietor.

He also wouldn't give out any information regarding other guests. Closing his eyes for a moment to quell his temper, Tony relented. "Fine, I'll speak with him first thing in the morning. Turning to Lou and Dominic, he suggested, "Let's get something to eat. I could use a drink."

Later that evening, while the men sat in the courtyard listening to the music and having an after-dinner drink, a lone figure moved up the back stairway to her corner room. She could not bring herself to face the crowded courtyard.

Morning broke into Annie's nightmare, again. By this time, she prayed for daylight each night. With activity, people talking to her, the children, and her long walks, she was able to keep the pain at bay. It was the nights that were unbearable. Stepping from the shower, she began her routine. Pulling on a dress Mama had provided, Annie piled her hair atop her head. The dress was a soft cashmere and silk material that swirled gently around her when she walked. Slipping into her sandals and setting her sunglasses on her head, she stepped out of her room and slowly walked downstairs.

Today, as in the days before, she had to face Mama, Poppi, and food. Maybe this time she could have something besides the coffee that Rhino always told her would put hair on her chest. Thoughts of her dear friend made her sad. "Rhino. Look at me. I can't even think anymore. I've got to find a way out of this quagmire. I just don't know what to do. What would you say to me now?"

When she sat down, Mama came again. This time she simply poured the coffee, slipped a plate with a hunk of cheese and a hard roll next to the cup, and sat. "Annie, you have to start eating. You gonna kill yourself. That won't help anyone. That won't help you. I'm your Mama now, and I tell you to eat and move on. No man is worth what you do now. Eat a little, walk more, and pretty soon you ask why you're sad. See?" She kindly patted Annie's arm, stood, and kissed her head. "The children come tonight. They all know you're here. You can't be this way with them."

Inwardly, Annie groaned. How could she deal with the kids again tonight? Unable to think from one moment to the next, she picked up the cheese and roll, pulled her sunglasses down over her bloodshot eyes, and headed for the trail. Her trail. It used to mean peace and tranquility, now it only meant she could cry unnoticed.

Tony watched her leave through narrowed eyes. She looked broken. His angry heart began to soften. He had already learned from the old man how fond they were of Annie. She had been coming here for many years and was well known in the village. Tony also learned what Annie's routine had been during this stay.

He could tell the old man was worried about Tony and his men. He knew Tony's type. "I know how you work, Mr. Tuscano. Annie is special. Maybe you should leave her be." Tony simply nodded politely to the proprietor. Tony would try to get her to come willingly; if not, well . . .

Anthony Tuscano stood, tossed his coat over his chair, and quietly followed Annie. Lou and Dominic exchanged glances and ate in silence as they watched their cousin leave. One way or another, this mess would end today.

"If he screws this up, I'm gonna miss that lady. She got me in a lot of hot water, but she's something else," Lou said, shaking his head. Dominic nodded in agreement. He was secretly enjoying this trip. The music, the people, the food—it was all home. She had been too easy to find, however. He needed to talk to her about that.

Annie walked along talking to the birds as she broke off bits of the roll and scattered them about. The birds immediately began to peck at the pieces. The sun splashed over the vineyard and on down the road ahead of her. Flowers were beginning to lose their summer clothing, and the night's dew had left its print on plants still under protective shaded areas. The road was dry, but not dusty yet. Annie walked on. She stopped once, staring at the hills. Slowly, she continued her walk.

When they were far enough from the villa to not be heard even if she should scream, Tony stepped up his pace. Annie could feel someone behind her. She heard the footsteps. Frowning, she wondered who would dare to interrupt her. Then the familiar tremble swept through her. "No, this can't be. Please let it be some kid, not him," she prayed silently. She stopped walking and slowly turned around. Tony was rapidly approaching her—his face dark, his eyes flashing, his mouth hard. She whirled back around, pulled her dress up over her knees, and fled. Her mind raced.

Tony was prepared for her reaction. Annie ran as fast as she could, but she was no match for a man who lived not only by his wit but also by his physical prowess. He reached her quickly, knowing full well what she was thinking. Grasping her he held on tight, jerking her around. "What the hell are you doing? You're still running from me?" he fumed, outraged. "You think you can just run whenever things get a little tough for you? I'm going to talk, and you're going to listen, Annie." He yanked her sunglasses away from her face to peer into her eyes. He was startled to see her face. Her eyes were red and swollen, and there were dark circles beneath them.

Quickly regaining control, he continued, his voice low and powerful. "First, you will never, never run from me again. Is that clear, Annie? Never!" Annie was too shocked to respond immediately. She had never seen him like this. He had been angry with her before, but not this way. "I'm talking to you, Annie! Never again, do you understand me? Never again!" he persisted, his voice menacing.

She stood as one frozen. His hold on her, in anger, was harsh. It was clear he had no intentions of letting her go. Her breathing quickened, her heart was pounding. She was not frightened of him, she simply felt trapped. "I hear you," she whispered.

His voice was cold, his fury unmasked. "Now listen to me, and you listen carefully. I know that woman, but not in the way you think. She is one of the women I would see on occasion in New York. I had someone bring her to the hotel. When I was finished, she was taken away." Annie shuddered at the arrangement, trying to back away from him. His hold tightened as he forced her closer. "An agreement, by the way, that suited her just fine. She never had any way to contact me, never was in public with me."

Tony's eyes pierced Annie's. He towered over her. "She chanced upon me. She sat down *seconds* before you came in. Uninvited, Annie, uninvited. I have had *no* contact with her since I've known you. None whatsoever." His voice began to soften. "Since the first time I saw you, outside the post office in Aguilar, I have had no contact with any woman except you." As always with her, he could feel his anger dissipate. "I told you that before. I love you Annie. I will *always* love you. There will never be a rendezvous with anyone. I don't need anyone else. Only you. I will never hurt you. At some point in time, you have to trust me, Annie. That's what happens when you love someone.

"You didn't let me to talk to you. You ran, *again*. Even a condemned man has a chance to speak. You wouldn't grant me that. You ran." He finished speaking, his eyes no longer flashing with anger but filled with love and tenderness. She stood without speaking. Her eyes sought his; pain washed over him at the sadness in them. Slowly, he loosened his grip, slipped his arms around her shoulders, and pulled her to him. Gently, he brushed the stray ends of her hair away from her face. As he expected, she began to cry.

"I thought I had lost you. I felt this ugly hole in my heart. You hurt me, beyond description, Tony. I had to get away from you."

"You didn't have to hurt, little one. If you had just let me speak with you, we both would have been saved a lot. Annie, you have to stop running from me. You have to know by now I would never let you go. You cannot get away from me." He tipped her face to him, gently kissing her lips. "I'll always find you, Inamorata." He spoke softly. "My family is not like other families. Remember?"

With her head resting on his chest, wrapped in his arms, Annie felt her heart begin to lose that awful ache. She turned her face to him, whispering. "Take me home, Tony."

His heart leapt. He was filled with emotion. He held her tightly, unspeaking. For a long moment, they stood as one. Turning around, they slowly walked back to the villa in silence. Entering the courtyard, he sat her with Lou and Dominic. "No more coffee, Annie. One of you order something light for her—scrambled eggs, maybe. You have to eat, Annie."

He left to look for the old couple, intending they should know she would be fine. He could tell they were fond of her. In his heart, he knew Annie and he would be back. Soon. He couldn't keep chasing after her. He wanted her badly. He could not believe how deeply he loved Annie.

The table was silent. Annie was uncertain what to say. She hated that these men had had to traipse across the globe to get her. Dominic spoke first, quietly. "If you ever do something like this again, Annie, you'll have more than Tony to answer to. You're family, now, whether you like it or not. We don't treat each other like this. In our business, we're all we have . . . each other."

Annie looked up, expecting to see him angry. He was not. Instead, he looked at her with sympathy. "I'm sorry you guys were dragged here, Dominic." She closed her eyes. "I had no one. I couldn't tell Lynn. She's just getting used to the idea of Tony and me. I couldn't jeopardize that fragile relationship, with Sam feeling the way he does about Lynn. I certainly couldn't call my brothers." She leaned her elbows on the table, holding her head in her hands. "And it's not like I could go to any of you and say, 'Your boss just stomped on me.'" She looked at both men. "Like you would or could help? I came to the only people I knew who could comfort me."

Lou idly tapped his spoon on the table. "Annie, you have to understand something. You really are part of our family now. I'm with Dom. Don't do this again."

"Another thing," Dominic continued, this time his voice was stern. "You made mistakes. We have to correct that. You never go to the same place to stay or rent a car unless you are absolutely certain those places are protected for you. Don't be predictable. You always let someone know where you're headed. You can't ever tell what may happen on the other side. Your room? Corner with two entrances, maybe. The best would be inside for a woman. We're involved with too many things now for you to move around normally. You and I need to spend some time doing a little training. Soon."

He looked around the courtyard, "Why did you come here anyway?"

"I've been coming here for years. I always stay in this place. It's home, almost. I've come here whenever I needed to clear my head, like after Mom and Dad died. I stay here whenever I'm searching for Italian art. I sit with the old ladies and gossip. It's a great place. It's my place. I never dreamed Tony could find me here." She smiled wearily at the two men sitting with her.

"Hmm, I can't think of *anyplace* he couldn't find you, girl." Lou grinned back at her, shaking his head. Thoughtfully, he added, "I would imagine you speak Italian very well."

"Yes, matter of fact, I do." She admitted.

"What else are you keeping from me, Annie?" Tony's voice sounded behind her. She jumped. He looked down on her with affection. "When we get home, you and I are going to have a long talk. There is no pass, this time," he added, gently chiding her.

"I'm a little surprised you missed this. It's probably the most regular thing about me. After this, I think that's about it." She shrugged.

The little band had set up for the afternoon and was playing

"Ritorna-Me" in the courtyard. "Come dance with me, Annie." Tony
ordered softly. Pulling her close, he moved into the center of the area.
They danced. The pain in her heart began to slowly fade.

Long after midnight, Tony walked Annie up to her room. "I love you,
Annie" He held her face, looking deep into her eyes, his voice thick with
passion. He kissed her, slowly, gently, melting her into his arms. Annie
handed him her room key. Tony locked the door behind them.

Annie's face, turned up to him, shone in the moonlight now flooding
the room with a soft breath of light. Slowly he slipped her dress off her
shoulders. His eyes never left hers as he let the dress fall to the floor.
Annie's breath caught at the touch of his fingers on her skin. Taking her
face into his hands, he kissed her again. His hand moved down to caress
her breasts. As always, she trembled at his touch. Annie began to unbut-
ton his shirt. His shoulders were smooth and broad.

Tony lifted her easily and laid her onto the bed. Annie's heart pounded
and she closed her eyes, responding as his touch ignited her passion.
Unhurriedly, ever so gently, he explored her body. When she opened
her eyes, she looked into his dark eyes filled with love and desire. The
night wrapped around them, their passions mounting with every movement. Just when Annie thought she could take no more, his gentle touch
lit a fire within her again. Night carefully tiptoed into dawn. The lovers
finally slept.

As morning light flooded the room, Annie slowly awoke. The night
had been like a wonderful dream. She could hear Tony's easy breathing.
She could feel him watching her. "What if I had not wanted to go back?"
she asked quietly, rolling onto her side to look at him.

A smile on his lips, his eyes caressing her, he said, "Oh, you'd go back.
Willing or not, you would go back. I keep telling you: I never give up
what is mine. I meant what I said, Annie," he continued in a soft voice,
"You are never, *never* to run from me again." Annie smiled in response.

"I'm not going anywhere, Tony. I'm through running from you. I'd
much rather be with you." She smiled at him tenderly. He rose up on one
elbow, tracing her jaw with his finger. Leaning over, he kissed her. "I do
love you, Annie," he whispered, before rolling back over to get up.

* * * *

Settled in her seat on the airplane, Annie leaned back quietly for a moment. Tony sat relaxed with his eyes closed. "Just how *did* you find me?" she whispered to him. He opened one eye to look at her; smiling he shook his head.

"I wonder what else you're going to find out that you didn't know. I've had a lot of fun in my life, you know." Her voice was teasing.

He smiled, his eyes still closed. "I have the rest of our lives to find out. No doubt, the journey will be interesting, love." He slept.

CHAPTER 61

A thought hung around Annie's mind, pulling at her consistently. Back in New York one evening, as Tony walked with her around the paths that filled the estate, she decided to broach the subject. "Tony," she began, "I need to understand something. It bothers me and I don't want anything between us." She paused to gather her thoughts. Tony looked at her, fondly. He guessed at her problem, but waited for her to ask him. She liked not having any boundaries. He knew it still bothered her to think she could not just leave. She was happy here, and happy with him. The nature of his "business" took some of life's liberties away. This was necessary for them. The trade-off insured liberties for the people they tried to protect.

"I have to be honest with you. I am still a little uncomfortable with the idea that I can never leave. I mean, what if I have to? No one has ever said I couldn't go before. I don't mean run away, I just . . ." Annie was pensive.

"Hmmm, having trouble with commitment are we, Annie?" he asked, his eyes full of mischief.

Annie quickly responded, "Your definition of commitment is a little stringent." She frowned. "I have never been this happy in my life, Tony. Still, the idea that I can't leave is bothersome."

Tony walked along with her for a few moments. She would have to understand where he stood, eventually. "Annie, this isn't the movies. You aren't held here because of some blood vow." He looked at her smiling. "You could leave this place and my protection, but you would be an easy target for some. Remember, I'm not protected by the government. It's conceivable someone could use you to get to me or us. You know nearly everything about my family, Allen and Earl's work, and you are becoming an expert at the information game. So perhaps part of the reason lies with what we do, yes."

Serious now, he stopped walking and turned to her, "The greater part lies with how I feel about you and how you fit into my life. What I do requires that we give up some liberties. We have to, to keep everyone in the family safe. Remember Annie, my family is not traditional. Simply put, we could be thought of as a gang. We are what we are."

He walked along again, his head down thinking. "You cannot just walk away, Annie. You're in my family. Frankly, you know too much to just leave. I can't change how you feel about the control issue. You have to deal with that. If someone doesn't take charge, we run amuck, as the saying goes. I'm in charge. Someone has to make a final decision. There really never is a fifty-fifty relationship. There must be a give and take on everyone's part. Sometimes it is thirty-seventy; sometimes it's sixty-forty. Whatever. Because of what I do, I have the responsibility of more than you and I. So, the short answer would be, you must learn to deal with it. Is it so awful, to let me take care of you, Annie?" He asked quietly. They walked along in silence.

"Well, yes. It is, sort of." Annie shrugged. She smiled up at him. His eyes were filled with tenderness, as she struggled to explain her feelings and keep some independence. "I do feel a little like I'm deserting the 'old' me. I'm not certain I can do that. I mean, look at me. I'm not a young thing anymore. I've been on my own for ages."

He stopped and walked her to a nearby bench, sitting down, pulling her onto his lap. "I love you, Annie. Neither of us planned on this union. Now that you're here, will I ever let you go? Never. I am making it my life's work, to be certain you never want to leave. Fair enough?"

She leaned against him. "I suppose, Mr. Tuscano. So tell me, just how did you find me so fast?" She turned to him, quizzically.

"Hmm . . ." He smiled back at her. She could tell he had no intention of telling her.

They sat for several moments, in comfortable silence, each in their own world. Annie snuggled closer to Tony. He smiled, as his arms tightened, "I love you, Annie." He whispered into her hair.

"I love you, too, Tony. I do so love you." She turned to him again, kissing him, gently.

CHAPTER 62

Rhamidid stared at the television, waiting impatiently for the six o'clock news to begin. His plot had already begun. He never spoke to the commander after the blowup and mess in Denver. He knew he really did not have approval to move forward. He also knew timing was everything in his line of work. Today, the news would confirm what his people had already known. Sleep had become an unknown pastime to him, exhaustion a constant companion. But he must be clearheaded in the days to come. Tonight would be better. He had one last meeting with his faction. When the news anchor began speaking, he listened intently. The informant was right. The final chapter would begin. Fate spoke to him, or everything would not have fallen into place so well. This night, he slept.

* * * *

Riyadzi splashed along, a lone, dark figure hunched over against the rain that pummeled him. His loafers sloshed through water puddles in the trashy unlit alley. It didn't matter; he was already soaked to the bone. His anger at Rhamidid flared then waned, only to blaze again. For years the two men had worked toward this; now he was left to find his own way . . . to what? He had done his part every time. From Spain to Turkey to India to London. Now he was to leave the group. "What group?" he asked himself sarcastically. Since when do two men make a group? No matter, he was headed out of this country anyway. He had been sent to the Netherlands. Rhamidid wasn't coming. Good, he could work better without him! One final job and he would be able to leave.

Rounding the last corner, turning onto the dimly lit street, he stepped under an old faded awning. Its edges were unraveling and torn. The cables, once strong and straight now rusted and bent, pulled the awning down in acknowledgment of the condemnation order fixed to the front door. Riyadzi glanced around the area, grasped the knob, and pushed the door open. Silently, he removed his soggy shoes, carefully placing them beneath the worn stairs. Sliding out of his thin jacket, he used it to wipe the droplets of rain from his face. Standing motionless, he listened. Only the rain, the distant thunder, and the creaking awning could be heard.

Softly, ever so softly, he took the stairs. Like everything he did, this was planned carefully. He knew which boards were loose and where to step. There was no need to hurry on this trip. When he reached the second floor, he paused. He could hear the sounds of men in deep sleep beyond the closed door. Carefully, he slipped the copied key into the door, pausing with each movement, listening, stealthily opening the door.

The room reeked of old food, sweaty bodies, and soured clothes. He noticed none of this. He counted—five, not four. Fine, what was one more? With the expertise of one who knows well what to do, he slipped the long narrow blade from its scabbard. Riyadzi moved from man to man, soundlessly. When he had finished with the last one, he removed a large candle from his pants pocket. Setting it in the sleeping room, he lit all three wicks. Calmly, he walked into the kitchenette. Scraping food and other debris aside, he pulled the windows down tight. Standing over the kitchen stove, he turned every burner on. Slipping out of the apartment, he closed the door, immediately pushing an old blanket under it. Swiftly retrieving his shoes and jacket, he stepped into the night.

When the building exploded, he was long gone.

* * * *

Rhamidid sat in a dark room. Closing his eyes, he reviewed the diagram yet again. There could be no mistake. The men with him were fanatics . . . willing to die for a cause they knew little about. Trained in Afghanistan, tied to no one in their homeland, they were the perfect team. He knew they could get in; they just had to get close enough to reach their goal.

He met with the rest of his group at a small coffee shop, and they all started toward the target. No one spoke. Each carefully melted into alleyways, changing into nondescript clothing. They mustn't draw any attention to themselves. By the time they reached the blocked-off area, they appeared to be just like any of the number of suited men wandering about with a validated pass. At last, they reached the entrance. A man disguised as a security officer met them and waved them past security after checking their IDs.

Once inside the building, Rhamidid spoke quietly to the man, "I'm ready to change." The false security man slipped him to the side, and into a large restroom. Careful to be certain they were not seen, both men stole into the back stall. Rhamidid retrieved the pack from the ceiling cache, while the guard kept watch. Once his pack was wired and in place, Rhamidid quickly stepped behind the unsuspecting man and, with one twist of his powerful arm, jerked the man's head. The guard's neck snapped, and he sagged. Rhamidid propped him onto the commode and secured him in place with bungee cords from his pack. Quietly, he rolled into the next stall, and left.

Finding this man had been a gift. He was a brother to one of the four men Rhamidid recruited. As a member of the security team contracted to watch over the building, he had easy access. It had taken months of work, but bit by bit the weapons and backpacks had been brought in and hidden in prearranged locations. Each of the four men was obtained by using Tina's information. It was a simple matter to provide IDs, passes, and papers; they were granted entrance as media personnel. Ah, the beauty of his plan. The camera equipment, carefully screened by security today, was easily disassembled, replaced by explosives to be carried into the crowd gathering in the hall. No one would suspect.

Rhamidid was certain Riyadzi had done his part; he always did.

Eliminating the men who had provided the fake IDs and hidden the explosives was crucial.

One by one, the rest of his team retrieved their packs, split up, and mixed with the crowd that was moving slowly forward. Rhamidid was calm. The only one left alive, after today, would be Riyadzi. He was already out of the country. With the information Rhamidid had mailed anonymously to the district attorney's office today, Riyadzi would never be allowed back into this country. Rhamidid gave himself a moment to think of his family and Tina, martyred because of her work. He would be with her again. It was time.

CHAPTER 63

The Democratic National Convention was held in October. As expected, every news channel covered the event. From the beginning, Annie and Lynn watched as the various speakers gave their push to excite the crowd. Flags flapped everywhere, images of elephants covered the walls, and the great convention hall full of excited men, women, and children was filled with blaring music. Images of "blue" states flashed across a mega screen. Streamers floated merrily to the floor, blown from some unseen vent, while confetti spewed across the crowd at irregular intervals.

With Rhino's warning blinking off and on like a neon light in their heads, Annie and Lynn watched a logistic nightmare. So many people and so much activity. Every camera available was focused on the convention from different angles. Some cameras constantly panned the crowd. Others focused on the stage, entrances, and exits. It looked like mayhem to the sisters. After months of studying photos and films, they had developed a technique to quickly pick out notables. It was something she and Lynn practiced daily.

So far, most attention had been on people arriving at the event. Security was tight. Annie had just turned to the screen panning the crowd inside the convention. Suddenly, her head shot up. "Lynn, look, that's him! That's Rhamidid!" Frantically she called Tony as Lynn scrambled to her side. "He's inside the Convention Hall with you, Tony! He's walking toward the front. Do you have the picture on?"

"Who, Annie? Who are you talking about?"

"Rhamidid."

"Take it easy, keep talking, I've got it on. Where?" His calm, controlled voice settled Annie quickly.

"He's on the right side of screen six that shows the stage and front crowd, about halfway up. See the guy with the beard carrying the camera or something? He's tall and dark. Look, now he's moving toward the center. He's looking for someone! You can see his face clearly. Do you have him?"

Rhamidid moved closer toward the podium. To be the most effective, they must take out the speakers, the candidates, and their families. Anyone close to the front must have a special pass, he surmised. That's where he wanted to be. He could not see the other four men with him; the crowd was too thick. With this many people crammed together, he knew the effect would be contained by those smashed against him. He wanted a greater pattern. He wanted more damage. He pushed forward, struggling against the people dancing and yelling around him. He must get to the front somehow. Even with his height, it was nearly impossible to see over the crowd of waving supporters. Everyone carried a banner, a flag, or a sign. Doggedly, he pushed forward.

"Annie," Tony's voice was quiet. "I have a man on the floor. I'm patching you to him; tell him exactly what you see. You're talking to Eddie. I am still on the line with you."

"Eddie, where are you? That guy is about midway to the stage; he's moving toward the front. He's wearing a brown suit, has a dark beanie thing on his head. He has a beard and a camera. He keeps looking around for someone."

"I'm headed toward the center, keep talking. You should see me. I've just looked up at the lights. I have on a black jacket and a red baseball cap. I'm about five rows from the front. Tell me where to go," Eddie replied.

* * * *

Annie repeated everything he said to her so Lynn could follow. "There," Lynn pointed excitedly. "There's your man. Now let's get him to Rhamidid." Annie gave clear directions to Eddie, steering him directly to Rhamidid. Tony's men were moving toward the center, watching the crowd, listening to Annie. Eddie spotted Rhamidid. Slowly, he moved toward him.

Several men dressed like Rhamidid had moved together, ahead of him, all talking excitedly. Rhamidid tried to yell to them but the noise was deafening. They needed to spread out now. Instead, he found himself slowly pushed backward. He tried in vain to shove his way through the crowd. Suddenly, he was jerked back. Cursing, he looked at the man closest to him. Their eyes locked, and he saw the victory in that man's face. It was over. All his hopes of martyrdom gone. His arms were grasped away from his body, and Rhamidid was quickly removed from the area. Allen's team covered Tony's men as they hustled their prisoner away. People around were confused. Things happened so fast no one saw anything. One of Allen's men made a comment about drunks causing problems. That rumor spread, and no mind was paid to them.

"I'll call you." Tony touched end on his phone.

Annie turned to Lynn, "Did you see that? What if he's not alone? Surely he isn't."

"Keep watching. Did you notice that bunch ahead of him? I'm certain we've seen them before. They are part of this fun little gathering." Lynn turned back to the screens.

Annie and Lynn watched riveted. The group of men Rhamidid tried to reach had spread out, positioning themselves in each quadrant of the room. Annie dialed Tony again. "There are four more. One toward each corner of the room. Someone had better move fast."

"That's okay, they're with us," Lou interjected.

"No, they're not. We know these guys. Move it!" Lynn countered.

Speaking rapidly, Annie tried to direct the team toward the men. Three of them were removed. In horror, Lynn and Annie could see the last man pull at his vest then throw his arms up. By this time, Tony's men were on him. A struggle ensued and the crowd began to split. People started scurrying away, and panic began to set in. Still the struggle on the floor continued. Allen's men circled the struggle, protecting participants from the view of Convention attendees. Shots rang out. Official security people tried to gain control of the crowd and get everyone out. Tony's cameras stayed on the men wrestling on the floor. Suddenly, the terrorist went limp. Security people were moving toward the scene, but the man was whisked away before they could get close. The entire team was lost in the crowd. What felt like an hour had taken only a few moments. It was over. Annie and Lynn sat frozen, staring at the television and each other by turns.

None of the media knew for certain what had just happened. Shortly thereafter, a man in fatigues came to a microphone and stated, "Four heavily armed men were apprehended at the DNC convention. All have been taken into custody. I have no further information. Thank you." He walked away amid security personnel. The room erupted into mayhem.

Turning off the set, Annie sat back down slowly. "There were five. How are we ever going to stop these people? This can happen anywhere. We were just lucky tonight."

"We've spent hours looking at and learning about them. Maybe that's how we help. We keep adding to our files. It's better than nothing. With Rhino's help, we've got a good system here. I'm sure Allen or Sam or whomever can add to it. It's a huge step. Every scummy one of them should come up on our screen at one time or another, and we can let the whole world know just who and what they really are. Well, maybe not the world, but at least the people like us, in every corner of the world."

Annie and Lynn followed the news reports carefully. Not one report could identify who did what. People were in various states of fright. Eventually, the director of Homeland Security released an official statement: "The department, with the assistance of other federal agencies, has thwarted an attempt to disrupt DNC activities." He went on to say, essentially, everything was under control.

CHAPTER 64

*T*hree days later, Tony arrived, waking Annie up at five in the morning. He was followed by the rest of his team, Allen, and Earl. The sisters' room became a conference room.

"Rhamidid wasn't alone, but he should have been. I don't know what they're giving the feds, but he's giving us lots." Tony was pleased with the progress.

"He's talking? I find that amazing. What did you do to get him to talk?" Lynn asked.

"Don't ask. There are those of us who realize we have to fight them in the same way they fight us . . . without pity," Allen said. "For us, the good news is the feds think there were a total of four involved; our man was not counted. That helps us keep him longer. Until one of the four spills the beans. On another note, we've got a proposal for you two." Allen grinned.

"Let me guess. You're taking us to some beautiful island somewhere, you'll fix us wonderful drinks, cook for us . . ." Lynn smiled dreamily.

"You'd like that?" asked Sam.

"I have no idea. Can you cook?" Lynn asked.

"No, he can't!" Everyone answered with much laughter.

"Get a robe, come with me," Tony bid Annie, smiling at her. Taking her arm, Tony led her out the door and onto one of the paths winding around the property. "Annie, I could never let you leave, you know that. We have discussed that ad nauseam. You know who I am and what I do. You know I love you. I know you love me. Will you still marry me?"

Annie looked into his eyes, so full of emotion. She felt her heart skip; deep within she felt that tremor. "Yes," she answered softly.

He grasped her tightly, held her almost desperately. Tipping her face up to his, he continued, "Your life will never be the same, Annie. I swear to you, I will do all in my power to protect and care for you. You've brought me to another place . . . I'm not even certain where that is, but I am happy and content. I have never been this way before. You're the first woman to see my world and anyplace else we have been." He smiled at her tenderly. Leaning down, he kissed her.

Holding her hand, he led her along the path. Neither spoke for several moments. "There is something else, Annie. I am going after another man. Dominic is going with me. This guy, Riyadzi, left the country. That makes it a lot easier; we can get at him now. He's Rhamidid's counterpart. We have to get him now. The information Allen is receiving puts him in the Netherlands. He's got big plans we need to stop. I can't let him go, knowing what I know."

Annie's face clouded. "Just what do you mean, you're going after him?"

Seating her on one of the benches along the path, he squatted in front of her, his hands on her knees, looking squarely into her hazel eyes. "Look at me, Annie, please. This is what we do. That means me, too. Dominic is the best there is. He's never missed a kill. We have to stop this guy. With what we've learned these past days, we have to move now. This could take awhile, even after we find him. We'll stay with it until we stop him. We don't have the luxury of waiting for authorities to look for him then decide what to do. There's not anyone else; Dom and I are it. I leave tonight. We are asking you to stay here and continue the work you started. We're asking you and Lynn to join us. I know you're staying; I want you to stay because this is where you want to be." He reached up and brushed away the tear that was slowly creeping down her face. "Your answer will keep me until I come back. I *will* come back, Annie."

Standing, he pulled her to him. She held him tightly, her face buried in his chest. Finally, he continued. "In my mind, we're already married,

Annie. Do you feel that too?" His voice was hopeful as he looked down on her, lifting her face upward.

"No, Tony," Annie answered, looking up to see his face cloud. "Not in my mind. I feel it in my heart. In my heart, Tony." She placed her hand over his heart. His face cleared.

He kissed her tenderly and held her close. "We'd best get back, love." Yet, he lingered a moment longer, holding her, memorizing each detail of the woman he had grown to love so quickly with such passion. "Soon, Annie, when this is settled, we'll go to Italy for a wedding, ours. Until then . . ." he kissed her again.

* * * *

Late that night, Annie kissed Tony good-bye passionately. Tony held her face in his hands for one brief moment, then he was gone. She stood riveted to the floor until she could no longer see him. Standing in the empty doorway, listening to the sound of the vehicle moving slowly down the driveway, she closed her eyes. When the great gate closed, she was certain she could hear the clank. Minutes went by; still she stood. She could feel his kiss, his hand in hers, and see his eyes and smile. Her prayer was a simple one: "Please help him do whatever he needs to do, to protect the innocents, then bring him back to me. Please."

The first week went by easily. Annie and Lynn continued their work, responded to requests for information, and had dinner each evening with whichever of the men were around. After the house settled down, Annie had taken to wandering its halls. She found a gathering room where the men sat to play cards and share a drink. Sometimes, she sat with them to keep her dreams at bay. Whenever Sam was around, he and Lynn stole what moments they could, and Annie took care to allow them that small gift.

Often, Lou walked the halls with her. She never asked about Tony out loud; Lou would quietly shake his head "no" every evening. When she had done all she could to keep going, she found herself walking along the paths of the estate alone at night.

Unbeknownst to Annie, every inch of the estate was visible to the men in the control room. Monitors scanned the driveway, walls, rooms, halls, and, of course, the garden pathways. Lou always stopped by the control room on his last round. He and the crew operating the equipment sat, silently watching Annie walk alone in her sadness. "Maybe you should suggest she not go at night, Lou. It's getting damn cold out there. She should just wander around here, in the house. Heaven knows there is plenty of room."

"I don't think it's the same. I do think she needs warmer clothes, though. Keep an eye out for her, guys. Maybe I can do something about the clothes." He stood for a moment longer, watching. He knew the men would take care of her. They had grown fond of her; she laughed with them, fed them, used discretion in all she heard or saw. Annie had moved into the position reserved for the boss's wife, except each man also felt a heightened sense of loyalty to her on her own merits. She was one of them.

The next evening, after Lynn had gone to bed and was sleeping soundly, Annie pulled her heaviest robe around her and walked the long hall to Tony's office. She kept a pair of boots and heavy socks hidden beneath Tony's desk. Bending to retrieve them, her hand touched something soft. She grasped it, and pulled. It was a long tan trench coat with a down liner. A thick red cashmere cap, with an attached neck scarf, and a pair of red down mittens fell from inside the coat. The boots she had been using were replaced with heavy wool and faux-fur-lined high boots and heavy socks. Smiling, she donned everything and stepped out, much warmer, into the evening air.

In the middle of November, word came that Tony's mother was dying. Lou made arrangements for he and Annie to fly to Denver and drive to Aguilar. Although Mrs. Tuscano did not know they were there, they sat with her for four days before she finally died. Annie cried with a heavy heart. She really didn't know Tony's mother, but her spirit felt broken because Tony was not with them. Mrs. Tuscano's body was taken back to New York and buried in a private family plot on the estate. Sam and Lou felt the death deeply. She was the last of their parents' generation. Neither Dominic nor Tony was around.

For several days afterward, Annie took her walks in the private cemetery. There, she saw the headstones for Tony's father, his uncles, and what she assumed were several cousins, along with aunts and at least one grandparent. The area was well tended with manicured plots of grass, brown now with winter's cold. Soon, though, she stopped going; it only made her melancholy. Annie missed Tony terribly, more than she imagined possible. "Please come back to me, Tony," her heart cried.

Thanksgiving came and went, like so many days before. The weather was dismal. Snow and sleet assaulted the area, and dreary gray clouds hung close to the ground, refusing to give up encasing the earth. Still Annie walked. The very world seemed intent on pushing her mood further and further into torment. In spite of whatever else happened during her day, she continued to walk every evening. Walking was Annie's salvation. It was then she examined her heart. Could she do this again? And again? And again? Tony had been clear. "We will be apart many times" bounced around in her head over and over. She played his promise—"I will come back"—over and over in her mind too. Slowly, over time, she became calmer inside. Slowly, she began to move beyond the immobilizing dread. What would come would come. As she stepped out of the fog of anxiety that had enveloped her, she found a measure of peace.

* * * *

Christmas was two weeks away. As everyone gathered for their dinner, Annie entered the room. For the first time in months, she wore her familiar smile. While it still bore a resemblance to sadness, it hinted of her old spirit. "Do you all have families?"

For a long moment, no one answered. They looked at each other as if trying to decide how or what to tell her. The old man from the control room at last stood. He spoke quietly in a thick accent. "We all of us had families, but no more. This is our family," he waved his hands around the room. "These are my brothers, my cousins and my family. Everyone is here. You are here, also. You and your sister. Your brothers have been in our family many years. It's been good. Welcome to our family." He solemnly nodded to her. The table clapped, and many of the men cheered.

Annie was taken aback. She hardly knew how to respond. Recovering, she smiled graciously. "Thank you. Thank you all for everything you do for my sister and for me. Perhaps it is not my place, but I am going to have Christmas, this year, here, for anyone who would like to stay and join me."

The men looked at each other around the table, again not certain how to respond. Annie couldn't have known that the only people who might actually leave were Allen, Earl, and possibly Sam. The rest lived here, in this place. Lou quickly stood up and toasted Annie. "Here's to Christmas with Annie. This old place has not seen a Christmas in many years. It's about time, Annie. Great idea." Cheers sounded around the table.

Allen and Earl had come back only days earlier. They both looked at Lynn in surprise. She shrugged her shoulders and looked to Annie. The table came alive with suggestions for what to do, laughter, and a feeling of the coming festivities. It lifted the fog that had held everyone for so long. They would have a good Christmas. These were Tony's people, his family . . . now hers.

When Annie and Lynn returned to their suite, Allen and Earl came to join them. After pouring the ladies a glass of wine, the men mixed drinks and sat. Earl started, "Annie, we were planning on going back home for Christmas. We're ready for some down time, and truthfully, that's not here." Allen and Lynn agreed.

"You need to get away from here, Annie. You can't do anything for Tony here. We all need a break. Let's have an old-fashioned 'Kirk' Christmas. What do you think?" Earl pleaded. Annie sat silently, listening.

Allen added, "It would be great if you would come with us. You need to get away from things, too, like Earl says. You need some sense of normalcy. Believe me I know, if anyone does."

Lynn added, "Sam is going with us. We need it. Please say you'll join us."

Annie looked at these people she loved so much. Quietly, she responded, "I have given this hours of thought. I'm waiting for Tony. I understand what you all are saying, and think you should go on. Heaven knows that place needs to have someone check up on it. Right now, I belong here." She looked at them all and added in a voice so soft it was hardly audible, "My heart is here. I have to stay. Please say you understand."

For a moment, the room was silent. Allen stood and walked to the doors leading out to the balcony. As was the norm now, snow was falling. The lights shone on the tiny drifts already forming on the deck, reflecting rainbows of color. Turning back to his sister, Allen smiled. "We do understand. We may not like it, but we understand. You'd only be a mess if you came with us. We're heading out this week. Whichever of us hears anything, calls the other, got it?"

Annie smiled at her brother. As usual, he came to her rescue. "Got it. Lynn, why don't you give Sam a call? Get his body up here. He may as well join us. Allen, I have to know. Just how did you get to the house that awful night?"

"In a word, Adeeb. He was working Rhamidid in Denver. I had enough sense to have a GPS tracking device implanted when Jacko came on board. We always knew he would try something, just never knew when. Adeeb kept up with it and saw I was roaming around a little too much. I didn't answer when he called, so he came for me. That's also why Buster didn't bark when he dropped me off. Buster knew Adeeb's car, although Jacko never saw it. Adeeb was at the ranch a lot. I still miss him," he admitted sadly.

The rest of the evening, on into the night, all five sat visiting, laughing, and relaxing. The next afternoon saw Allen's Suburban loaded and ready to roll. They tried to get Buster to join them, but he promptly sat next to Annie and watched.

"He knows none of you would let him sleep with you," Annie explained. "He's got a big ol' soft bed here. Of course he's staying," laughed Annie. She waved them off. As the gate closed, she smiled to herself reaching down to rub Buster's ears. Somehow, things would be fine.

Under her direction, Annie's Christmas came alive. Tiny lights adorned every tree and bush. Small, lit trees sat along the paths and on the patios. The inside was decorated with live pine boughs woven throughout with vivid red ribbons, silver balls, and lights. Nearly every room had a tree. The cook began to turn out Christmas cookies, cakes, and candy, as the spirit spread. Annie snuck out one day, with Lou, and did her shopping. As they sat in a small coffee shop having soup, Lou commented, "You know he is going to be fine, don't you?"

Annie smiled a little sadly. "Yes, this time. Whatever comes, comes. In my heart, Lou, he's worth it."

By December 23, the estate resembled a wonderland. A large Nativity scene occupied one corner of the great room, complete with a manger, straw, and endless logs in the fireplace nearby. On the CD player, traditional Christmas music played softly. Against one wall, stood a long narrow table set with a variety of finger foods and beverages. The last corner held a large tree, complete with decorations and packages. Tony's men had been in and out all day absorbing the spirit of Christmas.

* * * *

Shortly after midnight on December 24, a black Hummer stole through the gates. Passing the front of the house, it moved slowly to the back. Lou stood expectantly waiting for the vehicle and its occupants. Both front doors opened at the same time. Men stepped up to the passengers, welcoming them and whisking the vehicle away. The two gentlemen walked slowly up to Lou. He affectionately gripped his brother and his cousin.

Tony was dirty, disheveled, and exhausted, and Dominic looked much the same. Both men had been through a long ordeal. The success was gratifying, exhilarating at some point. Now, it was simply over for the time being. "Where is she?" Tony asked, eager to be near Annie again.

"Come on, I'll show you." Lou led both men into the control room. Tony watched Annie with gentle concern as she moved along the shoveled pathway. Holiday lights throughout the area played off the snow and ice, casting dancing shadows around the benches and statues. Annie's figure moved steadily across one screen, to be picked up on the next one. Dominic smiled to himself. He slapped Tony's back and walked out. He had his fiends to fight before sleep would find him.

"Still?" Tony asked softly.

"Every night since you left, Tony," Lou answered. "We all watch, to make sure she's safe, but there's no stopping her. I wouldn't even ask it of her. It's her time."

Annie had stepped once more onto her beloved path. She had been walking for nearly half an hour. Music piped onto the patio floated softly through the frozen air. Lights glowing in the trees, bushes, and around the fountains, bounced off the fallen snow. Gazing upward, Annie was surprised to see it was so overcast. Another storm threatened. With her coat wrapped tightly around her, she walked onward, her mind on the only man she had ever loved.

"You shouldn't be wandering out alone, Inamorata."

Annie stood stock-still. Slowly, hardly daring to breathe, she turned to see him step from the shadows, a dark form against the white snow, lit by thousands of twinkling bulbs. His long overcoat flapped slightly as he walked toward her. "Tony!" She murmured, her eyes bright. Suddenly she had wings as she dashed to him, the red scarf flowing behind her while tufts of snow shot up from boots that flew along the path. His arms wrapped around her as she melted into his embrace.

"I told you I would come back," he reminded her, his voice deep with emotion. He kissed her deeply. At last, he took a step back, and reminded her, "I never give up what is mine, Annie."

As Christmas Eve officially began, Annie was again swept away by the gentle touch and passionate kisses of this man she had come to love. The man she would never run from again.

ABOUT THE AUTHOR

Born and raised in Colorado, I was the second of four children. I spent my youth on a ranch twenty-three miles from town. My high school class had twenty-nine graduates. Living so far from town, my family seldom made the trip unless groceries or other supplies were needed. During the winter, we traveled over frozen roads. Most days the school bus made it through, but occasionally we were snowbound.

It was a working cattle ranch: the steers arrived in early spring, were fattened up all summer, and shipped out early fall. Men arrived early in the spring, before the steers, to mend fences and make ready for the cattle. There were several large hay fields; the harvested hay was baled and kept for the horses through the harsh winters. The ranch was beautiful, with meadows, pine- and spruce-covered mountains, rapid flowing creeks, and great rock walls rising from the earth, remnants of past geological activities.

Mine was an ideal childhood. I rode horseback to help move cattle, drove a tractor pulling a flatbed of hay, and worked the garden. Although everyone did their fair share of the work, there was plenty of time to roam the country, both hiking and riding horses. Nearly every Sunday, after Mass and lunch, my older brother would ride with me beside every creek and past every beaver pond on the property. When he could not ride with me, I walked alone. As I walked the many, many miles on that ranch, stories traveled through my mind. Characters came and left, knocking on the door of my memory whenever a certain sound like the ripple of the creek or a familiar sight such as the quivering aspen awoke them. For much of this time, I felt as if I were an observer of life. Watching how people interacted, how animals interacted, and how what we do affects both.

My father worked every day, including Sundays. My mother kept a welcoming home for every cowboy, ranch hand, and child who found their way into our kitchen. There was always a pot of coffee and a kettle of beans on the stove while a pan of bread sat rising nearby. My mother never locked her doors. Not even when she and Dad moved into a small town in New Mexico. She believed if someone broke in, they needed what they might take more than she did.

When I left home to start nursing school, the youngest in my class, it was an entirely different world. Most notable for me was the fact that there were so many people in every class. And boys! Thousands of them! Unlike current living arrangements at colleges and universities, our school had male and female dorms. Since the school was a Catholic university with a history of being a convent, the boys were three miles off campus. Life was definitely interesting.

My first job as an RN was on the evening shift. I found myself observing people, as usual. Only now, the people were ill—usually very ill and frequently alone. We once let a dog come into the room of his owner, a tiny blind woman dying of cancer who was without family or friends. I'll never forget the look on her face in response to that simple act. The dog stayed all shift. He was taken back down the fire stairs before the night crew came. The lady died shortly thereafter, but at least she had had "family" with her for a while.

I moved to Carlsbad, New Mexico, in 1970. It is a small town, with a population of around twenty-eight thousand, with one high school and one hospital. It was there that I raised my only child. Lucky for me, my son shares my passion for baseball.

I continued to work as a nurse. My career choice provided a marvelous opportunity to observe human greatness as well as the depths of depravity we are capable of displaying. Nursing was, for me, a gift. I actually got paid to help people.

When my son went away to college, I was totally alone for the first time in my life. I stayed at work as long as possible to avoid the empty house. One can only wallow in self-pity so long. I began to write every evening. I hardly knew where the story should go or how to get it there, but go it did. The characters developed a personality of their own. They moved my story along, demanding additional twists or requiring that I leave some individuals by the wayside. They gave new life to me.

I remarried, and my husband made the decision to move back to his roots, so to speak. We moved to Edinburg, Texas, in 1998. Only forty-five minutes from Mexico, the change was dramatic. The language barrier, disease prevalence (more than 60 percent of the population is diabetic, bringing with it increased incidences of heart disease, kidney disease, among others), and horrendous poverty must share the stage with the violence along the Texas-Mexico border. Small but steady lights shining through these problems are the very strong family ties and the persistence to move forward and upward the area clings to. I have found the people to be kind, good-humored, and always willing to offer assistance to those in need.

I stopped writing for a period of about eight years while we set up my husband's medical practice and I settled into a new hospital. Eventually I took up my computer once again. How great it felt to be back at my desk. It was like seeing an old friend. However, my prospective on life had changed and so, too, did my book. It took on a new feel, a much more comfortable feel. My writing is no longer a way to pass time. My writing *is* my time.